D0375875

Acknowledgments

With grateful thanks to Fiona, who rescued her reading course material from the bin.

continued . . .

"High on humor and pithy exchanges between the aged and aging characters . . . A warmhearted and well-drawn portrayal of crime in the slow lane, with a good dash of naughtiness . . . English village mystery fiction at its best."

—*Shots Magazine*

The Measby Murder Enquiry

"This cozy will keep you guessing until the last page. A very fast story with a very unique main character in Ivy. Full of wit, animosity and friendships to keep."

—*Once Upon a Romance*

"A pleasant read, evoking Saint Mary Mead and Miss Marple with its atmosphere of surface calm and hidden demons. It's a solid book, cleverly plotted and tightly structured, with all the makings of a perennial favorite."

—*Curled Up with a Good Book*

The Hangman's Row Enquiry

"A delightful spin-off."   —*Genre Go Round Reviews*

"Full of wit, venom and bonding between new friends."

—*The Romance Readers Connection*

"Purser's Ivy Beasley is a truly unique character, a kind of cross between Jessica Fletcher, Miss Marple and Mrs. Slocum from *Are You Being Served?*—just a delightful, eccentric old darling that readers are sure to embrace. Pair this with Purser's charming storytelling technique, and you have a fast-paced tale that will keep readers guessing to the very end."

—*Fresh Fiction*

Titles by Ann Purser

Lois Meade Mysteries

MURDER ON MONDAY
TERROR ON TUESDAY
WEEPING ON WEDNESDAY
THEFT ON THURSDAY
FEAR ON FRIDAY
SECRETS ON SATURDAY
SORROW ON SUNDAY
WARNING AT ONE
TRAGEDY AT TWO
THREATS AT THREE
FOUL PLAY AT FOUR
FOUND GUILTY AT FIVE
SCANDAL AT SIX

Ivy Beasley Mysteries

THE HANGMAN'S ROW ENQUIRY
THE MEASBY MURDER ENQUIRY
THE WILD WOOD ENQUIRY
THE SLEEPING SALESMAN ENQUIRY
THE BLACKWOODS FARM ENQUIRY

Blackwoods Farm
Enquiry

ANN PURSER

BERKLEY PRIME CRIME, NEW YORK

THE BERKLEY PUBLISHING GROUP
Published by the Penguin Group
Penguin Group (USA) LLC
375 Hudson Street, New York, New York 10014

USA • Canada • UK • Ireland • Australia • New Zealand • India • South Africa • China

penguin.com

A Penguin Random House Company

THE BLACKWOODS FARM ENQUIRY

A Berkley Prime Crime Book / published by arrangement with the author

Berkley Prime Crime Books are published by The Berkley Publishing Group.
BERKLEY® PRIME CRIME and the PRIME CRIME logo are trademarks of
Penguin Group (USA) LLC.

For information, address: The Berkley Publishing Group,
a division of Penguin Group (USA) LLC,
375 Hudson Street, New York, New York 10014.

ISBN: 978-0-425-26181-1

PUBLISHING HISTORY
Berkley Prime Crime mass-market edition / April 2014

PRINTED IN THE UNITED STATES OF AMERICA

10 9 8 7 6 5 4 3 2 1

Cover illustration by Griesbach/Martucci.
Cover design by George Long.

One

"IF ANYONE ASKED me, I would say you are lucky to be alive!" Ivy Beasley, a fierce expression on her face, was facing her fiancé across a small table in the summerhouse at Springfields Residential Home in Barrington, a small village in the county of Suffolk.

"Of course, Ivy my love," said Roy Goodman, "but I was reminded by the church bells that but for my accidental confrontation with a combine harvester in the middle of the road, you and I would now be man and wife, and enjoying marital delights as a result."

The couple's wedding date had been postponed yet again, this time because of Roy's accident. He had been driving his trundle, a custom-built silver and black stream-lined version of the humble shopping scooter. He had designed it himself and was extremely proud of it. In this instance, he was on the road instead of the pavement, and amidst squeals of brakes and yells from passers-by, he had managed to steer hard left, but the huge machine had caught his rear wheel and sent him spinning.

He had broken a bone in his wrist, and although he was otherwise only shocked, bruised and shaken, Ivy had insisted on once more postponing the wedding. She had said at the time that if anyone had asked her, she would say an autumn wedding was much to be preferred.

Now, in early-summer sunshine, she and Roy were sitting out in the garden, drinking tea and eating cream puffs, licking their fingers clean and brushing the pastry crumbs onto the ground, where tame sparrows came to pick them up.

To the casual visitor, these two would seem to be a contented couple, spending their investments on a place of comfort and security to end their days. The proposed wedding was unusual in Springfields, but had yet to happen, and Mrs. Spurling, the manager, privately hoped it would stay that way.

Of course, the casual visitor would be wrong. Ivy and Roy were the senior partners in an enquiry agency that had brought them face-to-face with swindlers, thieves and even murderers. They had two further partners: Deirdre Bloxham, Ivy's much younger cousin, and Augustus Halfhide, a mysterious character, who was said to be ex-MI5, or something similar. He was a tenant of the village squire, and was unrelentingly and amorously pursued by his neighbour, Miriam Blake.

"They should be here soon," said Ivy, scooping up vestiges of cream from the plate with one knobbly finger. "We should perhaps order more tea. The new assignment will take a fair while to explain."

"They might even decide not to go along with it," said Roy gloomily. He was hoping this would not be the case, as Ivy was bored, and only a new case to tackle would curb her unfortunate habit of attempting to reorganise Springfields and everything in it.

"Hi, you two!" called Deirdre, appearing in the garden. She was a good-looking woman, very trim and well cared for, and behind her came Gus Halfhide, tall and gangling and with unruly sandy hair.

"Sit down, Deirdre," ordered Ivy. "And Gus, as you have a way with the girls in the kitchen, please go and order more tea and puffs."

"Puffs?" said Deirdre.

"Cream puffs," said Roy. "Ivy's favourites, and freshly made."

Gus walked off to give the order, and Deirdre settled herself comfortably out of the strong sunlight. She had fair skin, and burned an unattractive scarlet if too long unprotected. Her late husband, Bert Bloxham, had loved her smooth, delicate complexion, and had kept a close eye on her in the summer. But poor Bert had died some time ago, leaving Deirdre, after a suitable period of mourning, a rich and merry widow. Bert had made his fortune in the motor trade, owning a string of luxury car showrooms around the county, and Deirdre still kept an eye on the business.

"So what's this new assignment?" she said.

"Better wait until Gus gets back," Roy said, and Ivy nodded. "Too hot to explain it all twice," she added.

Then Gus arrived back, saying Katya would be bringing fresh supplies, and a piece of news. "I couldn't tempt her to tell me first, but she should be out in a few minutes."

"I hope it's not bad news," Ivy said. "We've had enough of that lately. I'm not uncrossing my fingers until Roy and me are safely wed."

Deirdre saw Katya approaching with a loaded tray, and jumped up ready to help. The care assistant, originally from Poland, had married a young law student a few months ago, and Deirdre reckoned she could spot significant signs of a pregnancy already on the way.

After all were served, Ivy took a sip of hot tea, and said, "So what's this news, Katya dear?"

The girl blushed a furious red, and said that in due time

there would be a new resident at Springfields. She was indeed expecting a baby, and Mrs. Spurling had kindly agreed that she could stay on in the home, restricting herself to light duties until the baby was old enough to go to a nursery.

So, the cast of characters was assembled. Ivy, Roy, Deirdre and Gus, all of Enquire Within; then Mrs. Spurling and her assistant, Miss Pinkney, and Katya, staff of Springfields; and last but not least, the late Bert Bloxham. He was now reduced to a photograph on Deirdre's beautiful grand piano, but was still a voice in her head, saving her from any second marital moves she might consider.

THE SUN HAD now moved round, shading the interior of the summerhouse, and in the cool of early evening Ivy and Roy began to explain Enquire Within's latest suggested assignment.

"We haven't agreed to take it on yet," said Roy, and Ivy added that they had told the woman they would have to consult their partners first.

"Woman?" said Gus, brightening, "what woman?"

"Relax, old boy," said Roy with a smile. "This one appears old, raggedy and lives in a house that has not seen a lick of paint or even repairs to its tiled roof for about two hundred years."

"And that goes for the woman, much the same," said Ivy, leaning back in her chair and folding her hands in her lap.

"Does she have a name?" asked Deirdre. "And where does she live?"

"Mrs. Winchen Blatch, and she lives here in Barrington. Twenty-five years a widow. Husband killed in a farming accident," replied Ivy. "The last house on Manor Road. It stands by itself in what was probably at one time a large garden. She is reputed to be wealthy, sleeping on a pile of notes under the mattress. You know, the usual unreliable gossip."

"And that's on the road before you come to the Manor House itself?" said Gus, who seldom ventured beyond the roadside spinney, where he walked his little grey whippet.

"That's her," said Ivy. "She turned up here a couple of days ago, and you could smell her a mile off. Mrs. Spurling was not pleased. But she insisted on seeing me and Roy, so we were banished to that nasty little conference room that's never used and has its own smell of damp and disuse."

"I'll carry on, shall I, dearest?" Roy said, and received the nod of assent. "She'd got it all worked out, and told us the most dramatic series of events, ending up with a threat to force her to commit suicide. She began with a lodger she had sheltered about twenty years ago. A young man named Sturridge, well spoken and neatly dressed, had come to her door one winter afternoon, and asked if she had a spare room for rent. She had thought quickly, and decided that it would be company for her and, anyway, she could use the extra cash. She said that contrary to rumour, she was not at all well off, managing on her old-age pension. The young man had apparently proved to be a charming lodger, careful not to impose on her privacy, but ready for conversation if she wished it."

"So what went wrong?" said Deirdre, her interest caught.

"They became very friendly, and were seen out and about together. She was said to look years younger, smartened up and with new clothes. Then he left suddenly, without giving notice, with rent paid up to date, but jewellery missing. The culprit had done a runner, and people were asked to keep an eye open for him. She has heard no more from him since, and relapsed into premature old age."

"Does this go on for much longer? There's not much of a point so far," said Gus.

"Patience, Augustus," chided Ivy. "The details are important."

"Mrs. Blatch felt sorry, having grown fond of the young man, and had not forgotten him. She had never seen him again, but only six weeks ago, she was awoken in the middle of the night by a voice calling her name. It came from outside in the garden, and she rushed to the window. But there was nobody there, and she decided she had been dreaming."

"Which she undoubtedly was, plus wishful thinking," said Gus. It was usually Ivy who spun out a story, but now it was Roy who seemed anxious to get everything right.

"Then the next night the same," he continued. "At exactly the same time, midnight. She knew it was that, as she heard the church bell. This time she ran downstairs and opened the front door. Nobody there. But she felt a rush of cold air pass her before she closed the door, and a faint shadow disappeared down the passage to the kitchen."

"Did she follow it?" Deirdre said, now sitting on the edge of her chair.

"Yes, and found nothing. But as she was about to leave, a voice said her name, and told her not to be afraid. She stopped and listened, and the voice, which she half expected to be that of her lodger, she recognised as her late husband's. He said that she was the only person he missed, and he wanted her to come with him to a far better place."

"Then she woke up?" said Gus.

"Oh, blimey!" said Deirdre, frowning at him. "So what had she got to do?"

"Kill herself," said Ivy bluntly. "And he told her how."

Two

GUS HALFHIDE AWOKE next morning from a dream in which Miriam Blake, his predatory neighbour in Hangman's Row, had come to him in the middle of the night and offered him her lottery win of two million pounds if he would take her, clad in purest white, to the altar in Barrington Church.

He staggered out of bed, dislodging his whippet, Whippy, and went downstairs to make a bracing cup of tea. Still in his pyjamas, the lack of buttons exposing his manly chest, he was about to retreat when a tap at his back door revealed Miriam, chiding him for getting up late, and reminding him of this morning's plan.

"Have you forgotten, Gus?" she said, with a long-suffering smile. "We were going to have a look at the Manor this morning. It's up for sale again, and I made an appointment with the agents for us to view."

Gus did not remember being included in this appointment, but agreed to meet her in half an hour's time outside in the Row. A couple of minutes later, he remembered that the Manor was a few hundred yards past the farm belonging to their latest client, Mrs. Blatch. He was not entirely convinced that there was a case to be investigated there. A middle-aged woman in her circumstances could well be suffering from all kinds of delusions. Nevertheless, he told himself, it would be useful to have a look at the house, and perhaps even see her working in her garden.

"Do they allow dogs to view the Manor?" Miriam asked sharply, as he came out to greet her.

"Of course they do. The Manor's empty, nobody living there, and, anyway, Whippy is fully housetrained."

"Mm, well, I suppose it will be all right. I was thinking of all those posh improvements the last people did. New parquet floors, and fresh paint everywhere."

"Odd that, wasn't it? I don't think they ever moved in, did they?"

Miriam, of course, knew the whole story. A couple had planned to live there, but the new wife had run off with another, and there was a divorce. "I call that really sad, don't you, Gus?" she said.

"Well, it happens," said Gus, unwilling to venture into another rerun of conversations he had had before with Miriam. He was a divorced man himself, and she was determined he should give matrimony another try.

They set off down the lane, and Whippy strained at the lead as they passed through a tunnel of trees. There were woods on either side for a quarter of a mile, and when they emerged in sight of Mrs. Winchen Blatch's house, Gus slowed down.

"Shall we dawdle here?" he said. "I am curious to know more about Mrs. Blatch. I heard her being discussed in the village shop yesterday. Seems she's a bit of a recluse?"

Miriam nodded. "Let's sit on that stile over there, and I'll tell you what I know. The Blatches were a farming family, and Ted Blatch used to climb over this stile to get to his herd of Jersey cows. Quite well known at the local agricultural shows, apparently. A handsome man in his youth. Won prizes for his cattle. His wife was left alone after he died, them having had no children. Most of the farmland was sold, and she stayed in the house. Had a sad love affair with a much younger man, so it's said, and that came to a sticky end."

Miriam could be relied on to supply such useful information, her own family having lived in the village for generations. Her father and grandfather had worked for the Roussels up at the Hall, and Miriam was said to have supplied certain services to the present squire.

"What do you mean, 'sticky end'?" Gus said.

"It was her lodger. They went out and about together a lot. I think they even talked to the vicar about dates, an' that. But the village noticed they hadn't seen him lately."

"Sad story," said Gus. "I expect she's a bit weird now, after shutting herself off for so long. Gets a bit mixed up in her memory, does she?"

"Goodness knows! I haven't spoken to her for years. I don't think she'd be of much interest to you, Augustus Halfhide!"

Gus did not answer. He now had a much clearer picture of Mrs. Blatch, and he changed the subject to the impending sale of the Manor House. "Looks like the estate agent is here already," he said. "Come on, then, let's go and have a look round."

The agent took one look at Gus, tall, shabby and austere looking, and Miriam, small, perky and undistinguished, and decided they were not worth much of his precious time. But then, he reflected, you couldn't always tell. Sometimes the shabby ones had money stashed away somewhere, whilst the ostensibly wealthy viewers who arrived in smart cars were deeply in debt and with nothing to sell.

After a quick tour round the ground floor and a cursory look at the many bedrooms on the two upper floors, Gus said that it had all been very interesting. But with the present owner having been determined to erase all traces of previous historical features, it would not be the house for him.

"Oh, I think it's lovely, Gus," trilled Miriam.

"Then I hope you've got the necessary loot hidden away somewhere," he answered, saying he must be off, as he had work to do.

THE AGENT GAVE them a barely polite good-bye, and then turned to look out for his next client, who was late. He had sounded keen on the phone, saying he was looking for a large house, with plenty of bedrooms, to set up a study centre. He hadn't said what his students would be studying, but that was of no concern to the agent. All he wanted was to make a sale. The old house, with its extensive grounds, stabling and servants' attic accommodation, had been on the market for some time and was something of a white elephant.

A large, shiny car pulled up in front of him, and a cheerful, round red face looked out.

"Hi, there! Good morning to you. Sorry I'm late. Traffic jams as usual. Still, you're here and I have plenty of time. Come on, Stephanie, let's do an inspection." This last was addressed to an attractive girl sitting next to him, introduced as his daughter.

Meanwhile, Gus and Miriam walked back into the village in a chilly silence. As far as Gus was concerned, it had been a waste of time, but Miriam could see herself as lady of the Manor, with children and their ponies, and she and Gus at the head of the family table.

"WHAT DID THAT cheery man say about his study centre?" Ivy asked Gus. He had given Ivy, Roy and Deirdre a short report on Miriam's revelations about Mrs. Blatch, and on their visit to the Manor House, and now he sat with his feet up on the small table in Springfield's summerhouse.

"That's all he said. Needed a big house et cetera for a study centre. Or so Miriam said. She was, as usual, eavesdropping when she went back to find a handkerchief she'd supposedly dropped."

"Sounds fishy to me," said Deirdre, sitting well out of the bright sun. Good weather was forecast to last for another week or so, and she was tired of skulking in shady corners.

"Our Miriam was quite excited, but I thought it best to keep mum in case she signed me up for something."

"Very wise," Ivy said. "Miriam Blake must be taken with a pinch of salt. If you ask me, I think the whole place should be knocked down, and a nice little development of affordable houses put up there instead."

This effectively halted the conversation for a minute or two, and then Gus returned to the fray. "It's a strange old place, that Manor House," he said. "I suppose the planning people have had their say. But inside, it's as if it was newly built. Quite a shock, actually, with its bleached wood and cheap brassy fixtures everywhere. There's even a telly let into the wall! In my opinion, the man who did all of that should be held in a secure place where he can't do any more mischief."

Deirdre laughed, and said she was thinking of having one of those giant telly screens fixed in her house. "Anyway, I must be off," she added. "Good hairstylists are scarce, so I don't want to offend mine."

"In my day," said Ivy primly, "the shopkeeper's wife used to cut our hair with blunt scissors from her kitchen drawer. Three shillings, she charged, and sixpence extra for a cup of stewed tea."

Three

SEVERAL WEEKS LATER, Katya, now with a decidedly rounded stomach, came into the breakfast room at Springfields, and approached Ivy and Roy with a big smile. "We saw people yesterday up at the Manor House with huge removal vans and big boxes—what do you call them? Full of all kinds of things."

"Tea chests, we call them," said Ivy. "I suppose they originally held tea, but now are used for packing crockery and glass, and all that stuff." Ivy, usually short on patience, had always been very kind and gentle with Katya, who had arrived at Springfields as a young girl with only a smattering of English.

In spite of a willingness to take on the Blatch case, Enquire Within had met with a sudden change of heart from Mrs. Eleanor Blatch. She had cancelled the investigation, leaving them to think of nothing very much but the new lease of life for the Manor House. Villagers had monitored several weeks of builders, electricians and decorators working at the Manor House, and Gus reported that

Miriam had said she couldn't imagine what they were doing, as she remembered it as being already perfect.

James at the shop had been able to answer that one. "He's converting the outbuildings into self-contained flatlets. The place will accommodate around fifteen or twenty students by the time it's finished," he had said to Gus.

Now Ivy shrugged. She had eaten an extra piece of toast this morning, and asked for fresh tea to wash it down. "So I suppose the village will be swamped with foreigners wanting to learn English? Still, I suppose it will be good for the shop. I hope James has got in a good supply of notebooks and pencils."

Katya laughed. "Don't forget I am a foreigner, trying to learn English," she reminded them. "And nowadays, students have iPads and electronic notebooks."

"I think you have lost us there," said Roy. "What else have you heard?"

"Well, having new people in the Manor House seems to have given Mrs. Blatch a new lease of life. She has been seen looking quite clean and tidy, working in her front garden, where she gets a good view of the Manor."

Katya returned to the kitchen, and Roy and Ivy were quiet for a minute or two. Then Ivy cleared her throat. "Um, Roy," she said. "I've been thinking."

"Oh dear," said Roy, with mock concern. "What has my beloved cooked up for us now?"

"Nothing for you, or Deirdre or Gus. This would be for me. I have decided that when the Manor House study centre gets going, I am going to take a course. I shan't need to stay overnight, as it is near enough for me to attend lectures and so on daily. Although I had an excellent education at my village school in Round Ringford, I do sometimes feel the need for some kind of further studies."

"Ivy! This is really out of the question! You have quite enough to do with planning our wedding, and Enquire Within, and, anyway, I can't see Mrs. Spurling agreeing to it. No, don't you think you might take up tapestry work instead? Or watercolour painting with that artist woman who comes here on Fridays?"

Ivy shook her head vigorously. "I mean real education," she said.

"Such as what, dearest?"

"Oh, I don't know. I shall decide when they put out their prospectus. As for Mrs. Spurling, she can only threaten me with expulsion, and there aren't that many queuing up to pay exorbitant fees to be cared for in this place. Our wedding, of course, takes precedence over everything else, but all the plans were made previously, and will be perfectly fine for our next date."

"Oh dear," repeated Roy. "As my late mother used to say, I don't know, I'm sure."

DEIRDRE AND GUS, arriving for a meeting of Enquire Within, found Ivy and Roy in the lounge, sitting by an open window, with long faces and clearly not speaking.

"Hi, you two!" said Deirdre, pulling up a chair and sitting between them. "What's happened? Is Tiddles missing again?"

Ivy's cat had a habit of vanishing for days on end, and then appearing with a dead, mouldering rat in its mouth.

Roy shook his head. He turned to Gus, who was still standing, nonplussed. "Good day, lad," he said. "Do sit down. It's very pleasantly cool today, and I saw starlings doing their amazing swooping flight out of my window this morning. Autumnal sight, do you think?"

Ivy took a deep breath. "Don't talk such rubbish, Roy," she said. "It's nearly autumn. Now, who's going to take the chair?"

"Shouldn't we go up to your room, Ivy? The lounge seems full of curious old parties today." Deirdre was a volunteer worker for social services, and often visited elderly disabled people in their homes. But in Springfields, the atmosphere was different. She always felt like an interloper, here under false pretences.

"Oh, very well," said Ivy, pushing herself up from her chair. "Come along, Roy, here's your stick."

WHEN THEY WERE all comfortable, Deirdre said she would take the chair for once, and begin with the first item on the agenda, what on earth was the matter with Ivy and Roy? They couldn't possibly discuss anything until that was settled.

Ivy looked at Roy. He nodded wearily. "Right," she said. "It is not a matter of huge importance, and really it's something to do with only me and Roy. But as you put it, Deirdre, we need to settle it. As you know, the Manor House will be a study centre, and I have decided to take up a course. On what, I don't know yet. When the prospectus is printed, I shall select something that interests me. I shall be a day student, obviously."

"And the problem?" said Gus.

"Roy does not approve," said Ivy baldly. She sat back in her chair and sniffed. "Now, Roy's side of the question, please."

But Roy shook his head. "I don't know what to think," he said. "I need help," he added, with the ghost of a smile. "I have always said that my Ivy is full of surprises, and I suppose this is the latest."

Deirdre took advantage of Roy's smile, and asked when Ivy was thinking of taking this big step.

Gus now chipped in with a sensible suggestion. "Terms for this sort of thing usually start in the autumn, don't they? That would really clash with your wedding, Ivy. Unless you're thinking of postponing it again?"

Red rags to bulls were nothing to the fierce reaction launched by Ivy. The colour rose in her usually pale face,

and she said loudly that she had in no way been responsible
for challenges to their banns, or accidents involving
combine harvesters. She was quite ready, and, indeed,
looking forward to their wedding day and honeymoon,
and intended to see what the Manor House college
suggested.

"If it means breaking off studies for two or three weeks,
then so be it. Does that answer your question, Augustus?"

Gus, completely flattened, did not reply, but turned
hopefully to Deirdre, who smiled consolingly at him. "I
think you'll find that these places do short courses all the
year round, so you'll be able to pick and choose, Ivy. I
think it's a nice idea. I might come along with you, just for
fun," she said.

"So what about Enquire Within?" said Gus, finding his
voice. "Do we go into abeyance, or continue to work
together?"

"Of course we shall continue. And we can do that right
now, if Deirdre will get us on to item two on the agenda,"
said Ivy.

Roy was quiet, digesting what Ivy had said. The discussion had changed his view somewhat, and he could now
see that her plan was more in the nature of a hobby than
a full-blown degree course. It could be quite enjoyable,
and he now fully intended to support her, recognising that
she wanted to do this alone. Something to do with being
tied into a couple with him? Women! Perhaps he should
have a chat with Gus privately. Although divorced, the lad
had always had considerable insight into the workings of
the female mind. But now, he told himself, we must put it
to one side and get back to business.

"Where are we at with Mrs. Blatch?" asked Gus. "She
cancelled our investigation, I know, but rumour hath it that
strange lights have been seen there in the middle of the
night. Has she shown any further anxiety about the mystery

of her night visitor? There's been a lull in activity, what with Deirdre's holidays and Springfields outings. Do you think some sort of contact would be a good idea?"

"Funnily enough," said Deirdre, "I have been asked to visit. I have met her once or twice, and she asked me in to see her improvements. Nice lady, I reckon. Apparently she went into the office the other day, and asked for help with grants. She wants to do up her house, but can't afford it. So they said. Anyway, I said I'd look in again, as I sort of know her, and make a report."

"Excellent!" said Roy, relieved that the air had cleared at last. "So you can tell us next week how you got on. She might well mention her earlier dealings with us."

"We really need something more challenging," Ivy said. "Mrs. Blatch has probably forgotten all about her phantom lover."

"Something will come up," said Deirdre comfortably. "It always does."

LATER THAT NIGHT, in the dark, silent house belonging to Mrs. Winchen Blatch, she sat up in bed suddenly, sweating with fear. The same shadow was materialising into a distinct shape. Ted! She held the bedclothes up against her chest, and waited for him to speak.

"Eleanor, my angel," he said. "You are looking as beautiful as ever. I have come for you, as promised. Come to me, my love, it is time to leave."

At this point, Eleanor Blatch made a near fatal move. She lowered the bedclothes, still half asleep, and began to laugh. "For God's sake, Ted!" she said. "You sound like a really bad B movie! Time to leave, indeed! It's time you left, right now. You've been gone these twenty-five years. And don't come back."

Through the darkness of sleep she saw a man in a dark

overcoat move menacingly towards her. Sitting up sharply, she put up her arm to defend herself, but failed, falling heavily to the floor and catching her head on the metal frame of the bed. As she began to lose consciousness, she thought she saw Ted, waiting with arms outstretched.

Four

IVY AND ROY were taking a turn to the shop to buy chocolates for her and postcards for him. He had decided to remind the most important of their friends of the wedding date, and Ivy had agreed. There had been such confusion over cancellations and refixing dates, and this time they were determined there would be no further hitches.

They emerged from the shop into a beautiful late-summer day, with a clear blue sky and everywhere still looking green and welcoming. There were fears lately that a stand of fine mature ash trees might be victim to the latest virus arrived from abroad, but so far they showed no warning signs.

"Morning, you two!" said Deirdre, arriving in her large, gleaming car to the front of the shop. "Lovely day! I'm just off to town to a meeting, but first I mean to drop in on Mrs. Blatch for a preliminary talk. All to do with social services, of course! Shall I call in this afternoon and report?"

Roy said that they were sure to be in. This morning's walk would stand them in good stead for the rest of the day, and they would be pleased to welcome her. Ivy said that around four o'clock would be fine. "Then you'll be in time for tea," she added. "Your usual time."

Deirdre grinned. "Thanks, cousin dear," she said, and drove on.

She had looked up the records of Mrs. Winchen Blatch, and found that her house had a name, dating from when it was a farm. Blackwoods, it had been called, and when she pulled up outside the shabby-looking house, she noticed the nameplate still there, hanging on a nail by the front door. She drove slowly through the farm entrance, its gate permanently open on rusting hinges, and stopped by the back door. A sheepdog, chained up to a kennel, emerged, barking spasmodically.

She could see that the dog was a poor old thing, and, squaring her shoulders, she knocked firmly on the door. She noticed it had been freshly painted, and felt more cheerful. At least the old girl was doing her best to smarten things up.

There was no reply to a series of knockings, and Deirdre frowned. She knew that Mrs. Blatch seldom went out. Maybe she was up the yard dealing with her chickens. She heard a shrill cockcrow, followed by a chorus of cluckings, and smiled. Eggs, too. So she was definitely looking after herself. She walked towards the gate out of the yard into the Home Close, and apart from a lame ewe snoozing in the sun, there was no sign of life.

Then she saw a side door, which had perhaps been an entry into the dairy. She pushed at it, and after creaking and cracking, it gave way and she was inside. Perhaps it had been a dairy once, but now it had declined into a junk room, where things not ready to be thrown away had been dumped, awaiting their fate.

After a quick look around, she noticed another latched door, and opened it, once more pushing against ages of swollen wood and grime. She found herself in the kitchen, and was embarrassed. Supposing Mrs. Blatch was deaf, and would be really shocked to find a strange woman in her kitchen? She called again, softly at first, and then loudly, from the foot of the stairs.

What was that? A distinct sound had come from upstairs. She steeled herself to what she might find, and started up towards the main bedroom where she finally found Mrs. Blatch.

Deirdre was a brave woman, and had seen many things in her volunteering, but this was something new. She knelt down beside Eleanor, adjusting her nightdress in an automatic attempt to make her decent. Then she touched her face, which was spattered with dried blood and vicious-looking bruises. Her grey hair was matted, and an evil wound on the back of her head still oozed.

But she was breathing. Not much, thought Deirdre, but faint breaths still came in and out, steaming up the handbag mirror held in front of her mouth.

Deirdre straightened up, took out her mobile and dialled the emergency services. Address? Now, she knew it a moment ago. Blackwoods Farm! That was it. Outside Barrington, on the way to the Manor House. She put her bag to one side, and began on a series of first-aid measures learned long ago.

When she had covered the poor woman, now definitely breathing better, with an old feather eiderdown, she sat back on her heels and thought. Before the ambulance could arrive, she would need help, she decided. Then she was honest with herself, and acknowledged that in fact she needed company, somebody to sit with her in this gloomy, crumbling old house with a half-dead body perhaps expiring on the floor in front of her.

She once more took out her mobile, and called Gus.

"THANK GOD YOU were at home," Deirdre said, taking Gus's hand. He was puffing, having run all the way.

"And now I'm here, you can relax and not worry. I've seen worse, Deirdre love, and the ambulance will be here in a couple of minutes. Did you alert the police as well? No? I'll see to that. I'm not sure, but I reckon she caught her head on the bed. It could have been an attack of some kind, but I doubt it. We'll know more when the medics have taken a look at her. You all right now? I shoved some instant coffee in this flask. Disgusting stuff, but it might help."

He released her, kissing her cheek and giving her a squeeze.

"You're a blessing," she said. She had a deep swig of the coffee, and agreed that it was disgusting, but hot and sweet. She drained the flask, and then said she could hear the ambulance siren, so one of them should be outside to meet it.

"Mrs. Blatch is not going anywhere by herself," she said, and burst into tears of relief and sadness.

Gus mopped her face with a reasonably clean handkerchief, and then went to open the door.

Once the paramedics had seen Mrs. Blatch, done some preliminary tests and wrapped her in clean blankets, they brought in a stretcher and loaded her straight into the waiting ambulance. By this time the police had arrived, and were working smoothly with the medical men. It seemed only a couple of minutes before the siren was on again, and the ambulance disappeared into the sunlit village.

"Now, Missus, er . . . Shall we sit down for a short while, and you can tell us how you came to find Mrs. Blatch in such a sorry state?" The policeman led them into the kitchen, and they found rickety chairs to sit on.

"First of all, Constable, our names are Augustus Halfhide and Deirdre Bloxham."

"Of course! Knew I recognised you, Mrs. Bloxham! Bloxham Car Showrooms, isn't it? I buy all my cars for private use there. I remember your husband well. Such a nice chap. Bert, wasn't it?"

Deirdre nodded, and said she still missed her Bert, but kept a firm hand on the business in the way he would have wanted. "I'll start at the beginning, shall I?

"I had made an appointment with Eleanor, as from social services, but after failing to get her to open up, I felt a bit uneasy and decided to push my way in. Finally I found her like she is now, and I did all I could for the poor thing," she said. "Then I rang Mr. Halfhide to come and give me support. I was feeling really wobbly!"

"And I came here as soon as I could when Mrs. Bloxham called me for help," said Gus.

After giving as detailed an account as she could summon up, Deirdre watched as the police finally locked up the house and left, saying they might need to talk to them again.

"So what now, Mrs. Bloxham?" said Gus, as they stood outside, watching the police car disappear round the corner.

"I still feel a bit unsteady," she said. "Don't think me silly, will you, but I'd really like to see Ivy and Roy. They make me feel safe, and we could tell them all about it. Do you mind?"

"I'll ring straight away and see if they're back in Springfields. Then we'll call, and get some good sound sense from our venerable colleagues."

"Should we have told the police about Mrs. Blatch's approach to Enquire Within?"

"Not yet. There'll be time for that. Come on, gel, let's be going. Do you want me to drive the limo?"

Deirdre nodded and sniffed. "Thanks for everything, and I'm sorry if I'm sometimes nasty to you. You're a love."

Five

"WHAT DID GUS say, then? Why so urgently coming to see us? We were expecting Deirdre at four o'clock this afternoon, anyway." Ivy frowned. Deirdre could be a bit of a drama queen at times. She shrugged. "I suppose it's something to do with the squire, and him and Gus being sworn enemies, fighting for her favours."

Roy chuckled. "No, dearest. Gus is with her, and he said it's to do with Mrs. Winchen Blatch. We shall soon know. I can see them in reception right now. La Spurling is no doubt warning them that lunch is imminent."

Katya was hovering, welcoming them, and brought up two chairs for them. She said she was sure that Mrs. Spurling would be pleased if they would stay for lunch. Anya had cooked chicken in a new way, and there was plenty for everyone.

"Thanks a lot, Katya," said Gus. "Very kind, I'm sure. But we shan't be staying long, and Mrs. Bloxham has a casserole in the oven, awaiting us."

Deirdre's eyes widened. There was no such thing, but she could see Mrs. Spurling's angry face looking at them through the glass partition, and realised Gus was being his usual diplomatic self.

"Another time, maybe, Katya," she said.

"WHAT HAVE YOU two been up to?" asked Ivy. She was aware that curious faces were turned towards them, and frowned. "Some people," she said loudly, "cannot mind their own business. Naming no names, of course," she added. "Now, gel, what's this all about?"

For the moment, this did the trick, and Gus and Deirdre spilled out details of the morning's tragedy.

"I really thought she had snuffed it," Deirdre said. "Though thank God she *was* alive when I found her, and the medics said they thought she had a good chance." As so often in Ivy's presence, Deirdre felt the weight of the morning's events lifting from her.

"And from the look of her," Gus said, "her injuries could well have come from falling out of bed. There wasn't much flesh on her bones, and it occurred to me that she probably wasn't eating properly. Almost starving herself. That can bring on hallucinations, can't it? Or maybe she was having bad dreams, and only half woke up." He added that perhaps when she was able, they could have a gentle talk with her.

"Deirdre would be the best person," he said. "She has a way with old people."

"So I've noticed," said Ivy. Then, realising that sounded a bit sharp, she smiled at Deirdre, and asked if she was feeling better. "It's soon our lunchtime, so why don't we leave it there," she continued. "You can come along and have tea as planned this afternoon, and we'll discuss the whole thing. Are you driving Deirdre home, Augustus?"

"Yes, he is," said Deirdre. "I do like to see a man at the wheel."

ALL THOUGHTS ABOUT further education had been erased from Ivy's mind by the sudden drama of Mrs. Blatch's fall. But now that Gus and Deirdre had left, she returned to the subject that she and Roy had been discussing.

"As I was saying, Roy, I rather fancy this course on creative writing."

The new Manor House College prospectus had been newly delivered to Springfields by hand, and Ivy had already been leafing through to see what she fancied.

"Why, dearest? Are you planning on writing a novel?" Roy was trying hard to be cooperative and encouraging, but for the life of him could not see the point of Ivy struggling over a number of unsuitable courses. They had between them ruled out Advanced Mathematics and Physical Geography. Ivy had dismissed out of hand Cookery for Healthy Eating and Knitting for Nimble Fingers, but had lingered over Creative Writing.

"I've had interesting times, dear," she said, "and I've often thought of writing my memoirs. 'Memoirs of a Useful Life,' I think. How do you like that?"

"Brilliant! And you've done the hardest part already. Found a title, and a good one. But do you really need to go on a writing course? Memoirs are so often boring, unless they are truly written in the subject's own voice. I reckon creative writing courses are a bit like art schools. They iron out talent into something ordinary."

"And boring? I expect you're right, Roy. I only fancied doing something outside Springfields, and this appealed."

"Of course, my love. Why don't we get more details, and talk some more about it. Whatever you decide, I shall be right behind you."

Roy smiled. He decided to leave it there. There could be no harm in it, and on second thoughts he could see that no amount of lectures and teaching could render Ivy's voice flat and ordinary.

AT FOUR O'CLOCK exactly, Gus and Deirdre returned to Springfields, and were ushered up to Ivy's room by Mrs. Spurling. "I will not have Mr. Goodman's afternoon nap in his room interrupted," she said sternly. "I have suggested to Miss Beasley that she wait until he taps at her door."

Gus raised his eyebrows, but said nothing. Mrs. Spurling herself tapped on Ivy's door, and it was opened by a sprightly Roy Goodman, beaming at her.

"Here we are then, Mrs. Spurling," he said politely. "We shall be fine up here, shan't we, Ivy dearest? And Katya has kindly brought up tea up for all of us. Come along in, Gus and Deirdre."

He opened the door wide enough to let them in one at a time, and then firmly shut out a red-faced Mrs. Spurling. The furious manager was forced to retreat down the stairs and into her office, where her assistant attempted to cool her down.

"Are we all settled?" Ivy handed round small fairy cakes, and leaned back in her chair. "Why don't you tell us again from the beginning, Deirdre?" she said.

Deirdre once more explained how she had gained entry into the Blackwoods farmhouse through the dairy, and found Mrs. Blatch on the floor of her bedroom, bruised and bloody. "There was a sharp corner on the bedside table, where she could have caught her head, and the metal frame of the bedstead stuck out from underneath the mattress. She could have bounced against that as well, I suspect. I suppose it could have been an intruder, but nothing seemed out of place in the room. I had a look around to see if I could see a weapon an attacker could have used.

But I was much more anxious to keep her breathing until the medics came."

"Did you look under the bed?" said Ivy.

"No, afraid not. She was stretched out right in front of it, and I didn't like to pull her about. But I expect the police did all of that."

Gus took over, and explained how he joined Deirdre, and they waited for the ambulance. "Deirdre was marvellous," he said. "There's no doubt Mrs. Blatch was on her way out. I reckon Deirdre saved her life. And that could be that, if it weren't for the fact that she had told us about the night visitor, and was scared of another ghostly manifestation from husband Ted."

"Ted? Yes, and then there was the other man in her life: the lodger, who ran off with her treasures. I think we need to know a lot more about him. See if we can find out what happened to him, and if he's still around here. We also want to know more about Mrs. Blatch's mental condition before she fell. Or if she *was* attacked. Any ideas how we do that?" Gus looked hopefully around at the others. As he expected, Deirdre was ready with a suggestion.

"Neighbours and friends are not going to be very useful, since she has been a recluse for so long. But in my offices in town there'll probably be some early records. Someone usually alerts us if there's signs. Curtains not drawn back in daytime, or newspapers being cancelled, doors not being opened to visitors, all that sort of thing. I have called in once or twice and had a chat with her. Not much of a chat! She seemed polite but confused."

"That's a job for you then, Deirdre love," said Gus. "Now, who's for ferreting about in the archives to find mention of a lodger? Ivy and Roy? You two are really good at that. Perhaps your faithful taxi driver might take you in to spend a couple of hours in the reference library?"

"Of course," said Ivy. "Roy, you can ring Elvis later and book the taxi for tomorrow. Ten o'clock sharp."

Elvis was the driver of a specially adapted vehicle which accommodated Roy's trundle and had been used by them on many occasions.

"Right," said Gus, "so that leaves me. Any suggestions?"

"Liaison officer with the local police," said Ivy. "One of us will most likely be questioned further by them, so we shall be ready for them. You'll be best for that, Augustus. Be very helpful, and say we'll keep them informed if anything turns up. Stress that we will let them know if we discover something really useful. Agreed?" she added, looking round the group.

All agreed, and Ivy said she could eat another fairy cake, and lifted the phone to order supplies from the kitchen. After that, she smiled beatifically, and held up the college prospectus.

"Changing the subject," she said, "Roy and I have decided what course I should do up at the Manor House College." She spoke as if it was already her alma mater. "Creative Writing. 'Memoirs of a Useful Life.'"

Six

ROY HAD SPENT the early part of the morning in Ivy's room, going through the Manor House prospectus once more. They had decided that she would start the course more or less straightaway, have a break for their wedding and honeymoon, and then restart when they returned to Springfields.

"Always supposing this fits in with the timetable of the course," said Roy now. He had been reading all the small print under Creative Writing, and had one question for Ivy. "Do you realise, beloved," he said, "what 'creative' actually means?"

"Of course I do," she said, in the immortal words of Harriet Morris. "It means that I shall be creating something. In my case, I shall create a memoir."

"It usually means making up something, creating a fictional story. Is your memoir going to be a fiction? Or the strict truth?" He was smiling now, and took her hand and kissed it. "I know you have a certain talent for embellishment, dearest," he added.

Ivy stared at him. Then she burst out laughing. "If you mean I'm a liar when it suits me, you're not far wrong. Anyway, it won't matter much either way. I'll just keep the reader guessing."

An answer for everything, my Ivy, decided Roy, and said that in that case, they should have a walk up to the college to see about signing on.

"It is a lovely day," Ivy said. "Elvis will be here soon to take us into town, but can we go up to the Manor after lunch, and be back for tea? I would like to take a quick look at Blackwoods Farm on the way. Perhaps we'd better go downstairs and fraternise with the grim lot in the lounge now, else we shall be getting another lecture from the old dragon."

ELVIS ARRIVED SOON after this, releasing them from a group of well-heeled old ladies whose favourite topic of conversation was the quality and variety of food in Springfields.

"Off we go!" said Ivy gaily, as Elvis made sure Roy was safely locked into the back of the taxi. "The central library, please, Elvis. We shall be there about an hour or so, and then we'll have a coffee in our usual café. Could you pick us up about twelve o'clock, to be back here in time for lunch?"

"Right you are, Miss Beasley, outside the café about twelve," he said. "I was thinking about you two this morning. Only a few weeks to go, isn't it?"

"You mean our wedding? Yes, it is really going ahead this time, and you are still free to be my best man, I hope?" Roy had asked Elvis some time ago, and the taxi man had been delighted to be included in what Katya persisted in calling the wedding of the century.

Once in town, Elvis drove slowly to the central library, where he stopped and unloaded his cargo. Roy was whisked away to the special entrance for wheelchairs, and Ivy followed him. Inside the reference library there were rows of desks with computers, and a respectful silence was broken by Ivy saying they would need a desk with two chairs and the computer switched off.

"No, no, dearest," Roy said. "We shall need the computer. An excellent research tool, so I am informed. Now, let's ask for the assistant, and then we can begin. This is rather exciting, isn't it, my dear?"

"I suppose so," she said. "I don't know how we're going to find out much. All we know is that he was a young lodger in Barrington, at the Blackwoods farmhouse, about twenty years ago, "

"And we know that Mrs. Winchen Blatch and he got on together very well, until he disappeared suddenly, never to be seen again."

Unfortunately, the library had not produced much in the way of information. The only brief reference they had of a young man in Barrington was one around that time who had won a Try Your Strength competition at a Barrington Church fete. And his name was Green.

Ivy was irritated by this. Forging ahead, she had looked forward to reporting their findings to Gus and Deirdre. "I think we should assume it might be the same one," she said firmly, as Roy shook his head in disagreement. "Newspapers are notorious for getting names wrong."

"Where do we go from here, then?" he said. "May I suggest our local café?"

By the time they agreed to pack up and go for a coffee, the sun had gone behind heavy clouds, and they emerged into a shower of heavy raindrops. Well provided with umbrellas, they reached the café, and were welcomed inside as old friends.

Roy covered his trundle, and went in first, manoeuvring with the help of his stick into their usual corner, while Ivy stood in the entrance porch, shaking her umbrella until it almost shrieked for mercy.

"Not really a good morning's work, eh?" she said, as they tucked into jam and cream scones, and large cups of milky coffee. "I hope we do better this afternoon. Do you think Mrs. Blatch will be home from hospital yet?"

"Good heavens, I shouldn't think so. Not if she is as damaged as Deirdre said. Poor lady will be in there for a while yet, I'm sure. Why, Ivy? Were you thinking of calling on her?" Roy was already thinking the afternoon's plan should be postponed until tomorrow. A quiet snooze with his feet up would be very nice. But Ivy did not feel in the least tired, and would not hear of postponement.

"I could go to the college on my own, if you like, now it's stopped raining," she said. "After all, it is my own decision to take this course. I don't expect you to nursemaid me along everywhere, you know."

Roy sat up very straight. "Ivy," he said firmly, "if you are going to a new place, meeting new people that neither of us has ever met and committing yourself to a course of action quite new to you, then I certainly wish to be there with you this afternoon. Is that clear?"

Ivy blinked. "Um, yes, dear. Quite clear. So shall we compromise, and ask Elvis to take us up to the college and wait until we're through, then drive us back?"

Roy nodded. He had quite surprised himself in his new role of husband-to-be. "Good suggestion," he said. "Here he is, drawing up outside. I'll settle the bill, and then we'll be off."

Elvis was pleased to be given another fare this afternoon, and agreed to pick them up about two thirty. "I expect you'll make an appointment, Miss Beasley?" he said.

"As soon as we get back to Springfields," Ivy said.

"You never say 'back home,' Miss Beasley," Elvis remarked.

"Home is where the heart is," said Ivy simply. "And my heart is with Roy. Wherever he is, my heart is there also. Ah, now we're back at Springfields. And there's dear Miss Pinkney looking out for us."

IN HIS NEWLY decorated study at Manor House College, the high master, as he called himself, picked up his phone.

"What name did you say? Beasley? *Miss* Beasley. Yes, I've got that. How can I help you?"

"I wish to talk to you about your creative writing course," said Ivy. "Will a quarter to three this afternoon suit you?"

"Um, ah, well, nice to talk to you, Miss Beasley. We do usually have a form of application for young students wishing to take the courses, which we require to be filled in before fixing an appointment."

"No need for that," said Ivy firmly. "I live down the road, at Springfields Residential Home. And I am not a young student, though my age is of no account. I shall see you, then, at a quarter to three this afternoon."

"AN *OLD* LADY, Pa? How old?"

"She said her age was of no account," answered the high master, chuckling. "Our first student, and she'll probably be about ninety in the shade! But what fun! Why don't you sit in on the interview, Steph? You can take notes."

"So how is she getting here?"

"Taxi," he said. "And her fiancé—yes, I did say fiancé— will be coming with her in his trundle."

"Trundle?" said Stephanie, his daughter and private secretary. "What the hell is that?"

Seven

IN THE DINING room, waiting to be served with baked sea bass and petit pois, Ivy and Roy smiled happily at each other.

"I'm quite excited, Roy," Ivy said. "Haven't done anything educational since the top class in the village school."

"And I bet you were top of the class," said Roy.

"Well, actually, I was. Most years. Until a new girl came. Elizabeth Jones, her name was. Now, how's that for a memory!"

"And did she supplant you?" Roy had a quick mental picture of Ivy as a child, plain and fierce, and felt sorry for Elizabeth Jones.

"Only once. After that, she came second, most years."

"Well, I'm sure you haven't lost the knack," he said, and then patted his stomach. "Goodness, Ivy," he said, "I'm really full. Shouldn't have had that second scone in town! Anyway, let's get ready for Elvis, and then sit and digest in the lounge. If, as is most unlikely, my eyes should close for a few seconds, please give me a nudge, won't you?"

* * *

ONCE MORE ABOARD Elvis's taxi, they rode slowly up to the Manor House College driveway. "I'll go to the front entrance and drop you off there, and then wait for you round the back," he said. "I'll be perfectly happy with my library book. It's due back tomorrow, so I'll get it finished."

"Oh, look, they must have seen us coming," said Ivy. "There's a cheery-looking character waiting at the door."

"Good afternoon, come in, come in," said the man, all smiles. "This way, please. We're completely accessible to wheelchairs. Met all the regulations, you know. Now, into here, please make yourselves comfortable and I'll order coffee."

"Tea, please," said Ivy, not at all overawed. "We're awash with coffee from this morning. Now, you sit there, Roy, and I'll take this chair, thank you, Mister, er . . ."

"Rubens. Peter Rubens. And you are Miss Beasley, and this gentleman is?"

"My fiancé, Mr. Roy Goodman," she said. "And did I get your name right, Mr. Rubens?"

"That's right, and this is my daughter and secretary, Stephanie. And this," he added, indicating a tall, pleasant-looking man coming through the door, "is my new tutor, Rickwood Smith, who will be in charge of your course. Some of your fellow students have already arrived, as we have an optional settling-in period, enabling them to get to know one another."

Rickwood Smith nodded across the room to Ivy, with a confident and heartwarming smile. "Very pleased to meet you, Miss Beasley," he said. "We shall be pioneers together."

"That remains to be seen, Mr. Smith," she said.

IN THE ODD surroundings of the restored Manor House, it was a little while before both Ivy and Roy could concentrate on what was being said, but then tea arrived, and they settled down. Rubens explained the form of the creative writing course, and said that if Miss Beasley would not object, she could start the course right away, with the students already arrived for a couple of weeks' bonding time, then take a break for her wedding and honeymoon, and a period of settling down as a married couple. After that, she could catch up easily enough. He looked across his desk at Stephanie and Rickwood Smith. "And if Miss Beasley likes us," he said, smiling broadly, "we might be lucky enough to receive wedding invitations!"

"Family and friends only," said Ivy coolly. "Now, how many others will be on the course? I am sure it takes more than two pioneers to make a wagon train?"

Mr. Rubens confirmed that a number of others had signed up. "Always a popular course," he said. "Once people get to know the college, I expect larger classes, of course. But by then, Miss Beasley, you will be an old hand!"

Roy cleared his throat. "Ivy dear," he said, "wouldn't it be more sensible if you waited six months, and then joined a new lot of students and took it through to the end?"

"No, of course not," Ivy replied. "I am quite happy to do the first half twice. I shall shine over the other students, don't you think, Mr. Smith? And thank you, Mr. Rubens, for not charging me twice for the first half."

"As you will be part of the very first course at Manor House College, I shall be happy to do that," he said nobly.

Ivy fired a number of other questions at both men, Rickwood Smith in particular giving very smooth and satisfactory answers. He then handed over a bunch of introductory leaflets. "Just general stuff, but useful for you to know our background," he said.

"It all sounds most interesting," she said, snapping shut her handbag. "I shall order the books on the reading list, and start practising my writing skills. Postcards from day trips to the seaside are all the writing I have done for many years. I might even treat myself to a new pen."

"I think you'll be using our computer, dearest," said Roy gently.

Ivy nodded sagely. "Of course," she said. "And my dear Roy will be my amanuensis."

"Never heard of him," said Roy, smiling widely. "Now, Ivy, we mustn't keep Elvis waiting. Are you ready, my dear? Don't forget we're calling on Mrs. Blatch to see if she's home."

"Ah yes," Ivy said. "Blackwoods Farm. Do you know it, Mr. Smith?"

Rickwood Smith nodded, but before he could answer, Rubens jumped in. "Not yet, Miss Beasley. We mean to seek out all our neighbours, you know, once we are up and running. And I must locate the vicar of this parish, in case any of our students require the services of the church."

"I doubt if many of them will be churchgoers, Pa," Stephanie said. "Take you and me, for a start. Haven't darkened the church doors since my christening! Still, leopards can change their spots. Isn't that right, Rickwood?"

"SO HOW WAS it, Miss Beasley? Are you going to be the next J. K. Rowling?"

Ivy chuckled. "It was quite interesting, Elvis," she said. "But I have no intention of writing anything more exciting than the memoirs of an old spinster. I shall enjoy digging up the old days, and Roy is going to help me."

"What was the college principal like? I've heard he's quite a jolly soul. I picked up one or two people who are going to study there, and they sounded optimistic. What's his name, anyway?"

"Rubens, and his daughter is Stephanie. She seemed a very pleasant girl."

"Very pleasant, I thought," said Roy enthusiastically.

"That's as may be," said Ivy. "We met the new tutor,

too, Rickwood Smith. But if anyone asked me, I would say it's early days to be getting too friendly with any of them."

"More importantly, Elvis," said Roy, "my Ivy has parted with a large cheque for the complete course. So we do hope it all comes up to scratch."

"I know you've always lived in villages, Miss Beasley," said Elvis. "And you know what? I was looking at my diary while you were in there, and I realised that in a few weeks I shall have to say Mrs. Goodman! Don't you forget about that, you two! It is going to be the best day of your lives."

They had arrived outside Blackwoods farmhouse, and Elvis brought the taxi to a halt.

"I think it would be best if you stay in here with Elvis," Ivy said to Roy. "I shan't be many minutes. In fact, even if she is there, she very likely won't answer the door."

Roy was reluctant to agree, saying it was a waste of time, as Mrs. Blatch was almost certainly still in hospital. But Ivy said that if she was not back in a quarter of an hour, Elvis should come in and find her. Roy watched her small, sturdy figure marching purposefully through the gate and saw her knock firmly on the front door. As he expected, nothing happened. Then she walked along the front of the house and disappeared round the corner.

"She's very determined, Mr. Goodman," Elvis said. "You'll be taking on a very strong-minded wife!"

"Ivy is the most wonderful woman I have ever met," Roy answered, "and I've had my days as a lusty young farmer, I can assure you." This prompted a series of romantic tales from Roy's youth, and Elvis was an attentive listener.

Meanwhile, Ivy had arrived at the back door, and knocked even more loudly. There was still no answer, but when she explored and found the dairy door, she discovered it to be unlocked. She pushed it wider, and stepped inside, just as Deirdre had done so recently. The door swung back on creaking hinges, and when she turned from surveying the piles of junk, she found she could not open it to rejoin Roy and Elvis.

It was stuck fast, and there was only one thing to do. She saw the door leading to the house, and saying a little prayer to the saint of locked-in elderly ladies, she pushed against it as hard as she could. It gave way reluctantly, but she was able to get into the kitchen. Mrs. Blatch could be having a rest upstairs, Ivy thought, and walked through into the hall.

"Coo-ee!" she shouted, but there was no reply. She shivered. It was damp-smelling and cold. And, she now decided, the house was empty. She made her way into the front room, where she found furniture covered in dust, and curtains hanging in shreds. She quickly rubbed a window-pane of glass clear with one of her gloves, and with some relief could see the taxi waiting for her.

"SO THERE I was, considerably the worse for wear, and with a girl on either arm, attempting to get up onto my old shire horse to take me home. Mind you," he continued, but Elvis interrupted him. "Excuse me, Mr. Goodman," he said urgently. "Isn't that your Ivy? I can see her face at the window. To the left of the door? Yes, it's definitely Miss Beasley."

"Get me out at once," snapped Roy. "Come on, jump to it!"

Elvis did not panic. "Um, no," he said. "I think it would be best if you wait here and I'll go and get her out. It'll be quicker if I go on my own."

Roy, feeling useless and unhappy, agreed, and watched as Elvis reached the front door, heaved at it with his shoulder a couple of times, and then disappeared inside.

In minutes, he was back, with Ivy holding his arm. He opened the taxi door for her and she climbed inside. "Roy?" she said. "Are you all right?"

"Of course I'm not!" he said. "What on earth have you been up to? Really, Ivy, I'm beginning to wonder if you are in your right mind. First taking on a college course designed for aspiring journalists, and now trapping yourself inside an empty house. And a haunted one, at that."

Elvis, in an attempt to pour oil on troubled waters, said that it was a bit unfortunate, and he thought Miss Beasley was not to know that nobody was at home. She had come to no harm. He said he would take them straight back to Springfields, and they could sort themselves out and forget about it.

Roy took a deep breath. "You're right, Elvis," he said. "Give me your hand, Ivy." She reached across and offered her hand, which he held and kissed. "I do love you," he said. "Pax?"

She nodded, and as they pulled up outside Springfields, Elvis sniffed and wiped away a single tear.

MUCH LATER, WHEN they were sitting comfortably in the lounge, Ivy touched Roy's arm. "Dearest, are you asleep?"

"Of course not," said Roy. "Only resting my eyes."

Eight

DEIRDRE HAD GONE to bed late, and was not pleased to be woken by an early call from Theo Roussel, the village squire. In her youth, Theo had been one of her hopeful boyfriends, and was now not much more than a good friend, with occasional warmer relations. He was a confirmed bachelor, and as she had no intention of letting any aspiring husband get his hands on her considerable fortune, their relationship was a permanent stalemate, which was fine by both of them.

"Watcha want?" she said sleepily.

"Deirdre darling, could you possibly come up to the Hall and do your usual elegant hostess bit? I have a dinner party to organise, with the local Inspector Frobisher and his wife, and a couple of other worthies. It will be boring as hell, but I promise to make it up to you after they've gone home. Any chance?"

"When? Tonight! Blimey, who let you down?" Deirdre did some quick thinking, and as she had once had a brief fling with said Inspector Frobisher, she decided it could be quite fun and agreed.

"You know I'd much rather our dinner party could be for two," Roussel continued. "But you never seem to have a free evening! Anyway, I'll see you about half six? You know the old trout who does for me is off sick. I am so grateful, Deirdre!"

The squire's voice was loud and hearty, and Gus had heard every word. He turned over in bed. "Ask him about the Winchen Blatches," he whispered.

"There is something you can help me with," she said obediently. "Have a think about what you can tell me about the Blatches up at Blackwoods Farm. You've lived here forever and must have some useful info. And no, I'm not going to tell you why I want to know. Later, maybe. Bye, Theo."

Gus made his usual protest about her double life, so she got up, showered and dressed, and went downstairs. She looked out at the rain teeming down and picked up her post and the local newspaper from the doormat. She saw under a photo of herself, a banner headline saying "Local woman saves recluse from certain death," and also an old photo of a small girl holding on to her mother's hand. The child's face was clearly that of Mrs. Blatch, and Deirdre felt a catch in her throat. Poor mite. She looked scared stiff.

She put her damp letters on the hall table, and began to read the news story. Mrs. Deirdre Bloxham, she read, had snatched Eleanor Blatch from the jaws of death. Mrs. Blatch was now in the General Hospital, and recovering well. Her home, Blackwoods Farm, was isolated, and it was pure chance that Mrs. Bloxham had called to see her.

"A lucky chance," muttered Deirdre, going through to the kitchen. "I hope to God they clean up her house before they let her go home."

"Talking to yourself again?" said Gus, coming up

behind her and putting his arms around her. "What's that? The local rag? Oh my goodness! You've made the front page, Deirdre love. And rightly so, if I may say so."

"You're beginning to sound like Ivy," Deirdre said, laughing. "Come on, let's have breakfast. I've got Enquire Within work to do this morning. I'm going to see what the office can turn up about try-your-weight champion Green, and then I'll have my hair done. Smarten up for tonight. Also, Gus old chap, my hairdresser is the biggest gossip in town, and who knows what he may have to say?"

IN THE HOSPITAL room allotted to Mrs. Winchen Blatch, she lay quite still under the pristine, clean-smelling sheets, and slowly opened her eyes. A nurse, coming in to check on her, gently touched her veined and blotched hand, and saw her eyes flicker.

"How are you, my dear?" she said.

Mrs. Blatch said nothing, but with the faintest of smiles, nodded her head and closed her eyes again.

The nurse refilled her water jug and went quietly out of the room. At the nurses' station she found the matron, and reported that Mrs. Blatch seemed very comfortable. "She smiled at me," she said, "but she doesn't want to talk. Closed her eyes, and that was that. But she did nod, when I asked her how she felt."

The matron said it was early days, considering what a trauma the poor woman had suffered, not to mention pain from wounds and bruises. "If there are visitors for her, tell them she's not allowed any today."

"Have you seen the local paper?" the nurse asked, and the matron nodded and asked that there should be as little gossip as possible amongst staff.

"Of course," said the young nurse. "But I don't suppose she'll get visitors. Seems she was a real Miss Havisham.

Lived in a house covered in dust and cobwebs, and never emerged. Ordered her groceries from the village shop and had them delivered."

"Very interesting," said the matron dryly. "Now get on with your work, please."

Nine

FIRST ON DEIRDRE'S list of calls was Bloxham's Luxury Car Showrooms, where she maintained a private office in order to keep a close eye on her late husband's business. She was reckoned by the staff to be pleasant, efficient and, if necessary, tough. Her purpose in calling this morning was to have a chat with the oldest member of staff, William Partington. He had lived in Thornwell all his life, and would very probably have come across the Winchen Blatches of Barrington.

"Morning, Mrs. Bloxham," he said, and sat down in the chair opposite her desk. "How are you keeping? This rainy weather doesn't do old bones any good! But you've a while to go before such as that worries you!"

"I'm fine, thanks, William. And you? You look exactly as you've always looked. I can remember my Bert saying that. Now, I won't keep you long, but I want to pick your brains. I wondered if you could recall anything about the Winchen Blatches? I think you said to me you had relatives in Barrington?"

He nodded. "Oh yes, them Blatches! I think it was that Mrs. Blatch who added the Winchen. When she were young, she were one of those who like to go up in the world, though I think she were no better than her husband, Ted. Snobby, though."

Deirdre laughed. "William, that saves me asking a lot of questions. You must have seen that ridiculous story in the paper? They certainly embroidered the truth there! It was not at all sure that she had been attacked. She fell heavily out of bed and as far as I could see, hit her head on the bedstead. I did what anybody would do in those circumstances. But can you tell me anything at all about the poor woman?"

"Oh yes, I remember her only too well. My nephew used to work on the farm at Blackwoods. They had pigs, all free range in one of their fields. You know, where there would be little old arks dotted about the field for the pigs at night. Some of the old boars were as big as a bull, and fierce, too. My nephew got damaged. Broke his leg, it did. He didn't get out of the way quick enough."

"How were the Blatches about that?"

"Mean as muck! Refused to pay up any compensation. The case went on for years, but they never paid out a penny."

"And the wife, Mrs. Winchen Blatch, didn't she want to keep on the farm after her husband died?"

"She tried, with what was left of it, but soon gave up. Stopped feeding the animals, and had the inspectors in. After that, she was hardly ever seen." Deirdre thought of stories of tangled grey hair and fingernails black with dirt. "So she gave up, did she?"

"Tha's right. My sister over there, she tried to befriend her, but she wasn't havin' none of it. O' course, it all changed after the boyfriend arrived," William said wisely. "Much younger, he was. But they was always about together after he moved in. Very lovey-dovey they were.

She changed then. New clothes, hair dyed, lipstick and that eye stuff. What a change!"

"But then the boyfriend left. I suppose she went to pieces again?"

"Oh yes, me duck. He was there living with her for quite a while, but then he did a runner, taking what jewellery she'd got, so people said. She went right back to how she'd been before he arrived. Folk tried to help her, but got the brush off every time. So they gave up in the end. And now she's been attacked, and you found her, Mrs. Bloxham. And just in time, the paper said?"

"Possibly," said Deirdre. "What can you remember about the boyfriend? He must have been a rotten so-and-so?"

William shifted in his chair, and a girl put her head around the door. "Would you like a coffee, Mrs. Bloxham?" she said.

Deirdre said that would be nice, and one for William, too, please.

"What about the boyfriend?" she continued. "Did people know his name?"

"It was Sturridge, I think."

"Did he talk much to local people, like your sister?"

"He was friendly enough, but seemed to fancy himself. After he'd left, the locals said they'd not known much about him. Never talked about himself or where he come from. None o' that kind of thing. Didn't really have a single friend, except for Eleanor Blatch. And they all reckoned he was more than a friend there!"

"And she was devastated after he left?"

"Suthin' like that. Went to pieces, like you said. He took a lot of her stuff with him. Silver and jewellery, that kind of thing."

Deirdre could see that William was fidgeting to be back at work, and so she thanked him and said how helpful he had been.

"And you look after yourself, Mrs. Bloxham," he said. "Your Bert wouldn't have wanted you to be too miserable."

AS DEIRDRE MADE her way to the hairdresser's salon, she thought how lucky she had been. That poor Blatch woman, left all alone, with few friends and little money. It must have seemed like a miracle to her, when an unattached man arrived on her doorstep.

"Morning, Deirdre!" said her stylist, taking her coat and seeing her to the seat she always had. It was by the window, and if she was bored, as she often was while the staff busied themselves around her, she could look out of the window at the life of Thornwell. It was only after she had mentally put together what William had told her that she realised she still had no idea what Mrs. Winchen Blatch was really like.

She looked at her watch. She had missed the time she would have gone to talk to her friend in the social services office, but now she thought of a better idea. She would take her out to lunch, ask her what she could discover in the records and have a general chat with her. She took out her mobile and dialled the number.

"Where were you? I thought you were coming in earlier?"

"Sorry, Jean," said Deirdre. "I got held up in the showrooms. A small crisis over tax affairs. I sometimes think I could do without an accountant! Anyway, are you free for lunch? Say in about an hour? Brilliant! See you then."

WHEN DEIRDRE INTRODUCED the subject of the Winchen Blatches to her friend, she immediately ran into another conversation about the newspaper item. Dealing with that as swiftly as possible, she asked if it would be possible to trace anything interesting about Eleanor Blatch or her lodger in the records.

"Tricky, that," said her friend. "Confidentiality, and all that, as you know very well. Still, we could get round that by keeping everything anonymous. Would that do? Mind you, I might not turn up anything about them. An awful lot of people never cross our path! How is the woman, anyway? The latest I read was that she would soon be out and back home."

"And home is a tumbledown farmhouse on the outskirts of Barrington. Knee deep in mud and worse. A few chickens in the yard. No heating, cold water and a primitive gas stove in what passes for a kitchen. That's all I noticed at the time, but I expect the rest is equally bad. You might very well be called in to work social services magic!"

They chatted on about this and that, and after a snack and coffee, left the restaurant. It was still raining, and Deirdre put up her umbrella to protect her expensive coiffure. They separated with warm good-byes, and Deirdre set off for Barrington and home.

ON THE OFF chance that Ivy and Roy would be in Springfields, she decided to call and compare notes on what they had discovered so far. She walked into reception and looked through to the lounge. Yes, there they were, snoozing in armchairs by the fire. Dear old things! It seemed a pity to wake them, but even as she thought this, Ivy turned her head and saw her. She immediately waved and got to her feet, shaking Roy by the shoulder as she set off to meet her.

"Sit down, girl, and get dry. I can see you've been into town and had your hair done. Are you sure those curls are suitable for a woman of your age?"

Ivy had been having a daydream. She was back in

Round Ringford, in her house next to the shop, and with a lodger who had been special in her life, but who had betrayed her. Seeing Deirdre in reception, she had jerked herself back to the present, but with a nasty cloud still depressing her. The parallel with Eleanor Winchen Blatch's circumstances was uncomfortably close, and she had begun to wish Enquire Within had never taken on the woman and her ghostly visitor.

"So things are moving, but slowly," said Deirdre.

"Slow but sure, my dear," said Roy huskily. "Mm, just had a bit of shut-eye after lunch. You're looking very pretty today, if I may say so. Very pretty indeed, doesn't she, Ivy?" he continued.

"That's as may be," said Ivy. "But she has things to tell us, so we must order some tea and repair to my room, where we can be free from wagging ears."

Tea was served by Katya, who added to the compliments paid to Deirdre's hairdo, and said she really loved the colour and the curls. "So elegant, as always, Mrs. Bloxham," she said. "Don't you agree, Miss Beasley?"

"Not bad. That will be all, thank you, Katya," Ivy said. "Now, to work. You first, Deirdre, and then I'll tell you about our visit to my new alma mater, as Roy calls it. The Manor House College, that is."

Ten

GUS HAD TURNED up at Springfields, and by the time Ivy and Roy had given a detailed account of their visit to the Manor House College, it was time for Deirdre to return home and get changed for Theo's party. Once back at Tawny Wings and under a wonderfully hot shower, she thought about what had been said. Ivy was obviously full of enthusiasm, but not without her usual dose of common sense, and Roy had been quiet and very far from enthusiastic.

She slipped into the little black dress, shook her apricot-coloured curls into a pleasant disorder and took a look at herself in the long mirror. Not bad, she thought, and twirled about on her high heels. I shall give those worthy old tabs with their henpecked husbands something to worry about.

When she arrived at the Hall, she realised they had been busy gossiping already. The wives were grudging in their praise of her timely rescue of Mrs. Blatch, and their husbands gathered round her, paying her compliments and anxious to hear more about the accident.

Inspector Frobisher hung back as they all downed their champagne cocktails, but Deirdre was delighted to see that Theo had placed her next to the law.

"Good evening, Mrs. Bloxham," he said, as they sat down. And then in an undertone he said, "I trust you can be discreet." It was years since she and the inspector had had at the most half a dozen pleasant afternoons. She could hardly remember how it had all happened, and now smiled widely at him and said how nice to see old friends gathered together, and would he like his glass refreshed?

Deirdre had told Theo that she was certainly not going to cook and serve, and had immediately found a suitable catering company who took care of the whole thing. She was there, she had told him, to shine amongst the dull guests and brighten their evening.

Having seen everyone happily served, Deirdre turned to the inspector and said, "Any new info on the Blatch accident? My guess, as you know, was that it was an accident."

Frobisher put down his knife and fork and turned to face her. "Off duty, I'm afraid, Deirdre. I never mix business with pleasure."

Undaunted, Deirdre said she agreed, and added that it would give her great pleasure to know if any further information had come up to substantiate rumours that someone had struck Eleanor Blatch a whopper with a hammer.

The inspector lowered his voice. "Your first guess, that it was an accident, was undoubtedly correct. But if someone had wielded a weapon, he is as yet unknown to us. We are following several lines of enquiry."

"Such as a burglar disturbed, or even a revenge killing attempt for some imagined insult in the past?"

"Deirdre, my dear!" shouted Theo from the other end of the table. "Do I hear you talking shop with my friend Frobisher? Talk to him about golf instead. Much more entertaining."

The inspector grinned, and immediately began an account of his last eighteen holes, played the previous afternoon.

As they got up to go to the drawing room for coffee, he held Deirdre lightly by the arm, and said quietly in her ear that she should ring him tomorrow, as he had a small puzzle to solve regarding Eleanor Blatch, and a meeting would possibly help him to solve it.

Alcohol and good food had warmed up the guests, and there were no embarrassing silences for the rest of the evening. Golf, investments, local politics, all were thoroughly chewed over, and finally, as they left with genuine thanks for a lovely evening, Deirdre kicked off her shoes and collapsed in an armchair by the log fire.

"You were marvellous, Deirdre, my darling," said Theo. "Quite the celebrity!"

"Mm, well, thanks for putting me next to the inspector. But he was like an oyster, clammed up for the evening. Still, he suggested a meeting with Enquire Within, so we may get further tomorrow."

"The caterers have gone," Theo said hopefully. "A little nightcap before bedtime, my sweet?"

"A hot water bottle would be more to my taste," she said, her eyes heavy with tiredness.

"No need for that, Mrs. B," he said. "I put on the electric blanket earlier, so up we go. Up the wooden hill to Bedfordshire!"

GUS, MEANWHILE, HAD heard about the dinner party, and wondered how Deirdre was getting on. He ate a solitary fish cake, drank a beer and turned on the television to watch a film about love on a motorbike. But he couldn't concentrate, and since he had no grounds for being jealous of the squire, he forced his thoughts into a more useful channel.

Mrs. Eleanor Winchen Blatch. Age? About fifty-five to

sixty, he guessed. Living alone, but not always alone, according to Deirdre. There had been a man on the scene for a while, a younger man named Sturridge who had left carrying loot, and was never seen again. Miss Blatch had been in despair, and relapsed into a sad, reclusive exist-ence, getting by on a meagre private pension. There were no real clues as to the background of the young man. There might be more information from Deirdre's friend in town, but other than that, it was difficult to know where to start. But if, as seemed possible, he had returned for more good-ies and had been given the boot by Eleanor, he might have been the one with the weapon.

Unlikely as it seemed, searching for evidence of the vanished lodger was the first and most important step to take. He had felt that Ivy's heart was not really in this investigation, and perhaps she was rather taken up with her new interest. Couldn't blame the old thing, really. She certainly had all her marbles, and, as she said, she would have plenty to write about. He wished her luck, but at the same time, felt that Enquire Within needed Ivy at the helm.

He switched off the television, and considered an early night. There was a light tap at his back door and he groaned. Miriam, with a friendly suggestion of a last glass of wine.

"I felt you were a bit down when I saw you coming home," she said. "Nothing like a glass of my old mother's primrose wine to cheer you up. Shall I bring it round, or will you come to me?"

Gus sighed. Given a real choice, he would have shut the door on her and told her to go to hell. But that wouldn't do. He forced himself to be neighbourly, and invited her in. He already had primrose wine left from the last bottle, and said they could share that. If he had had the courage, he would have poured it down the sink, since it was always followed by a dull headache, but he duly administered the poison and sat her down by the fire.

"So what's new in the village?" he asked.

"Nothing much," she replied. "Except they're still talking about Mrs. Bloxham's good deed. I must say I would not have liked to be in her place. That Blatch woman can be very unpleasant. I know everyone's feeling sorry for her, being hurt an' that, but I haven't forgotten how nasty she was when I took her a bottle of this wine last Christmas. I thought she would need cheering up, but she told me to get lost. Didn't want any charity, she said. So that was the last time I try to be nice to Mrs. Blatch!"

"What about that bloke, Miriam? The one who lived with her for a while. Nobody seems to know where he came from, or went back to."

"Well," she said, taking a good swig, "I remember hearing him talking to James in the post office one day, and I reckon he had no particular accent. I'm pretty good on accents, and he sounded slightly posh to me."

"That narrows it down a bit," said Gus with a smile. "No idea what part of the country?"

Miriam laughed, a throaty, primrose wine laugh, and said it certainly wasn't Edinburgh, because she had had a friend at school who had come from Morningside, and that was an accent you couldn't forget. Scottish posh, and he wasn't that!

"Can we change the subject now, Gus?" she added. "I'm feeling quite sleepy. How about you?"

Gus shook his head. "Watch the news, then work to do before bedtime," he said, but they had no sooner settled down to watch the television news than his head drooped and he was fast asleep. Miriam fetched a soft rug from the window seat, curled up beside him on the sofa, and closed her eyes.

Eleven

NEXT MORNING, AFTER breakfast, Roy received a message from Mrs. Spurling via Katya that Thornwell library had telephoned to say they had information on another mention of the strong young man living in Barrington, with the same description as the one previously found. The name was definitely Green. Would Mr. Goodman and Miss Beasley like to call in and go through some papers with the librarian?

"How very kind of her," said Roy. "Really kind to take so much trouble for a couple of oldies, don't you think, Ivy dear?"

"Just doing her job, I would say." Ivy pursed her lips and continued with instructions for Elvis to take them into Thornwell more or less straightaway. "But we are not really interested in Greens, are we? Still, I suppose it might lead us somewhere," she said, looking prim.

"Good idea," said Roy. "And then I'll give the librarian a ring to say we're coming in. Such a nice woman!"

* * *

WHEN THEY ARRIVED outside the library, a member of staff was waiting for them. "Nice to see you two again," she said. "Our chief was really struck with how keen you were to use our facilities! She's been glued to her computer ever since. Jacqueline, her name is. Come along now. I think there will be a cup of coffee waiting for you."

"Tea," said Ivy. "And thank you, that will be most acceptable."

Her voice was about as warm as a tinkling icicle, and she was silent from then on until they had reached the reference department and found the chief librarian waiting for them.

"How very kind of you, my dear," said Roy, at his most charming. The librarian, a pleasant-looking woman in her thirties, smiled warmly at him.

"Now, come along here and see what I've found," she said.

"Before we start," said Ivy, "could you tell me where the toilet is. One of the little trials of old age, I'm afraid. I expect you'd like to go, too, Roy," she added, well aware that old age was not what he wanted to talk about at this moment.

When they were finally ready to start work with the smiling librarian, Ivy touched Roy's arm. "Got your glasses, dear?" she said, with the sweetness of a stick of rhubarb. "Forgotten them again? Never mind, borrow my spare pair. Now, shall we begin?"

"Here we are, one Colin Green," the librarian said. "I remembered you saying there might be a sporting connection, and I found this in Sleaford football club records. But I am afraid there are dozens of Greens. I have listed them all, and printed them out for you."

"That is so kind of you," said Roy. "I know we have to

pay a small charge, but we do appreciate all the trouble you have taken."

His mobile began to ring, and he excused himself off to the other side of the room to answer it. Meanwhile, Ivy took charge of a sheaf of papers, all of which contained particulars of sporting Green families who might have visited Barrington.

When Roy returned, saying he had spoken to Gus, who had had a question or two, Ivy asked what had they had been about. "And didn't he ask for me?" she said.

Ivy was frowning, but Roy proceeded gently. "Afraid not, beloved. I think you have been rather taken up with planning your writing course lately, and Gus and Deirdre don't like to spoil your new enthusiasm."

"Rubbish! I am as concerned with Enquire Within as ever I was!"

Ivy's face was red with chagrin and annoyance mostly with herself. What Roy had said was true, and she was determined to put the writing course firmly in its place as a secondary interest.

As they drove home with Elvis at the wheel, he asked if their visit had been productive.

"Very," said Ivy. "We learned a great deal about dozens of men called Green, any of whom might be the one called Sturridge that we are trying to trace, and I learned a lesson on the way." She did not elaborate, but Roy took her hand and planted on it one of his gentlemanly kisses.

"Well done, my love," he said. "And here we are, back in time for lunch."

AFTER A VERY satisfactory meal, the two retired to Ivy's room for a short nap. This had become a comfortable habit for them, with Ivy stretched out on her bed, and Roy in a chair with a cushion behind his head.

Today, however, neither felt sleepy. The morning in the library had produced not much more than a large chunk of paper for them to go through, and Ivy sat on the edge of her bed with a pen and writing pad, making notes for Monday morning's meeting of Enquire Within.

"So, all we know is that out of this list of Greens, there might be one who visited Mrs. Blatch and stayed on for quite a time. Do you think this might be a waste of time, dear?"

Roy nodded. "I suppose it might be useful to look for local addresses," he said. "We might as well, since that nice librarian went to so much trouble. If we do find one, we can investigate and see if he ever appeared in Barrington, sweetening up lonely women, and then disappearing with their life savings."

"And clever with it! I think the others will agree that we need to find our particular Sturridge as soon as possible. He left Miss Blatch long ago, but there's a possibility he may have returned, especially if he had fallen once more on hard times."

Ivy closed her notepad and with difficulty wriggled round and lay down on her bed.

"And last but not least," she added, "was he ever wanted by the police? There is no record of him being violent. One for Deirdre to find out from her friend Frobisher. Now for a bit of shut-eye, and you, too, Roy dear, then we shall be fresh for our tea."

Twelve

DEIRDRE HAD BEEN much occupied since Friday, thinking about Mrs. Winchen Blatch and her life since the departure of her lover. "Lover" was probably the right word, she was sure, and when this younger man came into her life, teasing her out of her widowhood and changing her life, it must have seemed like a miracle. And when the miracle did not last, her new world of love and affection came to a cruel end. It was not surprising that she reverted to her old ways.

The telephone rang, and Deirdre arose from her solitary breakfast table to answer it. It was Gus, and she was determined to be especially nice to him.

"To the hospital? Well, yes, I suppose so. Is she still in there? They hope she will go home tomorrow, after the doctor has signed her off. Why did they ask you to go in?"

Gus was sitting with his feet up on his sofa, reclining back on a cushion. "Obvious, my dear," he said. "I was with you soon after you found her. And a man of my charm and winning ways is the obvious choice. But no, Deirdre love. They reckon I must have seen her around, at least. She has no friends or family, apparently. James at the shop suggested me, as a likely character to bring her out of her trauma. God knows why, but there it is. And I thought immediately of you, as I do frequently. So will you come? I could pick you up about two o'clock."

He said a fond farewell, and then got to his feet. He looked at his watch, and saw that he had more than four hours before he needed to pick up Deirdre. Plenty of time to walk up to Blackwoods Farm and have a snoop around. If the hospital was intending to send her home tomorrow, there would surely be some swift cleaning work necessary, something he was sure Deirdre could organise. He set off with his small dog, Whippy, on her lead, across the Green and over towards the shop, where a gang of twelve-year-old boys yelled obscenities at him. Whippy broke away from him and approached the boys, who immediately became warm human beings, making an excessive fuss of her.

I suppose there's a moral there somewhere, thought Gus, but for the moment he could not think of one. On then, and with Whippy returned to him, he walked up Manor Road, and came very soon to Blackwoods Farm.

The wind was sharp, and the previously blue sky clouded over as he approached the building. At first sight it looked completely derelict, and Gus's heart sank. But then he noticed new paint on some of the windows and doors around the back of the house. Perhaps Mrs. Blatch had continued to make some improvements. Inside was what mattered, and Gus took the route through the dairy and into the kitchen, where he looked around without much hope.

But after half an hour or so, he had made some notes on what could be done to make it habitable. She would need only the kitchen and bathroom, one sitting room downstairs and a comfortable bedroom upstairs. He was pleased to find that the stairs were solid and safe, and when he pushed open the doors of the bathroom, lavatory and the biggest bedroom, he reckoned that with the help of a good cleaning service, they could work wonders.

The big bedroom had been cleared of traces of the accident, and Gus opened all the windows to admit gusts of chilly wind. He stood looking out at the road which led to the Manor House, and suddenly heard a noise behind him. He turned around quickly, but could see nothing. Then Whippy began to whimper and whine, looking fixedly at the door.

Gus strode over to the landing which connected all the bedrooms, and sniffed. Cigarette smoke? He sniffed again. Yes, that was it. Or perhaps a cigar? Anyway, someone had been in behind him, and was having a smoke somewhere in the building.

It could have been a homeless person making use of the house whilst it was empty. Getting in had been easy enough. But homeless persons do not usually smoke expensive cigars, even small ones. He opened first one door and then another, until he came to a half landing with one closed door at the end of the short passageway.

The smoke smell was stronger now, and he had a shiver of unease. He knocked. No reply, but a rush of cold air passed him. Again he knocked, but there was no response, so he turned the handle and pushed open the door. The room was empty, with its one long window, almost reaching the floor, standing open. He walked swiftly over, and looked down to the yard beneath. Then he noticed the fire escape, leading to the ground below. The door of the cage at the foot of the escape was open.

Taking a deep breath, Gus perched on the edge of a neatly made bed. There were signs of occupancy all around. A small cigar, half smoked, but black and cold, had been stubbed out in a saucer.

Had someone been living here, using the fire escape as entrance and exit? Had he been living here all the time, and keeping his head down? Perhaps her lodger had returned, needing somewhere to hide. The dark clouds were overhead now, and a sudden burst of heavy rain beat down on the yard outside, sending hens scuttling for shelter and forming instant puddles and streams rushing out into the road. He closed the window, and decided he had seen quite enough. He needed Deirdre's commonsense reaction to all of this, and he made his way downstairs and out into the real world in Manor Road.

"A FIRE ESCAPE?" asked Deirdre, as they drove into Thornwell to visit Mrs. Blatch in the General Hospital. "That's unusual, isn't it, in a domestic building like that?"

Gus nodded. "But very useful for our mystery lodger. If it was his room, it was very neat and tidy, but he had left a smouldering cigar. Not the most sensible thing to do in a house full of old beams and rafters."

"Turn right here," Deirdre said. "We can park on the roadside. I've spent hours trying to find a place in the car park. And you don't have to pay here."

They walked into the hospital reception, and were directed to a lift. "First on the left, down the corridor we call the street, and you'll find Roussel Ward at the end."

"Must have been a philanthropic ancestor of Theo," said Deirdre.

Gus snorted. "Pity he didn't pass down his taste for philanthropy to our present Roussel. *He* could start with reducing my rent! Daylight robbery for that hovel."

"Talking of hovels," said Deirdre, "we must report what you found out this morning. It will surely affect her home-going tomorrow. Ah, here we are. In you go, Gus, and announce your charming self."

HAVING ESTABLISHED THEIR bona fides, they found Roussel Ward and hesitated at the entrance.

"Can I help?" said a young nurse.

"We're looking for Mrs. Blatch," said Gus.

Deirdre, meanwhile, had looked around the ward, but could recognise none of the old ladies, most of them asleep.

"The bed in the corner," said the nurse quietly. "We'd be very glad if you could get some response from her. Gently, of course. But your voices might bring some recognition. I am afraid the poor lady had a terrible accident."

They tiptoed down the ward, aware of one or two pairs of eyes following them. Then a voice spoke loudly across to them.

"You'll get nothing out of 'er! She's away with the fairies, that one."

"Thank you," said Deirdre politely, and took Gus's arm. "Come on, let's find the old dear. I shall recognise her."

"Let's do five minutes and then scarper," whispered Gus.

The bed in the corner was almost as flat as if nobody were in it. Only the grey head on the pillow disturbed its pristine appearance. The nurse drew up two chairs, one each side of the bed, and they sat down. Deirdre saw two pale hands resting on the cover, and gently covered one with her own.

"Mrs. Blatch," she said quietly. "Mrs. Bloxham and Mr. Halfhide are here to see you."

An eyelid flickered.

"Hello, Eleanor," said Gus. "I hope you don't mind my using your Christian name? Mrs. Winchen Blatch is a bit of a mouthful."

Another flicker. Then her eyes opened. Deirdre held her breath, and then Gus said in a loud, chatty voice, "Shame you fell over, my dear. Still, old age is a bugger, isn't it!"

A strange noise came from Eleanor Winchen Blatch. After a few seconds, Deirdre realised what it was. The poor old thing was trying to laugh!

"Gus!" she said. "You'll offend the other old dears."

"Not likely," said Mrs. Blatch in a much firmer voice. "Rough lot in here. Now then, young man, help me up on these pillows. I don't know what I'm doing in bed in the middle of the day, anyway." She added, "What day of the week is it?", struggled and looked around her. "Where is this place? Looks like a hospital ward to me."

Gus found it easy to lift her thin frame into a sitting position, and Deirdre went off to tell the nurse Mrs. Winchen Blatch was awake, and demanding food and drink.

Thirteen

MONDAY MORNING'S ENQUIRE Within meeting was well under way, and Ivy was in good form. "Do you really think, Gus dear," she said, "that it was your personal magnetism that woke Mrs. Blatch from her coma? Or has it occurred to you that she might have been conscious all along, and was just having a comfortable rest at the expense of ratepayers like you and me?"

Gus bristled. "I'm sure there was no doubt that Mrs. Blatch was seriously hurt. It is surely something to be glad about that she has been so strong and survived. And, may I add, the ward sister, or whatever they call them now, was amazed. She said it was the quickest recovery she had seen in a long time."

"There you are then!" said Ivy triumphantly.

"But Ivy," persisted Deirdre, "I think it is best to accept that Mrs. Blatch was woken by Gus's cheery voice. I was there, and I saw her reaction. Granted it could have been the next man who spoke to her, but it wasn't. It was Gus, and she was very grateful when she realised what had happened to her." Deirdre was on the defensive, and Gus put his hand on her arm.

"Very well," said Ivy. "But I've heard tales about that particular woman when she was younger, flaunting herself about in the company of a much younger man. You can't trust that kind of woman."

Seeing things becoming something of an impasse, Deirdre said brightly, "Time for me to make tea. With milk and sugar, Ivy?"

"No sugar, thank you. I'm sweet enough already," Ivy answered.

"Indeed you are, dearest," said Roy, "but I think we should continue to concentrate on the return of Mrs. Blatch to her house. The least we can do is to make sure it has been cleaned and warmed throughout."

"Done," said Ivy. "Deirdre organised everything yesterday, and the cleaners went in this morning. They said the door at the end of the passage leading to the little room where Gus said he found a cigar stub was locked. So they left that alone. Everywhere else is habitable, though badly in need of a fresh coat of paint and some curtain laundering."

"How about food?"

Ivy nodded. "Dealt with," she said. "Deirdre went to Waitrose and stocked up. At her own expense, I might add. I tried to get her to claim from social services, but she hasn't, have you, Deirdre?"

"Not yet," Deirdre said. "We'll see how things turn out."

"Well," continued Ivy, "the Blatch woman can't expect to be subsidised forever. Rumour is once more rife that she has a hoard of gold stashed under the floorboards."

"That will surely have been assessed and sorted out before she leaves hospital," said Gus. "But I did volunteer to keep a friendly eye on her. The police will be investigating her accident, but the last thing she said was that she wanted us to continue searching for evidence of an intruder. She now thinks, apparently, that her late husband's appearance was probably a bad dream. But she can't shake off the threat that somebody wants to kill her, and might try again. The police have probably put it down to demented wanderings."

"Mm," said Ivy, and then was silent. Her silence was eloquent, and Deirdre said that if Ivy did not want to be part of this investigation, she and Gus were willing to carry on alone.

"Don't be ridiculous, Deirdre! Of course I want to be part of it. But I think a little caution is in order when dealing with the likes of Mrs. Winchen Blatch. We are dealing with an old lady who is clearly confused. But if having us on the case helps with her recovery, then I suggest we go ahead."

"You may be right, Ivy dear," said Roy. "But perhaps we could make a polite call, when we go up to the Manor House College? You remember you have books to collect for your course work."

"Why not? It sounds like a good idea, Roy. We will take her unawares, and see if she can shed any more light on this attacker of hers. We'll go this afternoon. She should be home by then. We can also remind her of our fees, though I have to admit she did give us a hefty down payment. But we're not a philanthropic institution, and she needs to remember that."

"DO YOU FANCY going into town for lunch, Gus? I feel the need to get out of Barrington for a bit. I'll treat you. Shall we go to the Royal Oak?"

Deirdre felt the morning's work had been unproductive. Ivy's very evident dislike of Mrs. Blatch depressed her, and she felt in need of cheering up.

"Fine," said Gus. "But I'll treat *you* for once. A small insurance policy matured and paid me a few pennies this month. So I don't have to be a kept man. Yes, let's go and order a huge lunch and then go back to your place to chew over the facts that we now know about Mrs. Eleanor Winchen Blatch."

"I think I like her, you know," said Deirdre slowly. "She's got spirit, recovering from a really nasty accident. As for that, I know what I think," she added.

"What? That the great god Zeus came down in a tongue of flame, and when she resisted him he knocked her about a bit and then went back up to Mount Olympus in a sulk?"

Deirdre laughed. "Something like that," she said. "So is it lunch in town? Then we can call in on Mrs. Blatch on the way back. If we go reasonably early we won't bump into Ivy and Roy."

"And I can see if her secret lodger is back. A whiff of cigar smoke will give him away."

"Do you think it might be him who attacked her? If he *is* there, and you are right, you can hardly go in with all guns blazing. It's never a good thing to interfere between man and wife, or partner, or whatever. Come on, let's go, and we can talk about it over lunch."

AT SPRINGFIELDS, THE customary quiet afternoon was disturbed by an argument between Ivy and Roy. He felt like forgoing their usual nap, and was attempting to persuade Ivy that it would be a shame to waste the sunshine. "The forecast is rain approaching later on, so why don't we go out now? What do you think, my dear?" he said.

Ivy kissed his cheek. "I hate to disagree, but I think you and I should go upstairs and have our usual nap, maybe a bit shorter than usual, and then set off for the Manor House, calling on Mrs. Blatch on our way. I do not intend to stay there more than a few minutes, since she seems to have half the county running about after her."

"Oh, come now, Ivy," protested Roy, laughing. "I am sure she will be glad to see a friendly face."

"Mm," said Ivy, and led the way up to her room, where she and Roy tried to relax but failed dismally.

"Ivy? Are you awake?" asked Roy quietly.

"Uh-huh," said Ivy. "Shall we get up and go?"

"Sun's still out. I think we should be off."

"Right. Best put a warm coat on, just in case."

AS THEY APPROACHED Blackwoods Farm, Ivy noticed a large cream-coloured car parked outside. "Isn't that Deirdre's?" she said. "Looks like Mrs. Blatch has got a visitor with a friendly face already. If not two," she added, noticing Gus's hat on the backseat.

"I suppose we should call in on our way back. Too many visitors at once will not be a good thing," Roy said.

"Also," said Ivy, measuring her pace against Roy's trundle speeding up. "Also, by that time Deirdre will have sorted out any lingering problems, and we shall be able to get away after a couple of minutes."

"Do I gather you are not keen to visit this poor woman, Ivy?"

"You gather right. I have already said that if I thought there was anything I could do for her, then of course I would be there like a shot. We shall find out, shan't we?"

"How about Enquire Within? As a member of the agency, don't you think that having taken on the case, we should do all we can to solve it? And in my book, that includes visiting the most important witness, Mrs. Blatch."

"Thanks for the lecture, Roy. And yes, of course you are right. We will go there on our way back and see if we can pick up any vital clues. Sorry I'm such a miserable old grouch. It's just that there's something false about the woman. I can't put my finger on it at the moment, but maybe if we call I shall be able to grasp it."

"That's my Ivy." Roy sounded relieved, and turned into the Manor House drive with a flourish.

Peter Rubens was waiting to greet them, having seen their slow progress up the gravelled drive. It was not good for Roy's wheels, but they moved steadily on and were directed round to the side door, where Roy could park and follow Ivy into the high master's study.

"Lovely to see you again," Rubens enthused. "Now, before we start, I have asked our new creative writing tutor to join us again. We have a daunting-looking pile of what we call 'units' for you. Each unit requires a written or typed piece of work from you, Ivy. I hope I may call you Ivy? And there will be tutorials three times a week. This is a trial programme which we have devised, and will be adjusted according to how you are getting on, so that we shall have good feedback for our future day students."

There was a knock on the door, and Rubens called, "Come in, Rickwood!"

Ivy looked him over and decided he seemed personable enough. She then ignored him and took up the conversation where they had left off.

"Does that mean that I can argue with what you think of my work?" said Ivy, who had clear memories of arguing with Miss Biggs, her village school headmistress. "No stripes across the hands with a ruler, I hope?"

"I beg your pardon?" said Smith. "Sorry, I didn't quite catch that."

Ivy shook her head. "Doesn't matter. It all sounds tickety-boo to me. Which days are tutorials?"

"Monday, Wednesday, Friday. I hope these are convenient? We have a number of other students already, and subsequent applications have been accepted. We thought you would enjoy working with other students on the same material. Bouncing ideas to and fro, if you know what I mean."

"No, I don't," said Ivy. "I don't bounce."

Rickwood Smith smothered a laugh with his hand, turning it into a cough.

Rubens sighed, running his podgy hand through his luxuriant mane of grey hair. "I think I shall have to ask you to trust me, Miss Beasley," he said. "I have had a great deal of experience in running these courses, you know."

"How interesting," said Roy. "Where was that, then?"

"Oh, well, mostly language courses for students abroad. I've travelled the globe one way or another!"

Ivy did not smile. Instead, she turned her attention to Rickwood Smith. "Now, Mr. Smith, and where do you live? I don't remember seeing you around the village?"

"Probably not, Miss Beasley. But I expect you know my mother? Mary Winchen? She lives in one of the old persons' bungalows in Spinney Close. I am staying with her at the moment, until I find a place of my own."

"Winchen?" said Ivy. "Isn't that one of Mrs. Blatch's names?"

Rickwood Smith nodded. "They are sisters, but I am afraid they have little to do with each other. Shame, really, but it's one of these family feuds. Goes back years."

"So shall we leave it there?" said Rubens firmly. "There will be plenty of time to get to know each other when term starts."

After more pleasantries, and promises of individual help and encouragement from Rubens, Ivy and Roy departed, the bagful of units safely tucked away in the boot of the trundle. As they walked and trundled down the long drive, Ivy looked back. Rickwood Smith was still there, watching them. He raised his arm and waved vigorously, then turned back and disappeared into the house.

"An interesting development," said Ivy. "I'll tell you later, my dear, when we have time to take it in."

THE SUN HAD gone behind a cloud as they proceeded towards the village and Blackwoods Farm. When they were closer, Ivy could see that Deidre's car had gone. She wondered how long they'd been with Mrs. Blatch, and whether she was having a sleep to recover.

"Shall I go in first and see if she's up to receiving more visitors?" she said to Roy. "Then you won't have to alight if she's not."

He nodded, and watched as Ivy disappeared round the back of the farmhouse. After lightning visits of an army of workers, it was looking distinctly more lived in and cared for. Ivy came to the back door and knocked. She heard a distant voice call out, asking who was there. She yelled back that it was Miss Beasley and Mr. Goodman from Enquire Within, and pushed the door. It did not open, and was clearly locked.

"Key's in the dairy cupboard," came the faint voice.

Ivy went at once to the dairy door, which was, as expected, unlocked. She waved to Roy, who had come round to within sight. He clambered off his trundle and limped towards her.

"We can get in with this key," she said, having opened the cupboard and found it at once. "Not much of a hiding place," she said. "Go carefully, my dear. I expect we shall have stairs to negotiate. Sounds as if she is still in bed."

When they reached the bottom of the stairs, however, they looked up and saw Miss Blatch, tidily washed and hair combed neatly, wearing a clean dressing gown and signalling that she was coming down.

"Can't have you stuck on the stairs, Mr. Goodman," she said cheerfully. "We can go into the sitting room. Mrs. Bloxham lit a fire in there, in case I wanted to come down and watch the telly. Wasn't that kind? I must say I did not expect such service from an enquiry agency! And now here you are, both of you come to help me with the case of the disappearing attacker!"

She seems very chirpy for someone who may have been cruelly attacked in the middle of the night by an unknown villain, thought Ivy. It must have been the charm and charisma of Gus and Deirdre that did the trick, she thought sourly.

But Roy was at his most gentlemanly, and suggested they all sit down and have a little chat. He would not want to exhaust Mrs. Blatch, but perhaps one or two questions would help them in their enquiries.

Ivy looked around the room. It was the one in which she had waved for help through the dirty window, she realised. "Someone's done a good job cleaning up in here," she said. "I came to make sure your house was suitable for your return, but got shut in and had to attract Roy's attention through the window there. I expect you were out?" she said.

"Probably," said Mrs. Blatch. "I'm afraid I am not too clever on the sequence of past events of the last few days. And yes, I am so grateful to all those people who set to and cleaned up this place. I had let it all go to pot, I'm ashamed to say."

"Perhaps you should get another lodger?" suggested Ivy.

"Oh no, once bitten, twice shy, Miss Beasley! No, no more lodgers for me."

"It's quite a long time since your last one, isn't it?" Ivy asked politely.

Mrs. Blatch nodded. "Haven't seen him for years now. I doubt if I'd recognise the sneaky little so-and-so. Ratted on me, that one, you know."

"He's probably changed a lot since that time," persisted Ivy. "Let's hope you may not need to identify him in the future."

"What are you saying, Miss Beasley? Are you suggesting my attacker might be my long-gone lodger? I can assure you that it was not him. If I didn't know his face, I'd certainly recognise his voice. Age doesn't change that, all that much. If there was a real intruder, then he wasn't an intruder, if you know what I mean. The face I saw, and the voice I heard, was my late husband, Ted. There, over there on the bureau, you can see a picture of Ted. Good-looking man, he was."

"Handsome is as handsome does," said Ivy.

Eleanor Blatch nodded, leaned back in her armchair and closed her eyes.

Roy signalled to Ivy that it was time to go, and she picked up her handbag from the floor. "We'll be off now, Mrs. Blatch," she said, and saw that she was drifting off into sleep already. "I'll put another log on the fire, then you can get some rest in here. My old mother always used to say you feel better sitting in a chair than propped up in bed. I am sure your nephew will be looking in to see if you need anything."

Mrs. Blatch did not move a muscle, but Ivy heard a sharp intake of breath. So she had heard. Selecting a large log and placing it firmly on the fire, she set up the guard and turned to Roy. "It is a long time since my mother said things in my head, after she had died," she said quietly." Must be because I love you, Roy, and you fill my thoughts."

Eleanor Blatch opened one eye, and shut it again quickly. Silly old bat, she thought, but did not say a word.

Fourteen

"NEXT TIME WE go to see her, I am going to ask straight out about that locked room at the end of the passage. We know it leads to the fire escape on the end wall of the house, and we also know the escape was not locked when Gus went in. But a locked door would be very difficult to negotiate in the event of a fire."

Deirdre had been thinking about their visit yesterday, and had come to the conclusion that Mrs. Winchen Blatch was a courageous woman who had, in the past, and without any support, finally given up, become confused and lonely and allowed her home to deteriorate.

The only really well cared-for thing in the whole property was the small hen ark. Deirdre had peeped inside, and seen clean wood shavings for bedding, with feeder and water trough close by. Everything was spotless, which was unusual for chickens. With their scratching and churning, their quarters were usually reduced to a mud bath. But these all looked well fed and had an attractive sheen on their black feathers.

In the distant past, Deirdre had kept chickens. They were bantams, and in her idle moments she had amused herself watching the antics of a feisty cockerel and his reluctant hens. In the end, a deputation of neighbours had turned up at her door, demanding that the cockerel must go. His strident crowing in the early morning had driven them to despair, and they threatened action if she did not get rid of him. She had given the whole lot to a nearby farmer, and peace reigned once more. But she missed them.

Now, pouring more coffee for Gus, who had turned up unannounced with the morning paper, she said, "I've got it. Poultry is what we have in common, and I shall go up there and talk to her about them. I shall say I'm thinking of getting some more. I know enough about chickens to keep us going for at least an hour."

"I suppose you don't want me to come?" Gus said hopefully. He could happily leave chickens to Deirdre. "But don't forget the real purpose of your visit, Dee-Dee. We do need to know about the cigar-smoking visitor, and why his door is sometimes locked."

"Did you notice yesterday that from outside you can look up the fire escape to the window? I did, and the curtains were drawn across, so you couldn't see anyone moving inside. I suppose you could if the light was on. It looked creepy and dark."

"Perhaps you'd better leave the dark chamber to me, Deirdre," said Gus, taking her hand. "Can't have you captured and held hostage by a cigar-smoking villain."

"Oh, for heaven's sake," she answered. "Perhaps him with the cigar was having a sleep. Dark chamber, indeed! Sounds very medieval."

"I knew of one once. In a friend's house. A small room that had had its window bricked up when there was a window tax. It was used as a junk room, and when they finally opened it up, all kinds of treasures were found."

"Mm, I think I've heard tell of that before. But I'm not put off. I shall go up to the farmhouse a bit later on, to make sure she's having a good lunch. Then I'll stay for a chat. No need for you to come."

"You have my permission to ask about the dark chamber and the cigar smoke," Gus added, and received from Deirdre a sharp reply about being a pompous idiot.

"I was going to suggest you eat supper with me this evening," said Deirdre. "But I can't be doing with any more of your nonsense. I'll see you tomorrow some time and report back."

Gus sighed. "I might turn up, anyway," he said. "Cap in hand at your back door, asking for a crust."

"You'll get the boot if you do. So drink your coffee, and I'll go up and get ready to go up to Blackwoods."

ELEANOR BLATCH HAD arisen from sleep quite early, and had gone out into a sunlit yard to open up her chickens. It was chilly, and she drew her cardigan closer round her bony chest. She watched as the cockerel came out first, and then stationed himself by the door as his girls came out one by one. Shivering now, she went into the house and washed her hands under the kitchen tap. The clean stone sink now shone, and there was a pleasant smell of disinfectant everywhere. How had she allowed her home to get into such a dreadful mess? She supposed it was years of depression, living alone and becoming more and more a recluse.

Miss Beasley's mention of her nephew had taken her aback for a moment. She scarcely ever remembered her sister living in Spinney Close. Apart from paying her rent and giving her a small allowance, that is. As far as she was concerned, she had no sister nor nephew. They were dead to her, and she had no wish to be reminded of them.

She supposed the nephew had come to see his mother,

as Mary had lived alone and was now too crippled to go out. She could not even remember the nephew's name, and he would no doubt be gone again quite soon. She put them firmly out of her mind. That had been all finished years and years ago. If people in the village remembered it, they had the sensitivity not to speak of it.

She would be up and about, and start on redecorating and buying new things for the house. She might join a club in the village. The Women's Institute would not do. She remembered very sharp things said by them about her lodger!

A book group had been newly set up. Details were in the post office. She liked reading, and decided to find out more. As she began to clear away her breakfast things, she heard a voice. "Mrs. Blatch? It's Deirdre Bloxham. May I come in?"

"You are in, aren't you," Eleanor replied. "I've just got up, done the chickens, and had some breakfast. I could make you a cup of tea if you like?"

Deirdre appeared in the kitchen, put down her handbag and began to dry up Eleanor's breakfast dishes as they were washed. "Have you thought of a dishwasher?" she said.

"I can honestly say that I have never thought of a dishwasher," Eleanor said with a straight face. Then she burst out laughing, and Deirdre joined in, and then apologised for asking silly questions. "What *have* you been thinking of since you were brought back to life?" she said, hanging the wet cloth over the Rayburn rail.

Eleanor sobered up. "I have done some thinking," she said. "I see that I have been given a second chance, and I mean to make the most of it. How old do you think I am, Mrs. Bloxham?"

"That's a facer! I really have no idea," said Deirdre, taking the easy way out.

"I am sixty next birthday. And I am well aware that

when I was found unconscious on my bedroom floor, I looked at least ninety."

Deirdre smiled, but did not comment. Instead she looked around the big farm kitchen and asked if Mrs. Blatch had ever considered adoption.

"What? At my age? Dear me, no, Mrs. Bloxham. I know this seems a big house, but I manage to fill it with my various hobbies. I love tapestry work, and as you've probably seen, I read a lot. House is full of books!"

"No, I don't mean adopting a small child. It was just a thought, but there are many young people needing a good home, if only for a short time. Some have never known what a real home is. How many bedrooms have you, if you don't mind my asking?"

"Um, let me see. There's mine. That's the main one, and then there are three good singles, and a small box room that's almost never used. So that's five. But I really don't want anyone else in the house, Mrs. Bloxham."

"Does that include the little room at the end of the passage? When we found you so cruelly injured, we looked around at once to see if anyone was hiding. That one, which my colleague calls the dark chamber, bless him, was where access to the fire escape would be. Please excuse me if you think I'm being nosy, but this is an old house and would go up like a tinder box if a fire did start. It would be wise to have free access to the escape, just in case."

Oh lor, Deirdre thought to herself. I've gone too far. Her face has closed up, and the room temperature has dropped several degrees.

"The dark chamber, eh?" said Miss Blatch. "Well, it's a good name for it. I'll take a look, Mrs. Bloxham, and see if it can be fixed. And I see your point about the fire escape. Now, if you'll excuse me, I have work to do. And thank you for your help," she added. She put out her hand, and Deirdre held it for a few seconds.

"If you need any help, anything at all, don't hesitate to ring me. Here's my card. It's been nice talking to you again."

As she turned to leave the kitchen, she sniffed. Not fumes from the Rayburn, nor smoke from the fire newly lit in the sitting room. Bert had loved a small cigar, and the smell was like a shove in the stomach. Dear old Bert, how she missed him. Pulling herself together, she smiled at Mrs. Blatch and said she would see her again soon, and left.

Fifteen

AS SOON AS she was home, Deirdre rang Gus. "Hi, are you still speaking to me?" she began, and without waiting for his answer, continued, "Guess what? It was there again."

"What was? A hawk stealing the chickens? A stray social worker hiding behind the arras?"

"Oh, ha ha. No, there was a distinct whiff of cigar smoke. Without my even thinking about it, I suddenly remembered Bert, and Sunday afternoons, when we used to sit after lunch and read the papers and he would smoke a small cigar. It was unmistakable, Gus. Somebody in that house either was or had been smoking."

"Right, well, that is a small clue when we're looking for a possible lodger. Except that if it was him, surely she would not allow him to carry on living in her house? Might be an idea to ask James at the shop if he remembers selling cigars to a person in the village during the time the original lodger was here."

"I doubt if James had arrived by then, but we could ask around. As to kicking him out, if he has returned, it might not be that easy for her. Maybe he's blackmailing her, or threatening her with more physical violence if she tries to get rid of him. If you think about it, it would be very difficult for a rather frail woman to turn out a fully grown, strong-armed man."

"It could be the reason why she has asked Enquire Within to investigate her case. She might be hoping we will find him, without her actually ratting him out, and then we'd arrange for the police to storm the building without warning, and then send him packing for good. It's possible, Gus, isn't it?"

"It is certainly possible. But she categorically denied that her intruder was her lodger. She is sure it is her husband's ghost. I think we need to have a meeting with the others, and chew over this new development. It's not much to go on, but worth a mention. Ivy's a shrewd old thing, and I'd value her advice."

"Me, too," said Deirdre. "Shall we see if they can come up to Tawny Wings tomorrow afternoon? I have an appointment in town in the morning, but should be back around two. I'll give Ivy a ring."

YESTERDAY, AS SOON as they left Blackwoods Farm, Roy had wanted to know what on earth Ivy had meant by asking Eleanor Blatch about a nephew. "What nephew?" he had said, and Ivy had told him in detail what she had heard from Rickwood Smith, the new tutor at the Manor House College, adding that she was sure Eleanor blinked at the mention. They had tried to remember where Spinney Close was, but neither had been that way recently. "We'll ask Katya when she comes in," Ivy had said. "She's probably planning to take the baby for walks all round the village, dear little thing."

Now she and Roy were seated in front of a new laptop computer he had given Ivy for her birthday. She was already well accustomed to the simple tasks, and had suggested they look up Rickwood Smith on the Internet.

"I think I'm improving," she said to Roy, as she selected Internet Explorer and brought up Google on her screen. "I really love the different designs they have each day," she said. "Now, here we go."

Disappointed that nothing had come up connected with his name, she switched to Rubens. "Should have more luck here," she said.

"I think you're wonderful, my dear, even to attempt to switch the thing on. But I should know better than to doubt my Ivy's determination!"

Ivy and Roy peered once more at the screen. "There it is, up there under the College heading. 'Peter Paul Rubens, MA Dip Ed.' I knew the name sounded familiar."

Ivy looked at him. "Are you joking, my dear?" she said.

Roy shook his head, and Ivy sighed. "Peter Paul Rubens," she said with exaggerated patience, "was a famous painter four hundred years ago. Did portraits of buxom women. Among other things."

"Oh my goodness, Ivy. Of course he was! Well done, my clever Ivy. Shall we put Beasley in, and see what comes up?" Roy was beginning to enjoy playing with Ivy's new toy. But she closed it down firmly and said that was quite enough of that. They had work to do, and that meant a trip up Manor Road.

"To see Mrs. Blatch?" said Roy.

"No, to see Mr. Peter Paul Rubens, whose parents must have had a good sense of humour," said Ivy, with a smile. "I've gone through that creative writing stuff we collected, and there are already several suggestions I'd like to make to improve it."

"Why don't we wait until twilight," said Roy, "and see

if we can make out lights coming from upstairs at Black-woods Farm?"

"Especially from the small room over the fire escape in the end wall of the house?"

"You read my mind, dearest. Bodes well for our marriage. Now, try these spicy biscuits of Anya's. They're almost as delicious as you."

At that point, Katya came to refill the teapot and was alarmed and then embarrassed to see Miss Beasley perched on the bony knees of Mr. Goodman, giving him what was clearly a loving kiss. Amidst all the confusion, they forgot to ask Katya where they would find Spinney Close.

Sixteen

WITH A FAVOURITE programme on television at eight o'clock, Roy said that it would be advisable if they set off at six o'clock after an early supper. He was sure Katya could organise a few sandwiches for them.

"So are we going all the way to the Manor House, or only to have a peep at the windows of Blackwoods Farm?"

"Oh, I think out for an evening stroll in general, as far as La Spurling needs to know. You can say we're going to hear the blackbirds singing. There are some lovely evening birdcalls around that time."

"Mm," said Ivy, "don't you think she might be suspicious of a sudden interest in ornithology? I think we'll just tell her we're going out with our mobile phones, and won't be gone long. That should do it."

MRS. SPURLING WAS not at all happy. These two most difficult of her residents had now informed her—not asked!—that they would be going out for an evening walk and refused to tell her exactly where they were going and what time they would be back.

And this wedding of theirs coming up again! Thank goodness they seemed to have other things on their minds, and as soon as the ceremony and honeymoon were over, life at Springfields could go back to normal. With luck.

She stood at the door of reception, watching them negotiating the gate and disappearing off in the direction of Manor Road. Perhaps she should have gone with them to ensure their safety? She looked at her watch. It was already past her home-going time, and she turned away to fetch her coat. Home was in the opposite direction from where they had gone, and before she reached her house, she had removed Ivy Beasley and Roy Goodman from the top of her list of priorities.

As they approached Blackwoods Farm, Ivy, who was walking beside Roy's trundle, stopped, saying her shoe was loose.

"Shoelace come undone," she said, bending down. "I'll not be a minute, but it is very dangerous. Might trip me up, and then what would you do?"

"Pick you up, of course. But take your time, my dear. We have a good view of the farmhouse from here."

Ivy rested her foot on the footplate of the trundle and bent down. Her shoelace was not undone, of course, so she undid it and slowly fiddled with it, having a good look up at the house at the same time.

"The light's on," she said in a muffled voice.

"Yes, and the curtains aren't drawn yet," said Roy.

"Oh, look, there's somebody moving about. Can you see who it is?"

As Roy looked fixedly at the window, and Ivy still wrestled with her shoelace, there were suddenly footsteps approaching and then a brisk male voice rang out of the dusk.

"Can I help you? Having problems? I do believe it is my new student, Miss Beasley? And your fiancé, Mr. Goodman? How nice to see you out taking the air. Don't you love this time of the year? And there's a barn owl hooting outside the Manor. Wonderful!" It was Rubens, and with him his new tutor, Rickwood Smith.

Ivy had knotted her lace, and now straightened. As she looked up, she noticed the curtains at the lighted window were now drawn across. The tutor was going on about owls and blackbirds, and she hoped Roy had been able to see who had drawn them.

"Well, we're off to the pub for a quick one," Smith continued. "Can we tempt you to join us, either or both? The students have been quick to find the local hostelry!"

"Of course not," snapped Ivy. "We are only on parole, and have to be back in prison in half an hour's time."

"Oh, how jolly!" chortled Smith. "Then I look forward to seeing you again soon, Miss Beasley. Good evening to you both!"

Not bothering to wait until he was out of earshot, Ivy said it was bad luck they had to run into them just as a person had appeared at the little window.

"Did you see anything?" she asked Roy, who was trying in vain to tell her to keep her voice down.

"As a matter of fact, yes, dearest. I did see a figure, and as far as I could tell, it was female. But who it was I cannot tell."

"Turn around then, Roy. We'd better be going back."

"Not a very useful exercise, I'm afraid," he said.

"Oh, I don't know," she replied. "At least we can tell Deirdre and Gus to find out if Mrs. Blatch smokes cigars. Some women do, you know. Most unwomanly. Still, if that figure you saw was female, it would be worth asking. Deirdre seems to have struck up quite a friendship there, so she could do it."

* * *

LATER, WHEN THEIR evening drink had been brought, Ivy took Roy's hand. "Are you really sure it was female?" she asked.

"Quite sure. Well, almost sure. If the shadow had been a child's drawing, there was a round head with longish hair, then skinny arms and rounded at the front. We men, you know, Ivy, recognise these things."

"Then perhaps you men could elaborate a bit more," Ivy said. "Rounded at the front! Really, Roy, you can do better than that."

Roy laughed, and protested that it was only a glimpse, and he had told her all he could remember. He looked at Ivy's bright eyes, and realised that her new venture with the Manor House College had given her an unexpected lift of spirits. What a brave and lovely woman she was!

MONDAY MORNING, AND Deirdre had set out pads and pens on the desk in the Enquire Within office. Coffee was simmering away in the pot. She looked at her watch. The others should be here very shortly, and she wondered if they would have anything new to report. Her positive scenting of cigar smoke last time she was at the farm was certainly important, and since talking to Gus, she had had further thoughts. She realised they had more or less decided a lodger or guest was at least visiting Blackwoods. Whether he or she was newly on the scene was not clear.

"Deirdre? Where are you?" The voice was sharp. "You've left your front door open, you silly girl! Anybody could come in and steal your silver before you noticed. It's Ivy, anyway, all ready for the meeting. And Roy, of course," she said, as she saw Deirdre coming. "He's parking the trundle."

"Fine," said Deirdre. "I was in our office. Are you

coming straight in? Coffee's hot, and there's new biscuits from the shop. Shall I give Roy a hand?"

"No, thank you. He is quite capable of managing. Is Augustus here yet?"

"Here I am, Ivy," said Gus, coming in behind her. "You're in fine form today."

"As always," said Ivy.

When they were all settled, Deirdre opened the meeting from her desk, saying she would be glad if Ivy could give them a résumé of the case so far.

"Your memory is so good, Ivy," she said, "and we all know you can organise your thoughts."

"Flattery will get you everywhere," said Ivy, smiling. Then she gave a succinct account of what they knew about their client, Mrs. Winchen Blatch, and added the latest spotting of a woman at the lighted window of the farmhouse.

"And then," she said, enjoying the drama," there's Rickwood Smith."

"Who?" chorused Deirdre and Gus.

Ivy once more related how the new tutor at the college had turned out to be a nephew of Mrs. Eleanor Blatch, and what was more, he was staying with his mother, Mary Winchen, who lived in an old person's bungalow in Spinney Close.

Giving them time to take this in, she sipped her coffee before continuing. "And before you ask, no, they don't have any contact. A deadly feud between the sisters, apparently, and they have managed to live forever in the same village without mending it. I suggest we leave that for the moment, and get on to the shape at the window of Blackwoods Farm.

"Unfortunately," she continued, "by the time we had a good look, the curtains had been drawn and only a shape appeared. A shape which my dear Roy is quite certain was that of a woman. And before you ask him how he was so sure, he muttered to me something about bosoms. But I am sure he will tell you more."

"Good man," said Gus, smiling at Roy. "Anything to add?"

"Not really. I don't know if it was in any way important, but at the point where we were looking at the window, out of nowhere appeared Rubens and Rickwood Smith, the new tutor from the Manor House College. Rubens was at his jauntiest, and tried to persuade us to go to the pub with him."

"We refused, of course," said Ivy.

"Naturally," said Gus. "Now, Deirdre, time to tell what you discovered."

"Well, last time I went up to see Eleanor Blatch, we got on well. I think she trusts me. Anyway, while we were chatting, I noticed a familiar smoky smell. My Bert used to love those small cigars, and that was it. Same lovely smell, drifting in from another room somewhere in the house. Eleanor claimed she could smell nothing, but it was quite strong. So that's another time one of us has smelt it. When I asked her if she'd thought recently of having a lodger, maybe a young person who could be useful to her, she reacted against it very firmly. Said she was much happier living alone, and changed the subject immediately."

"Interesting," said Gus. "What do you think, Ivy?"

"Well, since you ask me, I would say that she's not to be trusted. I wouldn't believe a word she says. I'm sorry about that, Deirdre, because I know you like her, but there it is. I think this new factor, Mary Winchen and son, puts her in a different light. She was very flighty in the past, and won't have changed all that much."

"Maybe, dearest," said Roy. "But I'm afraid the fact that she was flighty in her youth has nothing to do with it."

Seventeen

THE MEETING HAD finally ended, after much disagreement between Ivy and Deirdre on the true character of Eleanor Blatch. The four had come out from the office and the trundle was ready for the off, when Deirdre's house telephone rang.

"Hang on, chaps!" she shouted as she ran in to answer it. "Probably someone trying to sell me double glazing!"

"More likely an assignation with the squire," muttered Ivy to Roy. He smiled. "Lucky fellow," he said.

But when Deirdre came out after five minutes, she looked pale and worried. "Better come back in for a bit," she said, helping Roy to dismount. "That was Eleanor, and she was in a panic. I said we'd help, so can we have a quick session?"

"Not an immediate emergency, then?" said Ivy.

"Not absolutely immediate, but she was very upset," Deirdre answered, frowning at Ivy.

When they were perching on chairs in the sitting room, Deirdre explained. "Well, she got up late this morning.

Overslept, feeling safe for the first time for months, she said."

"Get on with it, Deirdre, said Ivy.

"Well, you know she has these chickens and they're like children to her. All got names, and that kind of thing? Well, apparently she'd forgotten to shut them up last night, though she swears she didn't. Anyway, being bantams, they could fly, and all but one had flown up into a tree. All but one, and there was no trace of it."

There was an uncertain silence, during which Ivy folded her hands in her lap and looked fixedly at the floor.

"So, she'd more than likely forgotten to shut them up last night? And a fox had taken one?" Gus could see that Roy was having trouble nudging Ivy into attention.

"And a fox could have come back for the rest. Foxes do that. It might come back tonight. She is very upset," Deirdre repeated.

"I'm afraid I agree with Deirdre," said Ivy, to the surprise of the others. "Anybody could get into the yard and slide open the hen door. And nobody is going to believe that she *did* shut them up. This is a very nasty way of causing alarm to a defenceless woman, and since it could mean other similar tricks could happen, we have to speed up our enquiries. Meanwhile, Deirdre, if you are going up to see her now, I should suggest to her that she find some reputable person to lodge with her, if only for a short time, until we, and of course the police, have sorted it all out."

Deirdre managed a wobbly smile at Ivy, and said that she would certainly do that, and maybe Ivy would like to come with her? "The two of us might reassure her. What do you think, Gus?"

"Good thinking, Dee-Dee. Poor woman needs some support right now. What a pity her sister can't help her. Why don't you and Ivy go up to Blackwoods in your car, and I'll walk with Roy and his trundle back to Springfields."

* * *

ON THEIR WAY up Manor Road to the farm, Ivy and Deirdre discussed what could be done straight away for Mrs. Blatch.

"I could invite her to stay with me for a few days," Deirdre said.

"You might never get rid of her," Ivy replied. "Don't advise that one. No, but I think she might agree to your staying with her for a night or two, until she feels braver. What do you think?"

"Um, yes," Deirdre said hesitantly. "Er, I suppose that would be all right. I could kip down on a camp bed or something, to be there during the night. But what about the dark chamber? Suppose there *is* someone in there, coming and going via the fire escape? That someone might not feel too kindly towards me. Come to that, why won't that mysterious lodger, if he exists, do for a reassuring presence in the house?"

Ivy did not answer, pleased that Deirdre was seeing sense, and not being too carried away by her new friendship. "Come on, gel," she said. "Let's go and see if she's handing out chicken pie."

They walked round into the farmyard, and saw that the remaining bantams were all down from the trees, and Eleanor Blatch had fed and watered them. She burst into tears when she saw Deirdre, and thanked them profusely for coming round so quickly.

"All part of Enquire Within service," said Ivy firmly. "Now, why don't we all have a nice cup of tea and talk about what's happened to you."

Deirdre did not have much longer to think about her plan to move in for a day or two. Eleanor told them once more how she was sure she shut up all the hens, having counted them in, and this morning she found the door open and the rest up a tree. "They looked scared to death!" she said.

How can you tell what a chicken is thinking? Ivy was already sceptical. Then Eleanor continued, "If I paid a suitable fee, Miss Beasley, do you think Deirdre, I mean Mrs. Bloxham, would come and sleep overnight here? I could make a spare bedroom very acceptable, and it would tide me over this horrible panicky feeling."

Deirdre was frowning again, and willing Ivy to refuse, but then Ivy nodded and said she was sure that would be okay. However it would have to be an Enquire Within decision, with all partners agreeing. "We have never undertaken this kind of task, you understand," she said. "We can let you know later today, in time for you to make other arrangements if Mrs. Bloxham is unable to do this."

At this, Deirdre opened her mouth to speak, but Ivy jumped in and said that they must be going in order to have an emergency meeting. They would be in touch, she said, and more or less pushed Deirdre out of the door.

"Ivy!" said Deirdre, as they drove off. "How could you? Poor woman. I shall go back there this evening. We don't need to ask the others."

"Chairman's orders," said Ivy. "No such decisions to be made by individual board members. First we go and ask Gus, and then we can get Roy's reaction when you take me back to Springfields."

Secretly relieved, having thought twice about the creepy old farmhouse and the dark chamber, Deirdre did as she was told and drove down Hangman's Lane to find Gus.

When he heard what they had to say, he stood masterfully over Deirdre, who was sitting on the edge of a rickety chair, biting her nails.

"I've had a better idea," he said. "I shall go instead of Deirdre. I've met far more dangerous moments in my life than a confrontation with an unpleasant prankster. No, Deirdre, no arguments, I shall go this evening. Mrs. Blatch and I will watch television together, then retire to our separate beds, armed to the teeth. She might even talk to me about her sister. All fixed."

WHEN DEIRDRE HELPED Ivy out of her car and went with her into Springfields, Roy met them at the lounge door, looking anxious. They gave him the bare bones of Mrs. Blatch's request, and he looked even more anxious.

"Relax, Roy," said Deirdre. "Gus is going to do it. He'll start tonight at Blackwoods Farm and report back to us tomorrow. I must say I'm relieved, and I'm sure Ivy is, too. Maybe a coward's way out, from my point of view, but I think it is the sensible solution."

Mrs. Spurling appeared, hands on hips. "May I be permitted to ask if Mr. Goodman and Miss Beasley will be in for lunch?" she said, tight-lipped.

"Of course we will," said Ivy. "If we weren't, we would have told you earlier, as usual. Now, you two, come along in, and let's get Roy up to date."

"Yes, indeed," said Roy. "I need to know for a start if you formulated any opinion on what we do next. Apart from Deirdre going to stay with Mrs. Blatch overnight? I did take one step by myself, and hope it will be approved."

"What are you talking about, my dear?" said Ivy.

"Oops, sorry, Ivy!" he answered with a smile. "I took it on myself, and I hope you won't mind, and I gave the police a ring about the hens. They were not too impressed, and said that Mrs. Blatch had already informed them. They were, of course, carrying out enquiries, ho ho."

"As Deirdre is about to remind you, Roy," announced Ivy, "even small actions like one hen going missing are trivial to us, but a disaster to Eleanor Blatch. Of course you did the right thing." She patted his arm, pecked his cheek and said she did not know what they would do without him.

Eighteen

GUS LOOKED AT his clock and with a small sigh put on his jacket, took down Whippy's lead and said, "Walkies? Yes, I'm afraid it is," he said, patting the little dog. "But not as we usually know it. I'd better take some food for your breakfast and a water bowl. And a mat, in case Mrs. Blatch objects to you sleeping on my bed. Sorry about this, but should be for one or two nights only, until she gets her confidence back."

They set off, and Gus noticed Miriam Blake at her window. She waved and beckoned. But he kept going, making an effort to put thoughts of her delicious supper out of his mind. When he arrived at the farm, Mrs. Blatch was waiting for him, smiling and welcoming them both into the kitchen.

"So glad you brought Whippy," she said. "I've decided to get another dog myself. I've still got the old sheepdog, but he's so ancient and useless now. He's deaf as a post and lives in his kennel in the yard. Didn't even bark when that intruder sneaked in. I fancy a lively youngster, something a bit feisty. I've been told a Jack Russell terrier is the most frightening to a burglar. Goes for their ankles, you know. Anyway, I am sure Whippy can bark loudly, and that's a good substitute!"'

"Thanks," said Gus. "Is it okay if I put her mat upstairs in my bedroom?"

"Wouldn't she be better as a guard dog here in the kitchen?"

Gus had a sudden mental picture of Whippy facing a big man with a stick, and said that he would prefer to have his dog with him. "She senses a presence, even before I have heard anything," he said. "So I can be fully alert if anything happens. Which I'm sure it won't," he added, on a more optimistic note.

"Well, we shall cross our fingers," Eleanor Blatch said, and led the way upstairs. She showed him the bathroom and his small bedroom, clean and tidy with fresh linen. As they came out onto the landing, he turned and pointed to steps leading to the dark chamber. "More bedrooms down there?" he said innocently. "Must have been a big family living here at one time."

She nodded. "A farmer in the past had five daughters, and so built on a couple of extra rooms. They haven't been used for years. That one's locked most of the time, but I occasionally go in there to check on the mice. No need for it, you see.

So that accounts for the shadow on the lighted window, he thought. Checking on mice. He said that he would turn in early, as he intended to be up in good time for Whippy's prebreakfast walk.

"Oh, but do have a cup of something with me before you retire," Eleanor said. "Or a nightcap. I like a small whisky myself. What do you fancy?"

Not you, missus, he thought. Although with a good

haircut and some makeup she could look another ten years younger. He accepted her offer of a nightcap politely.

The bed was comfortable, and as Whippy landed on his legs under the covers, he relaxed and was asleep within ten minutes. A good hour later, he awoke to the sound of footsteps. They were soft and quick, and as Whippy pricked up her ears, he heard the main bedroom door shut. Eleanor needing a pee, he decided, and went back to sleep.

An owl hooting outside his window was the next interruption. He got out of bed and drew back the curtains. A bright full moon shone into his eyes, and he blinked. He had never seen the moon looking so huge. It could have been suspended a hundred yards away over the nearby field, and he looked up the road towards the Manor. To his surprise he saw lights at the upper windows. A student working late, burning the midnight oil, he guessed.

The owls hooted again, two of them answering one another. Gus yawned widely and padded back to his bed. Whippy raised her head to look at him, and then curled up tightly, disapproving of his restlessness. This time he found it difficult to go back to sleep, and wondered once more what could have caused such a complete rift between two sisters. Perhaps he would bring up the subject tomorrow.

His thoughts wandered on to the fire escape. Unusual in an old farmhouse, surely? Someone must have realised that the old wooden beams and occasional lath and plaster walls could go up in flames in a couple of minutes. Or did the dark chamber have a more sinister history? Was it a punishment room for one of those daughters? Being forced down the dizzying descent of the fire escape as an extra ordeal? And then, arriving at the cage exit, was there a man-eating tiger waiting for her?

For God's sake, Halfhide, he told himself, don't be so ridiculous. He punched his pillow and settled more comfortably. He wished now that he had succumbed to temptation and gone to supper with Miriam. He could be snoozing on her sofa now, with Whippy by his side. Finally he fell asleep.

IVY AND ROY had watched television in her room until later than usual, then they had kissed tenderly and separated, Roy going along the corridor to his room, and Ivy slowly undressing for the night. They had been talking about their coming marriage, and Ivy had said that it was going ahead this time, if she had to carry Roy up to the altar herself. Roy had laughed and put his arms around her and lifted her a couple of inches from the floor. "I shall do the lifting in our marriage," he said. "That's quite enough of that," Ivy had squealed, and then he had gone and peace reined over Springfields.

Before she fell asleep, Ivy had a recurring few minutes of anxiety. Roy had made it clear that a double bed was ordered, and that they would share it happily together. All very well, Ivy thought now, if you have the body of a twenty-year-old. But what would he think of wrinkly skin and droopy bosoms? And then there was her middle-aged spread controlled during the day by her mother's old boned corset. Should she ask him to look the other way whilst she unhooked it and leapt into bed? Well, slowly climbed would be more accurate. Her old legs were pretty good for her age, but she was well aware of knotted veins and spindle shanks.

And then, a voice that had been absent for so long returned inside her head. "Ivy Beasley! Don't you be so stupid! He'll be no oil painting with his clothes off, you can be sure of that. No good you expecting perfection at your age. Nor him neither! A good cuddle will be quite enough, so make the most of it. Now just you go to sleep, and let's have no more nonsense."

Ivy chuckled. "Thanks, Mother," she muttered, and her last thoughts before falling asleep were of Gus, struggling free from the encircling arms of Eleanor Winchen Blatch.

AT A QUARTER to four in the morning, Gus was once more woken, and this time by a very loud, shrill scream.

"God Almighty!" he yelled, tumbling out of bed. "What the hell's going on?"

Whippy was already at the door, barking and whimpering in turn. A second scream led Gus to the door of the main bedroom, and he knocked firmly. "Mrs. Blatch! Eleanor! Open up, please!"

Silence. Not even sounds of sobbing. Gus wondered fleetingly if she had been having a nightmare. But if so, it had been a terrifying one. He knocked again, and tried the handle of the door. He pushed, and seeing a dim light, he peered inside.

It was all shifting shadows, and he realised a figure was standing by the head of the bed, holding a torch. Without thinking, he snapped on the light, and saw Eleanor Blatch staring unblinking at the window.

He moved quickly then, taking the torch from her and gently moving her to sit down on her bed. Then he put his arm round her shoulder and began to talk quietly, while Whippy sat at their feet.

"Were you having a bad dream?" he asked, and she shivered. Then in a voice broken by choking sobs, she answered him. "He was over there," she said, pointing to the window. "Gone now. Doesn't like the light. A creature of darkness. That's what he says he's become."

"Is that why he used the dark chamber?" Gus was quiet, almost whispering.

Eleanor nodded. "I gave him hell, and he retreated up there. We stopped speaking." She struggled to stand up, and put her torch down on the dressing table. "He comes back, you see. Stands over me, with something like a hammer in his hand."

"And so you scream. I am afraid it was a nasty dream, Eleanor. Come along, back into bed. You'll sleep now. I'll make sure he doesn't come back. No wonder the hairs stood up on the back of Whippy's head! Still, the birds are beginning to sing, so let's have another hour or two, and you'll have forgotten about it by morning."

Eleanor hesitated, then began to get back into bed. "Would you like to stay and make sure he doesn't come back and get me?"

Alarm bells rang loudly in Gus's head, and he made for the door. "You'll be fine," he said, and went back to his own room, locking his door and making sure Whippy was at his feet.

IN THE MORNING, he pulled on his clothes and tidied the bed, and taking Whippy he went downstairs to the kitchen. As far as he could tell, Miss Blatch was not up yet, and he was pleased, hoping she had managed to have a good sleep after the ghostly drama.

"Come on, dog," he whispered. "Walkies, and then breakfast. No barking!"

Whippy often barked joyfully in anticipation of a walk, but this morning her tail and ears were hanging low. Gus unlocked the kitchen door, but Whippy held back, growling. Half turning, he stepped on something soft, almost tripping headlong down the steps into the yard. In fright, he pulled Whippy after him, and saw that what he had stepped on was a recumbent sheepdog. He retreated a few steps, and then turned to look at the kennel. A chain snaked across the yard, and at the end of it, the elderly sheepdog, deaf as a post and nearly blind, not moving. Before he could examine it, he saw Eleanor Blatch standing at her open kitchen door, looking down.

Nineteen

ELEANOR HAD GASPED, but regained her composure quickly, and in a strong voice ordered Gus not to touch the dog.

"I'm ringing the vet straight away," she said. "I want to know exactly how he died, and whether he was poisoned. Poor old thing, he's been in the family for so long I can't remember how old he was."

She shivered, and asked Gus to be careful with Whippy. "When you come back, if the vet hasn't been yet, can you step over him carefully? I'm sure Whippy will want to go nowhere near him."

"Don't worry, I'll tie Whippy up outside while I come in to get my things."

"But you will be back this evening, won't you? I'll pay double time, if money is an issue."

"That won't be necessary," replied Gus. "And yes, if it is a help, I'll come up overnight one more time. After that, I'm afraid I have other commitments."

He was reassured when Eleanor calmly fetched a small

blanket from the kennel and draped it carefully over the dog, then returned to the kitchen. Gus tied Whippy to a stable door, and followed her. She was busy with eggs and bacon, and asked if Gus would have time to eat something before he took Whippy. "She's settled in the morning sun," she said, looking out of the window. "Is she a greyhound or a whippet?"

"Whippet," said Gus. "And if you are sure, I'd love a quick snack. It smells too good to resist."

He was very struck by how serene and collected she seemed after her total panic in the night. She appeared less upset about the sheepdog than she had been about the missing hen. A hangover from the days of a working farm, when the sheepdog was part of the machinery? Or maybe because it was so old, it was a natural end.

In an easy silence, Eleanor placed in front of him a plateful of eggs, bacon, sausage and tomato, which he ate appreciatively, pleased to see that she too was eating normally.

"I'll be off now with Whippy, and I'll be back at nightfall," he said, getting to his feet. "If you want to ring me after the vet has been, this is my mobile number."

He wrote it down on a scrap of paper, and handed it to her. "I'm really sorry about the poor dog," he said. "I heard nothing, I'm afraid, but from what you say, he could easily have slipped away in the night. Gone in his sleep, as it were."

"More than likely," she said quietly. "His time had come, anyway. And there's only the old lame ewe for him to look after now. I'll ask the vet about local Jack Russell terriers. He'll probably have some suggestions. Have a nice day, then, Gus. See you this evening."

GUS FOUND HIMSELF scuttling back down Hangman's Row as if the hounds of hell were behind him. That was a very strong woman indeed, he thought, as he unlocked his door and went gratefully into his familiar cottage. She was like two people. One in terror in the night, and then the practical, steady farmer's wife next morning! He was not looking forward to another night spent in her company, and thought he would phone Deirdre for support. A conversation with a sane and sensible woman would be a relief!

"Dee-Dee? Ah, how are you this morning, my dear?"

"What's wrong?" said Deirdre.

"Nothing, nothing. Just thought I would like to hear the sound of your voice. Can I cadge a coffee from you this morning?"

"What happened? Did she try to seduce you? You're definitely not yourself, Gussy. Come up about ten. I have to go into town later on. See you then."

No sooner had he refreshed Whippy's water bowl than a shadow passed his kitchen window, and there was Miriam, frowning at him.

"You're a fly one!" she said. "Pretending not to see me last evening, and then my spies told me you were seen going into Blackwoods Farm. What are you up to, Gus? Wouldn't it have been polite to explain?"

"Sorry, sorry, Miriam," he said wearily. "I was late. And my mission was an Enquire Within duty. Not pleasure, I assure you."

"What's up with Mrs. Blatch, then? She does go round the bend every so often, you know. I could've warned you. She swears she sees a ghost of somebody, usually her late husband, Ted, coming to take her into the next world, brandishing a weapon. People reckon she does it to attract attention. She lost a nice grey cat once, and claimed it was somebody trying to frighten her."

"A hammer," said Gus. "Last night he had a hammer. Anyway, she had asked for one of us to stay a couple of nights in the house. You know she had a really nasty accident, so it was understandable." But what about the hens? Had she really shut the door?

Miriam was still talking. "Fell out of bed, didn't she? That can do a bit of damage. What did she tell you about that room? The locked one?"

"The dark chamber? Oh, she said it was never used, and she went in occasionally to see to the mice. Otherwise it was locked. Had been locked for years, and as the family didn't need the extra room, they more or less forgot about it."

"Lies, all lies. Did she tell you she used to lock up the lodger? Another of her stories was that he starved himself to death. Nobody believed her, of course. That room led to the fire escape. It was a safety precaution, when they built on the extension. Another of her stories was that she made the box room into a little workroom for the lodger, and he used the fire escape as his private entrance. This was all many years ago, of course."

"What *about* this lodger, Miriam? I've heard a lot of tales about them swanning around the village together, but nobody seems to know who he was, where he came from, or where he went when they fell out."

"That's about all anyone knew. He turned up in the village, was taken in by Mrs. Blatch, and went away again to God knows where."

"Do you remember his name?"

"He had several. Sturridge, I think."

"Honestly, Miriam, it is a pretty sordid tale, don't you think? I must say I didn't take to the woman. But when we agree to work for a client, it doesn't mean we have to like them."

Miriam looked at him, unshaven and miserable, and her soft heart melted. "Come on with me now," she said. "You look as if a freshly made apple turnover would buck you up. And a nice hot cup of tea. Come on, bring Whippy with you."

"Thanks," he said, running his hand over his chin. "Give me ten minutes, and then I'll be round."

She turned to go, then looked back at him. "I do remember one thing," she said. "That lodger was a lot younger than her, and a good head shorter. See you in a minute."

FEELING MUCH MORE cheerful, Gus washed and shaved, and put on some clean clothes. He was reminded of a song from *South Pacific*, and sang tunelessly as he came downstairs to find Whippy. "Gonna wash that girl right outta my hair," he droned.

That was it. He needed to clear away everything he had experienced at Blackwoods Farm. The dead sheepdog, the hooting owls, not to mention the shaking woman and her fearful vision! How could he get out of going up again this evening? He couldn't. The others would understand, but he would definitely go down several notches in their estimation. No, he would have to steel himself. It was for one night only, after all. He locked the back door and went across the gardens to be welcomed into the lovely warm smell of Miriam's baking.

"YOU'VE BEEN GOSSIPING with Miriam again," accused Deirdre, as he bent to kiss her cheek. "I always know. It's that scent she uses. Cheap, cheerful and very strong!"

Gus began to think he would not mind if he never consorted with another woman in his life. "She's a good neighbour, Deirdre," he said. "Rescued me this morning when I was feeling grim."

Deirdre looked at him. "It's that Blatch woman, isn't it?" she said. "I knew at once when you called first thing. Best sit down and tell me all." Once more, Gus did his best to give a dispassionate report on his night with the client.

But when he came to the sheepdog laid out on the doorstep, Deirdre gasped and put her hand to her mouth. "Oh, Gus! Poor woman. Not what she needed right now! It wasn't the prankster, was it?"

Gus shook his head. "No, it died of natural causes, more than likely. She's getting the vet, but she seemed to accept it without being too upset. Do you think we could go back a bit, and recap from the beginning? I'd like to sort out my thoughts, if you don't mind."

With Deirdre's help, they began. First, Eleanor Blatch had approached Enquire Within, with a request to investigate a mysterious intruder, find him and get rid of him. Legally, of course. Second, Deirdre had found Eleanor on the floor by her bed, unconscious and bloody. She had been taken to hospital, treated and released after a few days. Her house had been cleaned, and probably fumigated, ready for her return.

She had continued to ask Enquire Within for help, including some protection during the night for an unspecified time. Knowing that the police would not be likely to help on such flimsy evidence as a vengeful ghost, Gus had agreed, but very reluctantly.

"Don't forget the missing hen," said Deirdre.

"Do you mean she could possibly have made up the whole thing? Play-acted the ghostly visitor thing? She was very convincing." Gus had gone pale at the thought.

Deirdre shrugged. "There's no limit to what some people will do to attract attention to themselves. Especially middle-aged women living alone."

Gus took a deep breath and smiled for the first time since he had woken up. "Not like you, my lovely?" he said, putting out his hand to her.

"I may live alone, Gus Halfhide," she answered, "but I do have plenty of friends."

Twenty

WHEN GUS RETURNED to his cottage, there was a message on his phone. It was Eleanor Blatch, and her voice was firm. "Good news, Gus," she said. "The vet says the old dog died of heart failure. Probably on the blink, but had enough strength to climb the step to the back door. Do you think he was trying to get into the house? Poor old devil. But it was natural causes, I'm glad to say. I shall bury him at the bottom of the vegetable garden, where Ted's dad put the others. Over the years, of course. See you this evening! Bye!"

Gus shivered. The others? He hoped they were all canine. What should he do this afternoon? He was reluctant to stay by himself, watching the hours go by until it was time for duty at Blackwoods Farm. He looked out of his window. The sun had come out, and the sound of the Budd children playing in their garden at the end of the terrace cheered him.

"I know, Whippy," he said. "Let's go across to Springfields, and have a chat with Ivy and Roy. They'll want to know how I survived last night."

He did not really want to go over it again, but he would have to make a proper report sooner or later, so he set off across the Green. Halfway across, a ball from the foot-balling lads hit him in the back. He stopped, and was about to explode, when he thought that it had probably not been deliberate, and so lined himself up and kicked the ball very accurately into their makeshift net on the other end of the Green.

Applause greeted this, all the boys joining in. "Come and join us!" one of them shouted. He shook his head and continued on towards Springfields. What a day! What a night and a day! He quickened his pace now, feeling refreshed. Ivy and Roy were in the lounge, playing Scrabble, while most of the other residents snoozed. It was peaceful, and when Ivy welcomed him warmly and ordered tea, even including Whippy in the invitation to repair to Ivy's room and have a chat, he felt supported, restored, and ready to face the night.

"SO YOU ARE beginning to suspect that she's made it all up? Much as my beloved guessed earlier on?" said Roy.

Gus nodded. "Not all of it. I still think she's nervous about being there alone. Someone might have disliked her enough to frighten her years ago, and she obviously has bad dreams. Unless all that was a convincing charade."

Ivy nodded. "I must say I thought at the time that she was released from hospital sooner than I expected. Maybe she exaggerated her injuries. What do you think, Roy?"

"Very difficult to say. I can't believe she deliberately put her own chickens in danger, and now the vet said the dog died from natural causes."

"You said you heard footsteps in the night, Gus," said Ivy. "It could've been her going down to open the hen coop. As for the night visitor, more likely a nightmare. Always been one for histrionics, apparently. Nightmares can be very frightening, though. Especially the kind where you can't shake it off when you wake up, and it seems real."

"I suppose she couldn't be taking hallucinating drugs?" Roy had a sketchy knowledge of such things, but knew it was possible.

"Doubt it," said Gus. "Although she could be. There's so much we don't know about this case, so I suppose we'll have to carry on with it."

"As long as we think there's some truth in what she says," Ivy said. "We have every right to cancel our enquiry, if we are convinced she is misleading us with lies."

"Well said, beloved," said Roy. "Shall we see what information you can glean from her tonight, Gus? Then we can come to a decision."

Eventually, as twilight fell over the village, Gus set off from home once more, and, steeling himself, put his mobile in his pocket and headed across the green towards Blackwoods Farm. Whippy, showing marked reluctance, followed at his heels.

Halfway across, he caught sight of a group of people coming towards him and branching off in the direction of the pub. He sighed. He could do with a pint or two just now. Perhaps he could indulge himself with a glass of Old Hooky to blunt the effect of looking after a deranged woman? Even Whippy seemed to cheer up as they entered the pub.

"Evening, all," he said, as he walked to the bar. A chorus of greeting came to him from the young people. In no time at all, he was leaning on the bar and chatting to an older man, who told him that they were from the Manor House College.

These youngsters are my students," he said, and held out his hand. "Rickwood Smith, at your service, Mister, er . . . ?"

"Halfhide," said Gus. "And are they on the creative writing course, by any chance?"

"Yes, we are," said an attractive blonde girl with a friendly smile. "Most of this lot are in residence already, but I live locally. In Spinney Close. Samantha Earnshaw is my name. I'm joining in the getting-to-know-you stuff, so we shall all be best mates by the time the course starts in earnest."

"A colleague of mine will be on the course," said Gus. "It will be interesting to see how she is received. She's well into her seventies!"

"More the merrier," said Rickwood Smith expansively. "We shall welcome a different perspective on life."

"Another drink all round?" said Gus, privately hoping they were on halves of shandy. "And here's to success in the course!"

WHEN GUS ARRIVED as arranged, Mrs. Blatch seemed unwilling to talk. As before, she offered him a nightcap, but when he hesitated, she did not insist. "Early bed for me," she said. "I'm quite tired now. Not much sleep last night, as you know!" she said. "I promise not to disturb you tonight. I might leave my light on all night. That should fix the apparition."

"So you do now think it was a figment of your poor old sleepy mind," Gus said consolingly, trusting this would not annoy. He was not expecting a tantrum, but she banged the table and said if that was what he thought, she would leave him and his dog to find their own way upstairs. She then turned off all the lights except the one over the stairs, and disappeared into her room.

"Um, yes, well, Whippy, we'd better go up, too," he said. "Or maybe we could go home, and call it a day?"

"No, you couldn't," said Eleanor, reappearing at the top of the stairs. "I've paid you to stay here. So here you'll stay, thanks very much." Then she disappeared again.

Gus was not pleased, and felt he was being sent upstairs

to bed like a naughty boy. He put the sitting room light on, and took out a book from his bag. He would read until he felt sleepy, and then go up. He searched in his toilet bag and found two small earplugs, which he inserted firmly. The drama queen could yell herself stupid, but he would sleep on, aided by two pints of Old Hooky and a quiet night.

Nothing more untoward happened, and he fell asleep quickly, with Whippy keeping his feet warm. He was amazed when he awoke and saw daylight through the curtains. His travelling clock told him it was six thirty, and he got out of bed and pulled on his clothes. His head was thumping, but a shower and shave would fix that when he returned home. Whippy, still ill at ease, stood by the door, clearly wanting to be released.

"A better night, eh, dog?" Gus could see the principal bedroom door was closed, and tiptoed downstairs, unwilling to wake up his client. There had been no dramas in the night, and he would slip away without her noticing he'd gone. He could leave a note on the kitchen table, saying he would be back for a further consultation during the day. But not another night!

Remembering he had left his book in the sitting room, he went back, drew the curtains and spotted it on the sofa. He went across to collect it, glancing out the windows as he turned. He could see the fire escape, leading down from the dark chamber, and he hesitated. There was something curled up in the steel cage at the base. He looked more closely, opening the French window into the garden. As he got closer, his heart beat faster, and then he was sure. It was Eleanor, and she was no longer alive.

Twenty-one

GUS HAD HAD enough time to telephone Deirdre, and ask her to tell the others the grim news, before Inspector Frobisher arrived, accompanied by his assistant, an attractive policewoman in sensible shoes.

"So what time was it when you found her, Mr. Halfhide?" asked Frobisher. The inspector knew Gus from previous cases, and was well aware that his good friend Deirdre Bloxham had nobbled Augustus Halfhide soon after he arrived in Barrington.

"I suppose it was around six thirty this morning. I had woken early, and hoped to be away before Mrs. Blatch was up and about. But before we go any further, Inspector, I should tell you that Mrs. Blatch has a sister Mary, living in Spinney Close in this village. She is disabled, but has her nephew, Rickwood Smith, staying with her at the moment. I'm not sure this will be in your records, as they don't have anything to do with each other. A family feud, apparently. I expect they should be told as soon as possible, if only as a courtesy?"

Frobisher nodded, and spoke to his assistant, who disappeared, only to reappear five minutes later. She muttered something to the inspector and settled down again.

"So, now, you had been spending the night here? Are you a frequent night visitor to this woman living alone?"

Gus explained that he had agreed to spend a couple of nights at Blackwoods to help tide her over a panic attack and nightmarish dreams. "She is a client of Enquire Within, as you know, Inspector," he said. "I had no amorous intentions concerning Mrs. Blatch, I can assure you. She asked Enquire Within to supply this service, and I was the one who, well, who . . ."

"Drew the short straw, Mr. Halfhide?" supplied the inspector. "Were you intending to be back tonight, continuing your service of reassurance?"

Gus shook his head. "No, I'd had enough, Inspector. It is a creepy old house, with floorboards creaking at night, and cold draughts of air when there are no windows open. She's welcome to it!"

"Please continue," said the Inspector. "My team will be arriving very shortly to do the necessary investigations on and around the deceased."

"You'll have seen to this already, I'm sure. But there's a small room in this house," began Gus, "which is sometimes locked, though your chaps will be able to unlock it. It is the one that leads out to the fire escape. It's just that, well, on one occasion, when I first looked around the house when Mrs. Blatch was in hospital, the small room was open, and I walked in, only to find that it been cleaned, with no sign of cigars."

"Right, well, thank you, Mr. Halfhide. I can hear the team arriving, so that will be all for now. I shall, of course, want to talk to you further. Oh, and by the way, I suppose you couldn't remember the brand of cigar?"

Gus shook his head. "Not sure, Inspector. Looked expensive."

"Right, well, I shall want to hear more about those nightmarish dreams of Mrs. Blatch's, so perhaps you will not mind accompanying my assistant down to the police station where we can continue our talk."

"Me? Down to the station? You're surely not suggesting I am under suspicion! Really, Inspector, that is truly ridiculous!"

"Nevertheless, Mr. Halfhide, it will be necessary."

A SIZABLE CROWD had gathered outside Blackwoods Farm, brought by the sound of sirens, police cars and an ambulance with flashing lights arriving in Manor Road. As Gus was accompanied by the policewoman to a waiting car, he felt like Danton on the way to the scaffold.

"At least you're not suggesting we go by tumbril," he said. The policewoman did not answer, but stood by as he opened the passenger-side door, stepped in and anchored himself with the seat belt.

"All set, Mr. Halfhide?" she said, and they drove off. The crowd's heads turned as they went, and Gus was mortified to see the shocked face of Miriam Blake among them.

As they drove towards Thornwell, the policewoman made one or two fruitless attempts at conversation, trying, without committing herself, to explain the inspector's decision.

"No offence," said Gus, "but I do not intend to say anything at all until I make a statement. I need to phone my lawyer, but first can you please make sure my dog is taken to Miss Blake at number three Hangman's Row? She will come into the garden via the cat flap. This is very important, as she has no road sense and could easily be run over trying to find her way home. That is, the whippet, not Miss Blake."

The policewoman detected a break in Gus's voice, and

drew the car to a halt. In two minutes she had delivered
the message, and was able to reassure him that Whippy
was safe, and had been collected by Miss Blake, who was
already on the scene.

NOW REASSURED ABOUT Whippy, Gus relapsed
into silence, trying hard to think his way round this ridiculous situation. Barry Frobisher was one of Deirdre's former *amoureux*, for God's sake! He must know that she
would never befriend a potential murderer?

When he had cooled down, he began to see the whole
thing more clearly, through the eyes of a policeman. A
woman had been found dead, possibly murdered, and a
man, himself, had been found in her house, having spent
the night there, claiming he knew nothing about it.

But he had summoned the police. Surely, if he had done
the dreadful deed, he would have done a runner as fast as
he could? But then again, if he had constructed a good
enough alibi for himself, it could be a double bluff. So what
was his alibi? That he had spent the night in the house, in
a bedroom near the woman's own, had arisen early and
planned to exit the house before she woke. A sudden
thought had struck him. Mrs. Blatch had not shown up at
all that morning, and he had gone to take a look in the
sitting room, and had found her outside in the fire escape.
So what?

"Guilty as hell!" he said loudly, and the policewoman
looked at him in alarm.

"Sorry, what did you say, Mr. Halfhide? Don't upset
yourself. We are nearly there, and I'm sure that after the
inspector has had another chat with you, you will be free
to leave. And yes, of course you can phone your lawyer."

As she steered him gently, one hand under his elbow,
into the police station, she said quietly that if he'd been

guilty as hell, it was very unlikely she would have been allowed to bring him into town unescorted and sitting in the front seat next to a woman driver.

AS THE INSPECTOR finally came out of Blackwoods Farm, the crowd had dispersed but a large cream Bentley now stood outside the cordon. Inside, much to his dismay, he saw Deirdre Bloxham staring at him with a face like doom.

She opened her door and stepped out into the road to meet him.

"What the hell do you think you're doing, Barry?" she said, loudly enough to reach a couple of plods on duty by the entrance to the farm.

"Please, Deirdre," he muttered into her ear. "I can explain everything. I need to take a statement from you, and also Miss Beasley and Mr. Goodman. Perhaps the best thing is if I follow you to Springfields, and then we can worry them as little as possible. They must be very alarmed already."

"Not helped by your idiocy in arresting Gus and taking him off in chains!"

"Don't be ridiculous, my dear. He agreed to my request. That is all, and as soon as I have had time to talk to him again, I'm sure there will be no need to keep him."

Deirdre, with a face of stone, turned back to her car and waited for him to follow her down into the village and round to Springfields gate. She alighted quickly, and came to his window, rapping on it sharply. He opened it, and she told him to wait until she had prepared them.

"They are old people, Barry Frobisher!" she said. "Living in a residential home because they are frail."

"Though their spirits are strong," Frobisher said, "or so I believe."

"Wait here," said Deirdre, "until I tell you to come in."

"Yes, ma'am," said the inspector, and touched his forelock.

"Oh, for God's sake!" said Deirdre, and marched off towards Springfields reception.

Twenty-two

"DID YOU SAY the inspector was outside, Deirdre?"
Ivy's face was an angry red, and Roy reached out to her
and took her hand. "And what about her sister in Spinney
Close? And her nephew, Rickwood? Have they been told?"

"Let's listen to the rest of what Deirdre has to say," he
suggested quietly. "Losing your cool, as the young say,
will not help Gus."

Deirdre had been trying to explain what had happened
to Gus, but all she knew was what he had told her briefly
on the telephone after he had found Eleanor Blatch. The
bare facts were bad enough, but they were all he had had
time to give her before Frobisher arrived and ended the
call.

Then Katya had come in with their breakfast and said
the sirens and police they had heard were all on their way
to Blackwoods Farm, and rumours were rife. The gossips
in the shop said they'd seen Mr. Halfhide being taken
away. They now remembered they had always known there
was something funny about him, the way he'd arrived in

the village with nothing but what he stood up in, and a small grey dog.

"Everyone was talking about it," said Ivy, "and now you have come to tell us Gus has been taken off to Thornwell police station for questioning. What do you expect, Roy? Of course I'm angry. Anyway, what else have you to tell us, Deirdre?"

"Not a lot, unfortunately. I had a word with the inspector, and he said Gus would soon be released. Then, being a policeman through and through, he was all for storming in here to interview you two, and I stopped him. I said he could come in when we were ready. And Mrs. Spurling is already guarding the reception door, in case he should try a forced entry."

"Don't be so melodramatic, Deirdre," said Ivy, now calmer. "You said Gus phoned you before he left the farm. He must have had more to tell?"

"Well, it seems that he went to look for his book, and saw out the window that there was someone in the cage at the bottom of the fire escape, and it was Eleanor. It was early morning, and he had been going to leave before she got up. He was fed up with the whole thing, I think, before he saw her."

"And is she all right? Why the police?"

"I am afraid she was not all right. In fact, she is dead, Ivy. Gus said she was lying crookedly in the cage, and he reckoned her death must have been instant. Sensibly, he didn't touch her. He had called the police. That's all I know, I'm afraid."

"Well, that explains the police and the ambulance. Thank you, Deirdre, that was all very clear," said Roy.

"So you'd better let the inspector come in, Deirdre," Ivy said. "Perhaps he'll tell us more, and then we can decide what to do about Gus. I'll swear our Gus couldn't kill a wasp, let alone push a woman to her death in the middle of the night."

"He hadn't heard anything in the night, he said, though he admitted he'd had a couple of pints in the pub before going to Blackwoods." Deirdre frowned at Ivy.

"Of course, dear. Best get your inspector, and then we can start work."

Mrs. Spurling had warmed up the small conference room, and when Ivy, Roy and Deirdre went in, they found Inspector Frobisher already waiting for them. He stood up immediately and wished them a good morning.

"Let's hope it is a good morning," said Ivy, allowing him to hold a chair for her. Roy sat next to her, and Deirdre directly opposite the inspector.

"Before you start, Barry Frobisher," said Deirdre, "do we have your assurance that Gus Halfhide will be released and back here today?"

"You know very well, Mrs. Bloxham," he replied stiffly, "that we have to question very closely the man who found the deceased. Especially since he had spent the night in her house."

"That's very reasonable, Deirdre dear," said Roy. "Now, Inspector, we are really very much in the dark about what happened, so perhaps you would be kind enough to fill us in. You will appreciate that we are very concerned about a valued colleague, as well as being fellow workers with you on a case already involving poor Miss Blatch."

Thank God for Roy Goodman, thought the inspector. "Of course," he began, "we all know that Mrs. Blatch had engaged the services of Enquire Within to find out who, if anybody, was disturbing her sleep with ghostly manifestations and threats to her person. We all also know that this lady has a troubled history, when she shut herself off from everything and allowed her house to go to rack and ruin."

"Not quite a ruin," interrupted Deirdre. "I reckon me and my team cleaned that place up pretty well before she came out of hospital. Needs more attention, but it's certainly not a ruin, and she was doing her bit to help."

"Don't interrupt the inspector," said Ivy. "Else we shall be here all day. Carry on, please."

"Thanks, Miss Beasley. Well, we were first called in when Mrs. Bloxham found Mrs. Blatch unconscious on the floor of her bedroom, apparently having fallen out of bed and cut open her head on something sharp. It could have been the old iron bedstead, or something else subsequently removed. She was taken to hospital, where she recovered. Since then she has been a new woman. Deirdre has befriended her, and we have made certain enquiries about a former lodger of hers."

"So what have you found out?"

"Deirdre! Do be quiet, girl!" Ivy glared at her, and Deirdre subsided with a mutinous expression.

"Nothing, so far. We are still following several leads, but nothing yet. Apart from his name, which at that time was Sturridge."

Deirdre opened her mouth to tell him that Roy and Ivy had failed to find any trace of him in the library, but a furious look from Ivy quelled her.

"We—I should perhaps say I—had more or less decided that Mrs. Blatch had dreamt up the threats, but was now well on the road to recovery from delusions, and her future looked bright," said Frobisher. "You can imagine, therefore, how surprised I was to receive Mr. Halfhide's call this morning. I have already explained why we want to talk to him urgently, since he may have many details to remember from the previous twelve hours which will help us in our enquiries."

He cleared his throat and looked round the three. "Have you anything to add to that?" he asked. "Anything at all that you can think of that might be helpful?"

"I think you should know, Inspector," Ivy said slowly, "that although Deirdre here really took to the woman, I had my doubts. It seemed to me that she was not always telling the truth. Nothing important, but one of those people who can't resist the odd white lie, where necessary to make themselves appear in a good light. And, as you perhaps know, she quarrelled years ago with a disabled sister living in Spinney Close, and they haven't spoken since. As she was a client of Enquire Within, it doesn't matter what I thought of her character. It was a job for us to do. Whether we shall want to carry on, I must discuss with colleagues. Releasing Gus is vital. He knew the deceased better than any of us. He'd spent two nights there, you know."

The inspector stood up. "As you say, Miss Beasley," he said. "He may well have important details to tell us. Please rest assured that I shall do my best to do my job efficiently for all concerned. And we shall naturally be speaking to her sister, and her nephew, did you say? Perhaps you will kindly let me know if you think of anything else that might help us."

He nodded at all three and went swiftly out of the room. There was a gloomy silence for a minute or two, and then Ivy got to her feet. "Right! Come on, you two. I regard the inspector's farewell speech as a challenge. We have a great deal of work to do, and there's every reason to start straight away. I smell cooking, and I suppose we can fuel ourselves with lunch first. Open the door, Deirdre. You'd better go home now in case Gus wants to get in touch. We shall be up to join you at half past two. Let's hope there's good news by then."

AS IF TO help them, dark morning clouds had dispersed and watery sunshine lit their way up to Tawny Wings. By three o'clock they were settled and Ivy had taken the chair. "I've looked at notes I made after our visit to the library. Now, do we all think there was anything at all in Miss Blatch's suspicion that her former lodger had returned to persecute her?"

"Yeah, I think so," said Deirdre. "After all, there was definitely something going on in the dark chamber, as Gus calls it. Dammit! We should have asked Frobisher if his men had broken into that, and what they found. Anyway, I think it is a line still needing to be pursued."

"Gus went in once, didn't he? Found nobody, but evidence of recent occupation," Deirdre said. "He told me later that he reckoned you can tell when a room is being used, and in spite of what Mrs. Blatch said, that room was. Being used, that is."

"I'd like to take another look at the bottom of the fire escape," said Roy. "I think I remember that cage thing. Not locked up, most of the time, like when Gus went in and found the cigar butt. I believed we had mentioned the need for the fire escape to be always accessible, so perhaps Eleanor had remembered that. Perhaps we could take a look up there, Ivy?"

"Police won't let you anywhere near it. Still, we might be able to creep round and see what's to be found."

"The reason I ask is that it would be the obvious way for an attacker—if it really was an attack this time—to get away from the house without waking Gus, who was asleep upstairs, but in a room with a door very close to Miss Blatch's. But why? Lord knows why she was found at the bottom of the fire escape, unless either she tripped and fell, or she was pushed. It seems almost ridiculous to contemplate that, but it must be looked at as a possibility."

"And if the killer had lured her into the dark chamber and then done the deed, he could easily have scarpered out of the house and away. But, anyway, I'm sure with all that going on, Gus would have woken. That's probable, isn't it?" said Deirdre.

"Or," said Ivy, "maybe the lodger was already living there and sharing Mrs. Blatch's bed, creeping in after there was no risk of Gus hearing him. Then he could easily have thought of a reason for the two of them to go into the dark chamber and unlock the escape. It would have been easy for him. Lord knows where he's living, if he is around. I suppose it could have been him who left the cigar butt? Perhaps he stays out of the way while people are around. Skulks in the dark chamber?"

"Ivy!" said Roy, "My dearest girl, what a terrible thought! No wonder you have joined a creative writing class. We shall wait in trepidation for publication day!"

Deirdre did not laugh. She was impressed with Ivy's guesswork, and now asked her why a wayward lodger should do such a thing. After all, he was living in some comfort, perhaps blackmailing Eleanor Blatch into keeping him in food and drink. Why disturb what was a cushy billet?

She paused, frowning. "What's that noise?" she said suddenly.

Ivy drew in her breath sharply. "Sounds like someone trying to get in the French windows in your drawing room," she said.

Roy struggled to his feet. "I shall go and look. You two ladies stay here. It's probably nothing more than a bird flying into the glass. They do, you know."

Before he could get to the door, it opened and Deirdre moved swiftly to protect Ivy from an intruder.

"Sorry to break in, Dee-Dee," said Gus, half smiling, and unsure of his welcome. "I think your doorbell is broken. Anyway, I'm here. And before you say another thing, there's a development I gleaned from the nice police-woman. Our friend Eleanor Blatch was a smoker, and her chosen puff was a small cigar. An immediate inspection found a small pack in her pockets, apparently, and a strong smell of cigar smoke pervading her clothes."

Twenty-three

"THAT EXPLAINS IT, then. I suppose in her generation ladies didn't handle cigars, at least in public, and she would retire to the dark chamber for a quiet smoke. So did you escape, or did Frobisher let you go?"

Deirdre now sat on the sofa beside Gus, plying him with coffee and chocolate biscuits. She even offered one to Whippy, but was immediately thwarted by Ivy saying that chocolate was certain death to dogs.

"Oh, he was quite happy to let me go," Gus said, "and I must say he was very professional and decent with it. Good chap, Deirdre, I must say."

"Naturally," said Deirdre. "I don't consort with rotters. Anyway, enough of that. Tell us all the interesting things he said about what the police have found so far."

"I don't think he felt much like confiding in me—yet! But he did close question me about Whippy."

"Whippy?" said Roy. "I hope he was not suggesting she had a hand in the business?"

"No, but he did pick up from what I said that Whippy

had not barked or whimpered in any way once I was in bed. Which indicates that Eleanor Blatch was persuaded to go into the dark chamber by person or persons known."

"That's quite enough of those known persons, Gus," said Ivy. "If anyone asked me, I'd say that the big question is WHY? Surely, at her age, she wasn't up to participating in athletic high jinks? And dear Whippy would certainly have pricked her ears at any squeals of delight?"

"Yep, Ivy, quite right," said Deirdre. "Of course, now we know she is the smoker, I suppose if she couldn't sleep, say, she could have retired to the dark chamber for a quiet smoke alone."

Gus thought for a moment. "Not when I first went up to bed," he said. "I think it was quiet inside the house in the early morning. But I couldn't swear to that."

"I suppose you didn't think to look at the dark chamber door? No, of course not, why would you?" said Roy.

"And the back door, Gus, the one in the kitchen? Was that locked?" Deirdre had a clear map of the ground floor of the farmhouse in her head, and since she had helped clean up the place, she remembered the front door was almost never opened, as Ivy had found. The back one was in constant use. So it was either a good push at the front or the back kitchen door leading out into the yard.

"Yes, it was locked," he said miserably. "I'm quite sure on that one, because I unlocked it to let the inspector in, after I phoned. So nobody went out that way."

"Did Barry Frobisher ask you about the missing hens, or the dog?" persisted Deirdre. "I know you won't agree, but I think those horrible things surely meant that someone reasonably local intended to frighten her. First bantams, then a dog, and finally a vulnerable lady. She could have had another nightmare and . . . Well, it's difficult to guess what happened. There might well have been someone very cunning who chose their moment, knowing you were sleeping in the house and would be an obvious suspect."

Gus looked grim. "I have to confess that I took a sleeping pill when I got to bed. I couldn't face another hysterical session. She was in a lousy mood when she went up, as I've said."

"Don't worry," said Ivy. "None of us has reason to go back there. We can safely leave that to the police. One thing is definitely sure. The murderer is not likely to be hanging around there, waiting to be found."

BUT LATER THAT evening, as Ivy and Roy were sitting in companionable silence over a last cup of hot milk, Ivy suddenly spoke with urgency in her voice.

"Roy! I've had an odd thought. Do you think it possible that the villain who killed Eleanor Blatch *is* still hiding somewhere around the farm? He could wait until it all blows over and the police depart, and then take up his secret residence again and nobody any the wiser. What do you think?"

Roy shook his head. "Possible, I suppose. But very unlikely. I don't underestimate police searching powers. They would do a very thorough job."

"But think how many places on a farm there are for a person to hide. And that particular farm has not been modernised inside or out for goodness knows how many years. Perhaps worth a look, once the police have gone.

"Mm, well, perhaps. But right now, Miss Ivy, it is time for bed. Tomorrow is another day, and we shall see what it brings."

A light and tactful knock on Ivy's door heralded Katya. "Sorry to interrupt," she said. "I have Mr. Halfhide on the phone, and he says it is urgent. I have told him it is too late to bother you, but he insists."

Ivy took the phone from her, and Roy watched her face. She smiled at first, then frowned, and finally nodded after ending the call. She said they must all meet tomorrow. Ten thirty at Tawny Wings.

"Did he say why, dearest?" said Roy, getting to his feet and going across to hold Ivy's hand.

"Seems there's been another casualty. Very serious, this time."

"What could be more serious than murder?" Roy said.

"Whippy. She has been kidnapped."

"But she is only a dog," Katya said. "She may have run off by herself."

"Not with Gus looking after her," said Ivy. "He is very upset."

"Then we shall be at Tawny Wings at half past ten tomorrow, to supply consolation and support." He limped out of the door and took Katya's arm. "That dog is like a child to Gus, my dear. A child and close companion," he said. He patted her swelling stomach gently, and said he was sure she would understand.

Twenty-four

IT WAS A very gloomy Gus who accompanied Ivy and Roy up to Tawny Wings. He had seen them from outside the shop, and had run across the green to catch up with them.

"Morning, old chap," said Roy. "Any news?"

Gus shook his head. "Nothing. I've been asking around since early morning, and left a notice up on James's Lost and Found board in the shop."

"And a reward?" said Ivy. "That often brings kidnappers to their senses."

"Possibly," answered Gus. "But my bank balance won't permit much more than twenty pounds."

"If it's kids," said Ivy, "that could well be enough. Worth a try."

They had arrived at Deirdre's front door, and she opened immediately. "Gus?" she said. He shook his head, and helped Roy to alight from his trundle. "No, Deirdre. I've just been leaving notices around the village, and asking everyone I meet if they've seen a small grey whippet."

Deirdre said coffee was ready to pour and they should have that first, instead of their usual half-time break.

"So now we have two cases," said Ivy, when they had settled. "The unresolved death of one of our clients, and the cruel kidnap of one of our colleagues."

"Well, not exactly colleague," said Deirdre, "but one of us, nevertheless."

"Thanks, love," said Gus. "I don't expect you to spend much time on Whippy. She is, after all, my responsibility."

"But the two cases may be linked," said Ivy. She sat behind the desk, her grey hair neatly confined inside an invisible hairnet, and the barest dab of powder on her nose. She sat straight as a ramrod, her skirt pulled well down over her knees, and was every inch the chairperson. Gus was comforted by Ivy's confident, straightforward approach, and said that if it was okay by the others, he would sit by the window in case Whippy had escaped and come looking for him.

"There is one other thing we can do." Last evening, Ivy had a new idea, and one worth pursuing.

"Carry on, my dear." Roy nodded at her, urging her on.

"Well, it was when we were supposing a murderer to be miles away by now. Which, of course, he could be. If he exists. But then I thought perhaps he was working a double bluff, and in fact hiding somewhere on or around the farm, possibly with Whippy. It's a terrible derelict place, with outbuildings stuffed with old bits of machinery, sacks of rotting animal feeds, bales of hay and straw in the hay barn, half eaten by rats. There would be dozens of places for a man to hide, at least for a while."

Gus suddenly jumped to his feet. "That's her!" he said, rushing to the window and then the door. But the car had gone by, out of reach. "She was there! Sitting on the backseat! I'm sure it was her, Deirdre. Can we phone Frobisher and get the police to keep a look out for an old Peugeot? Faded blue. A woman driving! Go on, Deirdre, go and phone him. Promise him anything."

Deirdre frowned. "What do you mean by that, Gus?" she said, but he didn't answer.

"What do you think?" she said, turning to the others.

"Worth a try," said Ivy. "I seem to be saying that a lot this morning. But it is worth a try, Deirdre."

Deirdre left the room, and they heard her talking on the phone in the kitchen. When she returned she was very red in the face. "Job done," she said shortly. "He'll deal with it."

"Right, now let's get on," Ivy said. "First of all, back to the farm. Roy and I are going to have a sniff around when I come back from my first day at the college. The police will probably have finished there by then. The house will be locked up, of course, but it is the rest of it that interests me."

"So, Gus is going into town to give more Whippy details to the police. Would you like me to come with you?"

Gus nodded. "Love you to, Dee-Dee," he said. "Sorry if I offended you. All in a good cause. So that's this afternoon fixed, everybody. Meanwhile, we must all keep our eyes well and truly open. Even spotting the blue Peugeot would be a help. It was old, and, as I said, faded here and there."

"There is a possibility," said Roy gently, "that it was not Whippy. It could have been a grey whippet, but not ours. Best to bear that in mind, Gus, old chap. It might save a bit of disappointment."

Gus shook his head. "It was Whippy, I'm sure of that. I would know her anywhere. But thanks, Roy. And thanks, everybody. So shall we report back at Springfields early evening? Perhaps after your supper, Ivy?"

"Fine. We'll expect you this evening, then. Good hunting!"

AS DARKNESS FELL in the field behind Blackwoods Farm, far in the corner, under a group of beech trees, the old henhouse on wheels and with its few steps leading to a tightly shut door was well hidden from view. It had been there for fifty or sixty years, but not in use for a good twenty. Eleanor Blatch had housed her few hens in the farmyard, and the field, known as Home Close, had been given over to a pig or two and a lame ewe that had become a pet.

The police were giving it a brief last look, noting that it was as big as a small caravan on wheels, with a stepladder leading to the door, which was stuck fast. By peering through the window on one side of the door, they could see it was clear and clean. A single chair and desk on one side, and a camp bed on the other. Small curtains hung at the only window, and they looked clean and fresh.

"Could have been used by a crook, I suppose, but more like a play house for kids. Anyway, you can see there's nobody in there."

"Very unlikely he's still around, I reckon," said a young constable to his colleague as they walked back down the field. "Miles away, more than likely. What we need to find is a reason why he—or, I suppose, she—wanted to kill an old woman with no money and little in the way of valuables."

"Love," said the policewoman walking by his side. "A crime of passion, I reckon."

"What? With her in her fifties, and not even very attractive with it?"

"There's no accounting for taste," said the policewoman, and climbed into the police car beside him. "You'll see. I could put money on it. A *crime passionel*, as the French say."

Twenty-five

MRS. SPURLING STOOD in Springfields reception facing Gus and Deirdre, her face red and arms akimbo.

"My duty, Mrs. Bloxham, is to my elderly residents. Their health and strength are my primary concern. And in the case of Miss Beasley and Mr. Goodman, who are engaged to be married, don't you think it would be nice to make sure they both arrive at the church in good heart? And," she continued, as Deirdre was about to speak, "by good heart, I mean in the best of health in mind and body. Which includes resting after a busy day and retiring to sleep with tranquil thoughts."

Deirdre and Gus were stunned. They knew the old dragon disapproved of Enquire Within and all its activities, but her deputy, Miss Pinkney, who stood close behind her, knew equally well that Miss Beasley and Mr. Goodman were so incredibly well and active *because* the whole business of detection and contact with the outside world was largely responsible for their excellent condition. That, and the wonderfully good food cooked by Katya and Anya in the kitchen.

"Perhaps you would kindly check that Miss Beasley and Mr. Goodman are expecting us? I think they might be disappointed if you send us packing, dear Mrs. Spurling," said Gus.

"I'll go and check," butted in Miss Pinkney quickly. "Shan't be a minute," she added, and disappeared. Mrs. Spurling, meanwhile, somewhat mollified by Gus's charm, returned her arms to her sides and said they could wait in the lounge until Miss Pinkney returned.

"I know Miss Beasley and Mr. Goodman have gone upstairs, so I would not want to disturb their little snooze," she said.

Good gracious, thought Gus. What can the woman mean? Surely not rumpy-pumpy under the duvet? The idea was so ludicrous that he laughed out loud.

"Here comes Pinkers," he said. "What's the score?"

"All clear," said the plump deputy, puffing a little. "You are to go up immediately, if that's all right with Mrs. Spurling?"

Upstairs, Ivy and Roy had rearranged the room so that two extra chairs could be accommodated when Deirdre and Gus joined them.

"Katya is bringing hot chocolate," whispered Miss Pinkney, as she left them, and soon they were comfortably settled, ready to catch up with what had been discovered during the afternoon.

"You first, Ivy," said Deirdre. "You take the chair."

"My report will be brief," she answered. "Roy and I went for a walk and happened to find ourselves outside Blackwoods Farm."

"Only *happened*?" said Deirdre, and they all laughed.

"Anyway," continued Ivy, "we noticed a police car outside and we could see a young constable and a policewoman opening and shutting stable doors and storerooms at the back of the house."

"Still looking, then?" Gus did not ask if they had found Whippy. He knew Ivy would have told him by now if they had.

"Yes, it seems so. The last we saw of them was walking away up the Home Close. There's a spinney up there, and I suppose they were taking a look. Up there somewhere is Spinney Close. You know, the place where Eleanor's sister lives. We should maybe introduce ourselves at some point?"

"Agreed," said Roy. "But this time the light was going, so we carried on back here. We did also look back at the fire escape, but it looked exactly the same, and there were no lights showing anywhere in the whole house. It looked very empty and sad. Or so my Ivy thought."

"And then I told myself to skip such sentimental rubbish, and get on with matters in hand. We hadn't forgotten Whippy, Gus, but believe it or no, we didn't see a single dog. Not one. Or, wait a minute, I tell a lie. Wasn't there a snappy little terrier in the vicar's window? But it was nothing like Whippy, I'm afraid."

"Never mind, and thanks for looking," said Gus. "I plan to stay up most of tonight, roaming round the village and empty houses and barns where she might be."

"You'll get arrested," said Deirdre. "Loitering with intent, or some such."

"I think if it was me, I'd do the same, if that would make you feel happier," said Roy. "I should carry on, and risk arrest."

GUS SET OUT from his house as dusk fell. Most people would be indoors, he reckoned, and be unlikely to wonder what Mr. Halfhide was doing, peering into gardens and driveways.

As he went, he whistled. Whippy was very accustomed
to his whistling her to return to him when they walked in
the woods, and even if she couldn't escape, she was very
likely to bark. Her bark was sharp and high, and would
carry quite a way.

He circled the Green, loitering outside houses with outbuildings or garages and whistling loudly. Once or twice
curtains were drawn back and a head would appear, but
only for seconds, and he moved on. He arrived outside
Springfields and wondered whether to go in, but thought it
most unlikely that Whippy would be hidden anywhere
there. There was constant coming and going, and somebody
would be sure to notice if a strange—or even familiar—
whippet appeared.

Then he came to the farm. Everywhere was dark and
unwelcoming. He told himself that spooks do not exist, and
walked into the yard, still whistling. Silence. No acknowl-
edging bark, nor even a whimper. He knew that the police
had done a thorough search, looking for the murderer. Frobisher had said nothing had been found there, except a half
century's worth of old junk dumped at random.

He stood looking over the field gate, whistling as loud
as he could, and through the darkness saw a dim light.
That would be the new houses up towards Tawny Wings.
A small development of affordable housing had been built
in a field the other side of the Blatches' spinney, including
some old persons' bungalows. The spinney was mature,
with a leafy canopy over tall, bare trunks, so that lights
could easily be seen. Then the dim light went out, and he
moved across the road to the Manor House College.

No streetlights up there, and Gus put on his torch. The
footpath had stopped by the farm, so he walked close to
the verge. He decided there was no point in whistling as
he walked by a field, and so started again once the Manor
House was in sight. There were plenty of outbuildings
there, some of them half constructed in Rubens's plan to

turn them into flatlets for his students. Keeping as quiet as he could, he walked up the drive to the house, and then crept round and along the line of outbuildings, several of them clearly originally stables. He hesitated. Best not whistle so close to the house, but he couldn't resist a short, soft burst. Then, at the same time exactly, lights came on and blazed at him, and over one of the stable doors leapt a small grey whippet.

"Whippy! Whippy, Whippy, Whippy. . . ."

Gus gathered her up in his arms and put his cheek to the top of her velvety head. Then a door opened, and Peter Rubens strode over to where they stood.

"Exactly what do you think you're doing? Oh, it's you, Halfhide," he said. "You're trespassing. I watched you on my yard camera. Very useful piece of technology. You'd better come in and explain."

Once inside, with a glass of brandy, Gus gave Rubens an edited version of what had happened.

"She must have somehow run off, maybe followed my spaniel dog," said the high master with a fruity chuckle. "He's a terror for escaping when he sniffs a bitch in the vicinity. He probably brought her home to meet the family! One of my students, meaning well, must have shut her in the stable. But fancy her leaping over the half door! It's very high for such a small dog. She could only have done it when she heard her master's voice. Still, no harm done."

Gus sighed. "Well, thanks, Mr. Rubens," he said, draining his glass. "I can't tell you how much it means to me to have her back again. There's no danger of puppies, since she's been fixed. So sorry to have disturbed you, but at least you know your yard camera worked a treat! I must be going home. By the way," he added, as Peter Rubens showed him out, "a friend of mine is about to be one of your students. Creative Writing, I believe. Miss Ivy Beasley, from Springfields. She's looking forward to it."

"And we're looking forward to having her here," said

Rubens. "I like a challenge. No disrespect to your friend, but I anticipate a small upheaval! Miss Beasley is clearly not one of your run-of-the-mill students, and she has not been able to be part of our bonding sessions in the last couple of weeks. But from what I have seen of her, I'm sure she will very soon find her feet with us. I have every faith in Rickwood Smith, who has said he is really looking forward to the course."

"Very good! Best of luck, sir," said Gus, as he walked on his way.

Twenty-six

AFTER A QUIET Sunday spent reading and watching television, this Monday morning there was a general air of something about to happen in Springfields. Ivy and Roy had been up earlier than usual, and Ivy had eaten a hearty breakfast before going up to her room.

"To titivate, so she told me," said Roy, still sitting over his toast and marmalade, and answering Katya's question as to her whereabouts.

She smiled, and picked up his empty coffee cup. "Ah, she is having a wash and brush-up, as my mother-in-law says. Before going off to college?"

"More or less," said Roy.

"And you are down in the dumps? Would you like more coffee?"

"I've been deserted, Katya. That's what. So close to having a wife to keep in order, I am now merely the fiancé of a college student studying creative writing. Fate has dealt me an unexpected blow." He looked at her shocked face, and laughed. "I'm joking, my dear," he said.

"But surely you will support her? And be very interested in her memoirs? I believe she told me that is what she intends to work on? All kinds of things you could learn about your intended bride!"

"That's the trouble. I may learn all kinds of things I'd rather not know!"

"Rubbish," said a brisk voice from behind him. Ivy had put on her coat and hat, and looked exactly as usual, except for a brighter look in her eye and a bundle of books in a capacious bag held in her hand.

"Are you going to walk me up to the Manor House, Roy?" she said. "I'd like to go early and take a look at that stable where Whippy was found. Leapt over a half door as high as a five-barred gate, Katya! Gus is ecstatic, of course."

"And now I shall help you with the trundle, Mr. Goodman. Mrs. Spurling asked particularly to let her know when you leave. I think she is worried you might go off and never return!"

"Oh, Roy will be back quite soon, but I shall be home around half past three this afternoon. Ready for tea, I expect!"

One or two of the younger residents had gathered to see them off, half jealous of Ivy's break for freedom, half critical of a reckless plan that was bound to fail.

"If anybody asked me," she said, as she followed Roy in his trundle out of the gate, "I would say it's all a lot of fuss about nothing. I shall start with the best of intentions, but if I fail, or don't enjoy it, I shall stop. Simple as that. Careful, Roy, there's a dead hedgehog on the path. Poor thing. Still, they're covered in fleas, you know. Best not to touch it," she added, kicking it accurately into the ditch, where it unrolled and glared at her.

THE FIRST SESSION of the creative writing course began with a dozen or so chairs positioned casually around a pleasant room smelling of new paint. A real fire blazed in the hearth, with a large basket of logs ready for replenishing.

Ivy took one of the seats directly facing a large desk, behind which sat Rickwood Smith, who smiled familiarly at her, and said how pleased he was to see her again. He jumped up to help her, and she brushed him away like an annoying fly.

"I am perfectly capable of finding my seat, Mister, er . . ." she said sharply.

"Rickwood," he reminded her. "We met when you came for interview."

"And your surname again?" said Ivy, not smiling.

"Smith," he said. "Easy to confuse me with other Smiths, so Rick would be better. May I call you Ivy?" he asked.

"No," said Ivy, and began rooting about in her bag to find the first Creative Writing unit.

Fortunately for Rickwood Smith, other students began to arrive and were jolly and friendly, and did not mind in the least being called by their Christian names. One pretty girl of about seventeen sat down next to Ivy. She said nothing, and Ivy could see she was a little uneasy.

"Morning, my dear," Ivy said quietly. "Are you as new to all this as me? I am sure we're going to enjoy ourselves."

The girl visibly relaxed, and said confidingly to Ivy that she had been encouraged by her parents to sign on, as she had written some interesting stuff in English lessons at school. "And I've been together with the students who are resident here, though I am local. We've had great evenings in the pub, and our tutor"—she dropped her voice to a whisper—"is a lovely man. Really kind and supportive."

And sophisticated and handsome, thought Ivy. But she smiled and said that she was intending to write her memoirs. "As I am very old, I have a great deal to remember, and I'd like to put it all in order and in print for those who come after me."

The girl nodded. "Great idea," she said. "What's your name?"

"Miss Beasley. What's yours?"

"Samantha Earnshaw," said the girl. "My friends call me Sam, mostly."

"I shall call you Samantha," Ivy said. "Very pretty name. Our prime minister's wife's name."

"Um, now, if we're all ready?" Rickwood smiled round at the assembled ten students. All but Ivy were late teens or early twenties, and Rickwood asked them all to say their names and tell the group a little about themselves.

"What's the point of that?" said Ivy. "Surely we'll get to know each other even better over time?"

Rickwood sighed. He had been warned by Mr. Rubens, but had not anticipated trouble quite so early in the day.

"It is a nice way of getting together, Miss Beasley. Always done, these days."

"Not in my day," said Ivy, shaking her head. "But carry on, Mr. Smith. I am all ears."

After all had had their say, Rickwood turned to Ivy. "And are you going to tell us a little about yourself? I am sure the others would be most interested to know . . ." He tailed off, aware that whatever he said would probably annoy her. Sure enough, she snapped back at him that if he was implying that because she was old she'd want to talk about the past, he was wrong. And could they get on with creative writing, especially memoirs, which was why she was present?

Round one to Miss Beasley, thought Rickwood, and said he would begin with outlining the different kinds of creative writing the students might be planning. "Becoming a journalist is very popular," he said. "Also travel writers, novelists, magazine contributors, poets, biographers and so on. All are using words to express what they wish to say. And, as Miss Beasley has told me, there are those of us interested in writing our memoirs. And that is not a bad place to start."

Ivy nodded in approval. She felt she was making headway, and managed a small smile of encouragement for Rickwood Smith.

ROY, BACK AT Springfields, was feeling very odd. He had become so used to having Ivy as his daily companion, and now he was lost for something to do with himself. He was about to suggest a game of chess with old Fred, when his mobile rang.

"Roy? Gus here. Has our novice writer gone off to college?"

"'Fraid so," said Roy. "And she's been there a good hour and a half, so I must assume she's not giving up before she starts. That is what I suspected might happen, but no. Not my Ivy. Anyway, how are you, my boy?"

"I'm fine. I'm ringing to find out if you fancy a trip out this morning? I was planning to go into Oakbridge library, to see if we could broaden out our background knowledge of Mrs. Winchen Blatch. They are very helpful there, and I can easily take you plus a folding wheelchair in my vehicle."

"Oh, how kind! Are you sure you're not doing this to cheer me up?"

"Of course not! I have been thinking we still know very little about Eleanor Blatch, or her family and early life, and we could do with a new lead. We know her estranged sister is disabled and lives in the village. And that her nephew is a creative writing tutor. But who, for instance, were the Winchens, Eleanor's second name? You've lived around here all your life. Have you ever heard of them?"

"Come to think of it, no, I haven't. As you say, could well be worth a hunt. When would you be picking me up?"

"Now," said Gus. "At least, I'll be there in about fifteen minutes. I'm going to leave Whippy with Miriam next door. I shall never again be happy to leave her alone. See you very shortly."

Good lad, thought Roy. And he was right. They knew next to nothing about Eleanor Blatch's background. He limped out of the lounge and into reception, to tell Miss Pinkney he would not be in for lunch. He was going on an important mission with Mr. Halfhide.

Miss Pinkney smiled broadly. "How lovely!" she said. "Exactly what the doctor ordered. I do hope you'll have some success with your mission. Will you be back in time to meet Miss Beasley out of college?"

"Heavens, yes! It wouldn't do for me to be late for that! And with luck, I shall have something interesting to tell her, as well as listening to an account of her day. Which, you know, is bound to be amusing and informative. My Ivy, Miss Pinkney, misses nothing."

Twenty-seven

THE FIRST SESSION of Rickwood's creative writing course had, after a halting start, gone reasonably well. Several articulate students had spoken up, and one in particular, Alexander, had dominated the conversations. A lad to watch, Rickwood had thought. And then there was Miss Beasley, who had said at one point that in her school days, she remembered that the best learning was done by pupils who only spoke when spoken to.

All the others, including Alexander, had laughed, and Rickwood had begun to think that, if handled properly, Miss Ivy Beasley could be a real asset in the class.

Ivy, for her part, had listened carefully to everything he said, and made a few notes in a fat notebook she had bought from the village shop. The introduction Rickwood had made to the subject of memoir writing had been very interesting, especially his emphasis on being brutally frank with oneself! Who is going to be interested in reading your memoir? Have you a talent for humorous writing? Does your long life contain historical or dramatic episodes that are likely to move the story on?

The word "story" stuck with Ivy. She realised that she would indeed be telling a story, and she would need to sift and reject subjects that might be of great interest to her alone. She had a question or two to ask Rickwood, but decided early on that she would note them down and ask him at the next session, when she would have had time to think about them.

Lunchtime was held in a converted barn at the back of the house. It had been sympathetically turned into a kind of canteen, where the tables were small, six places at most, and the serving counter was colourful with fresh flowers.

Samantha, who had gained courage quite quickly, and made several sensible contributions in class, now asked Miss Beasley if they could share a table, and Ivy gratefully sat down next to her. Two more students joined them, including Alexander the pest, and talking was animated and easy. Then Rickwood Smith appeared, and took the last chair at their table. The conversation immediately stalled, until Ivy said that if she had known the teacher was going to join them, she would have brought him an apple. Alexander chuckled. "An apple for the teacher," he said. "Very good, Miss Beasley."

"And how is your mother, Mr. Smith?" said Ivy, in with both feet as usual. "I understand she has difficulty in getting about?"

"She has been disabled for many years, Miss Beasley. A riding accident, back in Australia, I'm afraid. The horse threw her, and she landed on her back on a large rock. But we are very lucky with caring help, so that she is able to stay in her own home."

"My mum calls to see her often," said Samantha. "She likes chatting to her. I expect she's very pleased to have you home for a while. Is it true that Mrs. Blatch, the one who died recently, was her sister?"

Rickwood nodded. "But we had no communication with Mrs. Blatch, unfortunately. Years and years ago there was an almighty row, and the serious feud was a result. I was forbidden by my mother to visit my aunt Blatch."

"Good gracious, Mr. Smith," said Ivy. "But a sister is a sister. Your mother must have been at least a little sad?"

Before Rickwood could answer her, Peter Rubens appeared, looking flustered. "Rickwood, old chap, could you spare me a minute? Unhappy parent on the phone. You'd think we were a nursery school sometimes!"

When they had gone, the students closed ranks and began to talk about the morning's work. "And how about you, Miss Beasley," said a nineteen-year-old, handsome and expensively turned out. "Did you enjoy your first morning?"

"Yes. Quite unexpectedly, I enjoyed it very much. And you? What is your name again?"

"Alexander," he said. "This is my second attempt at creative writing, and I must say Rickwood seems an excellent tutor. Unlike my previous one, who was a batty old duck who seemed to think Barbara Cartland was the goal towards which we should all strive."

"Ah," said Ivy, with a bland smile. "My favourite author. Wonderful storyteller, Alexander. When you have written as many books as she has, and had them published, you can call yourself a writer!"

By the time they had all assembled back in class, Ivy was feeling quite at home and looking forward to Rickwood's next session.

"Welcome back," he began, "I hope you have all charged your batteries with a good lunch? Good. This afternoon I plan to have a question and answer session. This will be the programme for all our day sessions, so it might be quite useful if you think of questions in advance. Who is going to start us off?"

The pest put up his hand. "I'd like to know," he said,

"what are my fellow students' opinions of the writing of James Joyce?"

Silence. None of them have ever read any James Joyce, thought Rickwood. He looked around, and Ivy caught his eye. "If anyone asked me," she said, "he ought to have been hanged. In fact, I'm not so sure that he wasn't. I never read anything he wrote, but I used to hear him on the wireless, trying to spread bad rumours over here during the war. Yes, I'm pretty sure he was hanged. Lord Haw-Haw, that was his nickname. What did he write, then?"

"Um, not sure if we've got the right man here," said Rickwood.

Samantha put up her hand. "I'd rather hear about Lord Haw-Haw than that Irish git who never knew when to stop. Go on, Miss Beasley."

Ivy was only too happy to talk about the traitor's broadcasts, and answer questions from the others about wartime, and how traitors were dealt with.

Rickwood sat back and listened. When he looked at his watch, he saw they had only ten minutes before they broke up for the afternoon.

"Time to shut up shop," he said. "I must say our first day has moved forward much more than I anticipated. You all showed great promise, and I look forward to seeing you again on Monday. Now, Miss Beasley, do you have a lift back to Springfields?"

"Nothing wrong with my legs, young man," she said. "And I see my fiancé is here, waiting in the yard to escort me back to base."

She waved through the window, and was relieved to see a happy smiling face. Roy had obviously had a good day, too.

MOST OF THE students were staying in accommodation at the college, but Samantha appeared on the drive as Ivy and Roy set off back to Springfields.

"Where are you staying?" asked Ivy. "Um, this is Samantha, and this is my fiancé, Roy Goodman."

"Pleased to meet you," Samantha said, offering a hand to Roy.

"Delighted," said Roy, giving her his kindest smile.

"I'm living with my parents. They live in one of the houses in Spinney Close. It's a new development, between the farm spinney and the big house. Tawny Wings, that is. Lovely name, isn't it, Miss Beasley?"

"And a lovely person who lives there," said Roy loyally. "Mrs. Deirdre Bloxham. Her husband sadly died some years ago, but she works very hard for people who need help."

"Also works with us," said Ivy. "We have an enquiry agency, operating from Springfields, the old folks' home down the road."

"Goodness! You certainly are busy, Miss Beasley! I must tell my mother. She will be very interested to hear about you. Wasn't it interesting what Rickwood had to say about his mother and his aunt?" She smiled, and said she had discovered a shortcut through the farmyard and across the field. "The whole place is deserted and falling to pieces. Such a shame. I should think it was a really nice house a while back?"

Ivy and Roy exchanged glances, Ivy almost imperceptibly shaking her head. "Spinney Close, did you say? Aren't there one or two old persons' bungalows there?"

"There are," said Samantha. "They are already occupied. One by the lady who is the mother of our tutor. Mrs. Winchen, she's named. Hardly ever goes out. My mum calls on her regularly to make sure she is okay, as I told you. Of course, now Rickwood is staying with her, she doesn't need Mum so much, but they have become quite good friends. Poor Rick escapes to the henhouse in the spinney, when his mother insists on television turned up loud. It's been cleaned up and quite sweet inside. He finds

it peaceful and quiet. I've taken him cups of tea occasionally. My house is only a step away."

"How interesting," said Ivy evenly. "Now, Samantha,
mind how you go, dear. We meet again on Monday afternoon. Enquire Within meets every Monday morning, so I
hope I won't miss anything important! Good-bye for the
present."

"Bye!" said Samantha, walking briskly into the entrance
to the farm. Ivy watched until she was out of sight, and
then said to Roy that they'd better be getting on. "La Spurling will be watching out for us," she said.

"And?" said Roy.

"And what, dearest?"

"And when shall we tell the others that we have found
out where Mrs. Winchen lives, and have a contact if we
wish to visit her?"

Ivy smiled. "You read my thoughts, Roy dear," she said,
and set the pace for him to follow in his trundle.

"NICE GIRL, THAT Samantha," Roy said, as they entered
the lounge for tea.

"Seems to be," said Ivy. "But you can't always tell from
first acquaintance. She was very shy at first, but soon came
out of her shell. Seems very attached to our tutor."

"And what about you, dear Ivy Beasley. How did you
get on?"

"Splendidly, Roy," answered Ivy enthusiastically. "Once
I had reorganised one or two things, and let the tutor know
exactly how I felt about the course, we got on splendidly.
They're all young enough to be my grandchildren, of
course, but I was myself, not trying to join in their youthful
excesses."

"And the memoirs?"

"We made a start. One or two good pointers, such as

keeping in mind who your reader is likely to be, and what will interest them."

"Well, I am your first reader," said Roy, accepting another piece of cake from a waiting Katya, "and everything about Ivy Beasley interests me. So you can choose what you like. Bad as well as good! Though I suspect there is not much bad in your past life, my love."

"All power to your elbow, Miss Beasley," said Katya triumphantly. Everyone laughed, and she protested that she had just learnt the saying from cook in the kitchen.

"And a very good one it is, too," said Ivy. "Now, no more talking, Roy, until we have finished our tea."

SAMANTHA, WALKING ACROSS the field, felt much more cheerful than when she had crossed to start her first real day at college. And she hadn't felt much better when they had all assembled. That know-all chap and his James Joyce! But Miss Beasley had put him firmly in his place! She pushed her way through the spinney undergrowth and came out exactly beside her mother's rear garden.

The houses were very well designed, and although the rooms were small, the windows were large and the sitting room full of light. She went in through the back door, and found her mother, with a familiar person smiling at her.

"Ah, this is my daughter, Mrs. Bloxham. Sam, this is our neighbour from Tawny Wings."

"Nice to meet you, Sam," Deirdre said. "I just popped in to welcome your parents to the village, and you, too, of course. She has been telling me that you are studying at the Manor House College? My cousin Miss Beasley has also started today. Creative Writing is her course."

"Oh, what a coincidence!" said Sam. "She befriended me today when I was feeling very nervous. She is a very kind old lady, and interesting to talk to. I imagine she is well loved locally?"

"Um, well, I wouldn't put it quite like that, "said Deirdre, smiling. "Interesting, certainly, but Ivy is known for her sharp tongue! Well loved, no; but certainly yes, by her fiancé, Roy Goodman. He is an absolute sweetie, and some people can't see what he sees in our Ivy."

"I can," said Samantha firmly.

Deirdre, highly amused at the girl's description of Ivy, got up to leave. "I have had a nice chat with your mother, my dear," she said. "I am sure we shall be seeing more of you, and do call in whenever you like. Good-bye both!"

TWO NEW FRIENDS in one day, thought Samantha, as she settled back in a chair. "Any interesting news from you, Mum?" she said.

"Only the visit from Mrs. Bloxham. So kind of her to call. She was telling me about her work for an enquiry agency in the village. Enquire Within, they are called. They do all kinds of work, from finding lost cats to solving murder cases. With the help of the police, of course"

"Murder cases! Surely there are no murders in Barrington? It seems such a quiet little place."

"You can never tell, Sam. Sometimes the quietest are worst. Anyway, let's have tea and you can tell me about your day."

Twenty-eight

"YOU HAVEN'T TOLD me how you got on in the library with Gus." Ivy was tired of answering questions from fellow elderly residents about becoming a student at her great age, and had escaped with Roy to her room straight after supper.

Roy smiled. "Thought you'd never ask!" he said. "Well, as a matter of fact, we turned up some very interesting stuff about the Winchen side of Eleanor's family. And this would be the Spinney Close Mrs. Winchen, also. They came from Lincolnshire, up on the east coast. Pork butchers in Boston, a port on the Witham, in the fens of Lincolnshire. They were quite wealthy folk, having been in business there for generations. Pork is a great specialty of the fens, apparently. Pork pies are especially delicious, so we discovered."

"Roy! I can't see how pork pies are going to get us any further forward with our investigations."

"Maybe so," said Roy. "But I haven't finished. We discovered that a local hostelry, now no longer there, had served its best pork to royalty."

"Roy!"

"Patience, beloved. We know Eleanor was a Winchen, and had added her name to Ted's when they got married. There were two sisters, and the other one, Mary, was the younger of the two. That's as far as the library records go."

"Good gracious, Roy. That puts my first day as a college student well into the shade. Really good work by you and Gus! You must remember the Winchen sisters when you were young? Maybe visiting Ted at his parents' farm?"

Roy shook his head. "Not that I can remember. There was only ever Mr. and Mrs. Blatch, and son Ted. I remember him bringing home his bride, but we moved in different circles. They didn't encourage guests. The old Blatches retired to the south coast, Eastbourne I think it was. Then Ted and Eleanor farmed, until he was killed when a tractor he was driving toppled into a ditch, and he died, and Eleanor was left a young widow. The rest we know."

"Oh, I don't think so," said Ivy.

Twenty-nine

THE TEAM HAD not been idle over the weekend. Gus had grilled Miriam Blake for her knowledge of the Winchens, whilst consuming with gusto her roast lamb Sunday lunch. Deirdre had agreed to go for a drink with the squire, to see if he remembered any particular references to the Winchen family, and Roy and Ivy went to church as usual, staying after the service to have coffee and cake, and talk casually to the older churchgoers about Mrs. Blatch's own family in Lincolnshire. Here they had drawn a blank, though one or two thought they remembered Mrs. Winchen, now up in Spinney Close, visiting her sister, Eleanor, at the farm when they were young. Although Monday was no longer wash-day, Ivy had spent much of yesterday sorting out her clothes into those she would need for the honeymoon, and others which could be packed away for next spring.

Now it was Monday morning, and all were assembled in the office at Tawny Wings. Ivy took the chair as usual, and said that each should in turn report on new developments.

"Shall I start, Chairman?" said Gus respectfully. Ivy nodded. "Off you go," she said.

"Miriam was very interested when I mentioned the Winchens. I asked innocently if she knew anything about that part of Eleanor's name, and she laughed. Said it was her maiden name, which she had tacked on to Blatch when she married Ted. She said everyone in the village laughed. Wasn't Blatch good enough for her, they had said. Poor Eleanor had had a tough time after Ted died, and had ended up more or less a recluse. Until her lover arrived. Miriam was very knowledgeable about that! Seems he came out of nowhere, asking for accommodation, and Eleanor took him in. Miriam seemed to think he was years younger, and said half the women in the village would have gladly taken him in!"

"Meaning herself," said Ivy acidly.

"Probably," agreed Gus. "Then, of course, when he left suddenly, everyone claimed they had always known what a bad hat he had been, and blamed Eleanor for being a silly old woman."

"Good heavens," said Deirdre. "You and Miriam must have had a fun lunch! What else did she say?"

"Not a lot, really. And she certainly didn't mention Eleanor's sister Mary, except that she had turned up as a mature lady living in Spinney Close, and severely disabled."

"And Deirdre, how did you get on with Roussel?" Ivy did not approve of Deirdre's assignations with the squire, but had to admit that the connection was useful.

"He was very superior, I'm afraid," said Deirdre. "Said how could he be expected to know the family trees of half the inhabitants of Barrington? But apparently when Ted had gone, and Eleanor had more or less given up, she had approached the Roussel estate, offering Blackwoods Farm for sale."

"But they didn't buy it?" This was news to Roy, who owned several farms in the district, and was not, as far as he could remember, approached by Eleanor.

"No. No money. The usual thing with landed gents. They live in genteel poverty, mostly. And Theo's lot were no different. Anyway, that's all he could remember, and we moved on to other things."

"Mm," said Ivy. "Now, since we all have the matter of Mary to follow up, I suggest we close the meeting now. I have a special dispensation to be at the college straight after lunch on a Monday. I told them that Enquire Within must come first, and they agreed. So, I'll be off now, and suggest we meet for tea tomorrow to see what has emerged. I mean to ask Samantha to introduce me to her mother, and then I shall bring up the subject of Mary Winchen. There will surely be a lot to discuss, including what plans Rickwood has for the farm. It has occurred to me and Roy that he probably inherits. Though with the feud between his mother and Eleanor, it is not at all certain."

AFTER IVY HAD gone, with Roy faithfully following in his trundle, back to Springfields for lunch, Deirdre took pity on Gus.

"I can't run to a roast lunch, I'm afraid," she said, as they arrived in the kitchen. "But there's cold pheasant and redcurrant jelly. And I can rustle up a salad of some sort. We'll open a bottle and think some more about Mary. I like the idea of Mary, the mysterious sister. I've said good morning to her once or twice, when she has been sitting in her garden in the sun. And her son, Rickwood, is always very polite. So come on, Gus, here's the corkscrew."

AFTER LUNCH, IVY walked briskly up the road from Springfields to the Manor House, with Roy in his trundle keeping up with her, urging her from time to time to take it more slowly. "It isn't a race, Ivy," he said. "They won't start without you."

Ivy said she had been sitting down all morning and needed some exercise before doing the same all afternoon. At the top of the drive to the Manor House, she kissed Roy on his cheek and disappeared through the front door.

Turning around and trundling back down the drive and into the main road, he approached Blackwoods Farm and slowed down. Perhaps he would take another look around, now the windows were boarded up and the whole place looked deserted and sad.

He shook himself. He mustn't fall into fanciful imaginings. That could be left to lovely Deirdre! No, he would mosey round the farmyard and see if anything odd caught his eye.

THE MONDAY MORNING session at the college had been taken up with a lecture on careful planning of material. Assuming that each one of the students did have something to write about, Rickwood the tutor summed up for Ivy what had been said, and stressed once more that serious planning was vital.

"And so, Miss Beasley, since I know you are intending to write your memoirs, you will, I am sure, have given some thought to organising your memories already. So shall we start with questions on this branch of creative writing, and see what thoughts we have?"

Teacher's pet, the know-all student Alexander, put up his hand immediately. "I'd like to ask Miss Beasley first why she thinks anyone will be interested in reading her memoirs?"

Ivy bristled, and Rickwood said quickly that he was sure Alexander would want to rephrase that more politely.

Grudgingly, the student said he supposed Miss Beasley

had had a long and fascinating life, and all his fellows would be curious to know how she would arrange her material. Would it be chronological or sequenced?

"Easy," said Ivy. "I shall sit down, begin at the beginning, and write, honestly and interestingly, until I get to the end. Which will not be too soon, I hope." Ivy folded her arms and stared at Alexander, who subsided in his seat.

Her friend from last week smiled, and said could she ask Miss Beasley about the honesty bit. "Do you think we do tell the real truth when we are remembering things from a long time ago?"

"Good point," said Rickwood. "This is a really good starting point, because in creative writing, of whatever kind, the matter of honesty is bound to crop up. Honest memoirs? Not necessarily. Many august memoirs have been spiced up or judiciously edited to make them more palatable to the reader. But it is a dangerous practice, vulnerable to being exposed."

"So watch it, Miss Beasley," said Alexander. "No bending the truth."

Rickwood ignored him. "In plotting a murder mystery, or a romantic fiction, you can lie as creatively as you like! But your characters must be convincingly drawn. Behave with some consistency. Rounded figures. They must be likely to have reasons for committing the crime, or for falling in love with unlikely people."

"But isn't that the fun of reading?" said another student. "We like to guess all these things, work them out for ourselves? Surely each reader forms his own picture of what the characters are like?"

And so the discussion caught fire, and lasted until Ivy said it would be time for Roy to escort her home, and Rickwood drew the session to a close. She gathered her papers together, and went quickly out to where Roy would be waiting. But he wasn't there to greet her with his lovely smile, and she walked all round the college and ended up by the front door with a sinking heart. What could have happened to him? She fumbled in her bag for her seldom used mobile phone and dialled his number. The message taker came on, and she said in a squeaky voice that she hoped he was all right and she was waiting for him.

The students left one by one, with Alexander offering her a lift in his vintage Morgan. But she turned him down and said to everyone that Roy would be there any minute. He must have been held up.

Finally, the high master, Mr. Rubens, appeared, and looked alarmed. "I will phone Springfields for you," he said. "They will surely know what has happened." He returned with a serious frown. "They thought he was up here with you," he said, adding that Rickwood would take her home in his car, and they would keep a lookout for Roy on the way.

Thirty

ROY SAT ON an upturned pail in a barn in Blackwoods farmyard, cursing himself for being an overconfident idiot. It had started to rain, but it promised to be a light shower only, and he had looked for a place to shelter for a few minutes. He had gone round to the back of crumbling cowsheds, out of sight of the road, and found a large barn, housing a vintage, if not antique, Ferguson tractor. He had been delighted, and parked his trundle outside with an electrically operated waterproof cover drawn over the seat.

Walking over to the tractor, he had stared at it, not noticing that the heavy barn door had swung shut behind him. Then he realised the light had gone dim, and was coming only from a dusty skylight in the roof. Never mind, he had told himself, the rain will soon pass over, and I shall open the door. It had been open when he came to it, so all would be well.

He had climbed stiffly into the tractor's worn seat, and long-forgotten memories had come flooding back. Had he been about four or five when his father first lifted him into

such a seat? He had always loved farm machinery, and
when others reminisced nostalgically about the days of
shire horses pulling the plough, he had defended the excite-
ment of modern machinery.

There were other relics of Ted Blatch's farming days,
and Roy had not noticed the time passing. Finally he had
looked closely at his watch, and seen that there was still
an hour to wait before Ivy would be ready to join him.

After that, things had not gone so well. When he came
to open the door, there seemed to be nothing to hold on to.
The latch was on the outside, and he saw a hole which
would take a finger thrust through to grasp the big wooden
bar. Roy was still strong in the arm, but even so he had
failed to move it. The weight of the door as it slammed
shut had wedged the bar tightly into place. Time passed,
and he had finally decided to ring Ivy on his mobile and
explain the delay.

Now he fumbled in his pocket, but it was not there.
Then he remembered he had put it for safety in the small
locked box that served as a secure place on the trundle.
He groaned, thinking of his precious Ivy standing alone
on the path from the Manor House, looking in vain for
him to appear.

IVY, MEANWHILE, HAD accepted a lift to Springfields
from Rickwood Smith, and they drove slowly through the
rain, staring out of misty windows to catch sight of Roy
on his trundle.

"He must have broken down somewhere and gone for
help," Ivy said. "But why doesn't he ring me? We both
always carry our mobiles with us in case we get stuck somewhere. Best thing ever invented for old people, Mr. Smith."

Rickwood slowed down as they passed Blackwoods
Farm. "Do you think he might have gone in there to shelter
from the rain?" he said.

"Oh, no. We've been there so many times, he wouldn't have done that. Anyway, Roy was a farmer, and a shower of rain wouldn't put him off coming straight to the college to meet me. He may be old, but he's tough as old boots."

Rickwood said nothing, though he doubted Ivy's description. He had noticed that Mr. Goodman had a slight tremor in his hands. And he had found it difficult to get out of a deep armchair in the high master's office at that first interview.

"I think the best thing would be for us to go on to Springfields, get you dry and warm and see if they have heard anything. Then I strongly recommend calling the police."

"Police!" said Ivy. "Certainly not! He would never forgive me. No, I know exactly what I am going to do. I shall call one of my colleagues, Mr. Augustus Halfhide. He will know exactly where to look. Ah, now, here we are, and there's our gaoler at the door on the lookout. Thank you very much for the lift, Mr. Smith. I shall be with you on Friday, as planned. Oh, and by the way, I should very much like to call on your mother, if she would like me to. I understand she doesn't get out much."

Rickwood assured Miss Beasley that he would certainly ask his mother, but she was sometimes reluctant to have visitors. "A bit reclusive, you know, like her sister, Eleanor. And now, here we are at Springfields. You go in and make yourself comfortable, and I'll continue to search. And don't worry! Mr. Goodman seems an eminently sensible gentleman!"

ROY SAT DISCONSOLATELY on the tractor seat, thinking of ways he could try to escape. He had walked round the barn carefully, looking for implements he could use to move the wooden bar, but had found nothing. He had even looked up to the skylight to see if he could use one of the old wooden ladders to climb up and open it. But common sense told him that would be foolish, and more than likely end in disaster.

Finally he had given up, and trusted that very soon someone would come looking for him. His thoughts had roamed around Enquire Within's latest discovery. Mary Victoria Winchen. He had a strange feeling about her, and now that he had nothing else to think about, he tried hard but failed to remember anything about her as a young woman.

He frowned. Stick to facts, he told himself. We need to turn up some hard facts about sister Mary. For a start, unless she married a cousin, or some such, was the "Mrs." a courtesy title? Shouldn't it be Smith?

A rustling noise from outside the door startled him, and he climbed down from the tractor with relief.

"Ivy!" he shouted, and then followed it up with a loud yell of "Help! I'm in here."

"Coming!" said a man's voice loudly. Then there was a noise as of hammering, and he realised someone was in fact slowly moving the heavy wooden bar.

"I'm still here, Ivy. Or Gus? Give me a shout to say you're making headway!"

"Nearly there, Mr. Goodman!" shouted the man's voice. Then the bar suddenly lifted and the door moved. "Ah, there you are, sir. No wonder you were trapped. This bar needs a circus strongman to move it! But here you are, and I shall accompany you back to Springfields."

"Thank you so much," said Roy. "It's Mr. Smith, isn't it? My Ivy's tutor? How kind of you. I have my trundle, and I shall be fine to go back to Springfields. I do hope Ivy has not been worrying."

"A little," said Rickwood. "But you wouldn't want it otherwise, would you?"

Roy laughed. "How true, Mr. Smith. How very true!"

*   *   *

FINALLY REUNITED, THE happy pair sat in front of a
roaring fire at Springfields, drinking hot tea, while Roy
went over once more his extraordinary experience.

"Mr. Smith was so kind, my dear," he said. "Very calm
and capable. An excellent fellow."

Thirty-one

AT BREAKFAST NEXT day, Ivy was pleased to see that Roy was none the worse for yesterday's adventure. She was relieved that he had resisted the temptation to scale a wobbly wooden ladder up to the skylight, and believed him when he said he had spent most of the time pretending to drive the Ferguson tractor.

"So what next?" she said, helping herself to another piece of toast. "We're expecting Deirdre and Gus to come after tea to pool ideas?"

"Good idea, beloved," said Roy. "You go now and confirm with them and I will meet you in the lounge to plan."

Deirdre had been looking forward to a quiet cup of tea and her favourite soap on the telly. She agreed reluctantly, said good-bye to Ivy, and dialled Gus. Engaged. He was probably receiving the same reminder. She put on the kettle for a quick cup of tea, and began to look at the newspaper, delivered ten minutes earlier by a straw-haired youth with the most engaging grin. George, it was, from an old village family, the Robsons. The father had a small business fixing the multitude of small failures in the inhabitants' daily lives. Nothing too small, was his motto, and he had been in and out of most houses, changing fuses, mending leaks, painting and decorating for years.

She looked out of the window at a blackbird consuming a worm on the lawn. Robsons, she thought. In and out of people's houses. The old grandmother would remember the Blatches when they were still farming, surely. Perhaps she would call and talk to her. The charity collection box stood on the kitchen table, and Deirdre saw an excuse to visit. She had yet to go up Robsons' lane. It would be something to ask the others about, anyway.

She was the first to arrive at Springfields, and Ivy said that Gus would be coming as soon as Whippy had had her walk. Meanwhile, the small conference room had been warmed up, and Katya was preparing a tray of tea and buns. It was Mrs. Spurling's day off, and Miss Pinkney had taken a scarlet potted poinsettia and placed it on the conference table.

Gus arrived, puffing from having jogged all the way from Hangman's Row to Springfields. "I shall have either sharpened my brain or exhausted my body. Or both. In any case, Roy, sir, what is it that gets us here this afternoon?" Roy gestured towards Ivy. "Ask the boss," he said.

Ivy then described what had happened to Roy in the old barn yesterday, and at the mention of the Ferguson tractor, Gus came to life.

"Wonderful!" he said. "Do you think we can buy it and get it going again?"

"Please concentrate, Gus!" said Ivy. "In spite of all our excitements, it has occurred to me that we are no nearer finding out exactly what happened to cause Eleanor to tumble to her death, or whether it was accident or murder. I am sorry to be so blunt, but these are the facts."

Gus reflected that he had never known Ivy to be anything less than blunt, but she was quite right. He postponed all further thoughts of the Ferguson tractor, and said that they had moved a little way forward, in discovering Mary Winchen. Eleanor, a woman with a sister and nephew, however much estranged, was a very different cup of tea from a sole widow with no apparent relations or friends. Or, he added, potential enemies.

"On another tack," Roy said. "I have been thinking about Rickwood Smith. He was on foot, without a car, when he found me. And as I turned to wave him good-bye, he was heading for the gate into the field. I do hope he didn't get too wet and muddy."

Ivy said she knew where he was going. Samantha had discovered a footpath from Spinney Close, across the field and out through Blackwoods farmyard, and then directly to the college. "Anyway, dearest, I shouldn't worry about him. He seems well able to take care of himself."

Then it was Deirdre's turn to make a proposal, and she told them about the Robson grandmother and what she might remember of the Blatches at Blackwoods Farm.

"Excellent idea," said Roy. "She worked in the farmhouse at one time as a kind of dogsbody, doing anything and everything. She could well have heard or seen something of the Winchen family, who must have visited once or twice, surely."

"As for me," said Gus, "I think I feel a trip coming on. A couple of days on the Lincolnshire coast, Deirdre? Do you fancy it? And some investigating into the pork butchers in town?"

"Be serious, please, Augustus," said Ivy. "You may be needed here in Barrington."

"Wait a minute, Ivy," said Deirdre. "I think Gus is being serious, even if he doesn't sound it, especially since we know about the existence of a sister. It's a really good idea, and we may find out much more about Eleanor's background. I don't think all the conversations in the world with Mrs. Winchen can guarantee giving us a clue to the reason for the feud. And that, after all, is what most concerns us at the moment."

Ivy was taken with Deirdre's mention of the Robsons. "Would it be a good idea if *I* called on Grandma Robson, and see what she remembers?" she said. "She and I must fall into the same age group, just about. I'll go later on." Ivy was smiling at Roy, who duly said Ivy must be years younger, if looks had anything to do with it.

"And then," continued Ivy, "I shall see Rickwood Smith tomorrow, and I can check that he is none the wiser for rescuing my fiancé!"

Gus and Deirdre then went into a huddle to decide on travel plans, and Roy left the room to, as he said, point Percy at the pavement.

AFTER THEY HAD disbanded, agreeing that useful things had been decided and nothing more needed to be discussed, Ivy said that as she would be going out later she would now sit comfortably for the rest of the afternoon with Roy and finish the rib in her knitting. "If you persist in getting shut in cold barns for any length of time," she said, "I must finish this warm jumper for you as soon as possible."

"Thank you, dear," said Roy. "You know, thinking about this day's work with the four of us, I realise that I have nothing in particular to do enquiry-wise. Gus and Deirdre are off to Boston, Lincolnshire, and you are bearding Grandma Robson in her den."

"Why don't you come with me?" Ivy said. "Your old-fashioned gentlemanly charm might work wonders."

Thirty-two

AGREEING THAT THERE was no time like the present, Ivy and Roy set off in the bright sunlight of a late-summer evening. Ivy knew where the Robsons lived, and as she stood waiting for the bell to be answered, she wondered how it had accommodated three generations of one family. She had got as far as mentally arranging for Grandma to sleep in the box room, mother and father in the best double bed, and George and his smaller brother in what used to be called the guest room, when the door opened. Ivy quickly said she had a message for Grandma, if she could have a word?

"Who are you, then?" said granddaughter Daisy suspiciously. "Aren't you one of them from up Springfields?"

Ivy announced herself, and said she would not be very long. She introduced Roy, and said Mrs. Robson would remember him, as he had farmed in the county for years. A few minutes would do.

"Who is it, Daisy?" came a voice from inside the house.

"A Miss Beasley and Mr. Goodman from up Springfields wants a word with you. Says she's got a message."

"Tell her to give it to you. I'm sitting by the fire!"

"You'd better come in, dear," said Daisy, obviously having decided Miss Beasley was not a burglar or selling anything, and she recognised Roy as a very respectable retired farmer.

"What's this message, then," the old lady said. "They're not thinking of putting me in Springfields, are they? She darted a look at her granddaughter hovering in the doorway. "Go on then, Miss Beasley," she added. "Get on with it."

"Well, first of all, my message was to tell you that we represent an enquiry agency, Enquire Within, and if you need our help—no matter what—we'd be pleased to oblige. And then, in connection with one of our present cases, to see if you remember any mention of the Winchens when you were working for the Blatches at Blackwoods Farm."

Mrs. Robson senior stared at Ivy with a frown, and said she couldn't remember what happened yesterday, so there wasn't much chance of her remembering the Winchens.

"But you did perhaps see one or two of them when Eleanor Blatch was young and just married to Ted?" said Roy. "She had been a Winchen, and some of the family might have visited the farm at that time?"

"Wait a minute, now," said Mrs. Robson. "Oh lor, Miss Beasley, I ain't going to be much use to you!"

"But there must have been Winchens of some kind visiting the farm? After all, Eleanor was a girl Winchen before she met Ted. Do you remember if there was one called Mary among them?"

Mrs. Robson senior frowned. "Mary . . . Mary . . . Now that rings a bell. Yes, I'm sure one of them was called Mary! But no, it was Margaret. Or was it Marion? Oh, I don't know, dear. It might have been the Wrights next door. I'm a poor old thing, as you see."

"I think you'd better rest now," said Daisy. "I'll show you out, Miss Beasley, Mr. Goodman."

"Come again, dear," shouted the old lady, when Ivy had reached the door. "We can talk about old times."

Ivy nodded her thanks to Daisy, and she and Roy returned slowly to Springfields. The old lady had been unreliable, certainly, and she seemed sure of Mary at first. But that was about all! A wasted journey.

Miss Pinkney was waiting for them. "Here you are then, fresh as a daisy from your walk. Come and have supper, my dears."

GUS AND DEIRDRE, still trawling through railway timetables and possible routes from Tawny Wings to Boston, Lincs, finally decided that the train connection was not good, and it was not that far away, so they'd go by car.

"We'll take the Bentley," Deirdre said. "You can drive, and I'll argue with the satnav. She's called Prudence, by the way, and is reasonably reliable."

Deirdre booked them in for a couple of nights into the Peacock and Royal Hotel in the main marketplace. "It looks a nice old place," she said. "And that amazing church called the Stump is just a few yards away."

"I hope the church clock doesn't chime all night, then," said Gus. "Could disturb our beauty sleep."

"No comment," said Deirdre. "Let's pack a few things, and I'll pick you up first thing tomorrow. We'd better tell Ivy and Roy, and also see if she had any luck with old Mrs. Robson. I'll give her a ring."

"SO YOU TWO are off on a jolly," Ivy said. "Well, try not to forget what you are there for. Pork butchers named Winchen, especially. And with an emphasis on the mystery of Eleanor Winchen Blatch's sisterly feud. If we can establish a reason for such a serious, almost lifetime estrangement, we might establish some answers."

Thirty-three

NEXT MORNING DAWNED with clear blue skies and puffy white clouds speeded along by a brisk wind.

"Wrap up warm, Miss Beasley, if you're insisting on going up to the college," said Mrs. Spurling. "There's a definite change in the weather. For the life of me I can't see why you cannot be content to stay in the warm with my other residents."

"I have explained many times," said Ivy, "and I don't propose to explain again. I know you are responsible for us, and if we go down with pneumonia it will be you who gets the blame, et cetera, et cetera. If it will help, I will sign a piece of paper saying I take full responsibility for myself in walking two hundred yards up the road to the Manor House College, and back again. Will that do? Oh, and no, I shall not be requiring lunch today. Thank you."

Mrs. Spurling could think of nothing polite to say, and so turned away and slammed herself into her office.

Ivy grinned, and went to find Roy in the lounge. "I am

off to college, dear," she said. "And there is absolutely no need for you come with me today. I know all the ropes now, and shall be back here, considerably wiser, around a quarter to four."

Roy, who respected Ivy's independent nature, agreed, saying that if she felt like having a companion on her way home, she was to ring him at once.

Once more, Ivy walked along Manor Road and stopped at Blackwoods Farm. It looked even sadder with the windows boarded up and weeds taking over the front garden.

Was it too soon for a will to be read and ownership safely established? After all, Eleanor, as far as they knew, had had no children and refused to acknowledge her sister, Mary, and nephew, Rickwood. There was the elusive lodger, of course, but he had vanished years ago, and they had turned up nothing to connect him with her demise. She thought hard, and as she walked into the front entrance to the college, decided to ask Roy if he thought Rickwood could have inherited so soon.

SAMANTHA ARRIVED IN the class ten minutes late, and was full of apologies. "Sorry!" she said, as she sat down next to Ivy. "Plumbing problems! You'd think it would be impossible in a new house, but no, this morning we had no water in the bathroom!"

Students had been asked to bring along the results of an assignment, and in particular, a short specimen chapter telling the story of an event in each's past life. Instructions had been to avoid a standpoint of everything being better in the good old days, and not always putting oneself in a good light.

Discussing this with Roy, Ivy had said that if anyone asked her, she would say everything *was* better in the good old days. He had tried to help by taking as examples things like cooking, travel and the national health service, and each time Ivy had given him watertight reasons why these had been much better years ago.

When it was Ivy's turn, the entire class waited in happy anticipation. Clearing her throat, Ivy began with a vivid description of Victoria Villa in Round Ringford, where she had been born and lived until coming to Springfields.

Far from giving the expected rose-tinted account, she described a battle-axe mother and browbeaten, henpecked father, and her own struggles to keep clear of both. And it was humorously written! By the time she related how her father had been scolded out of the house one night, and greeted the postman next morning from the garden shed in his pyjamas, Samantha and all the rest of the class were laughing aloud.

"So we couldn't say you were an indulged child?" said Rickwood the tutor.

"Good heavens, no. Mind you, my mother's favourite saying was 'spare the rod and spoil the child.' All the children in the village knew how to dodge, though. We knew right from wrong, and expected it."

At coffee break time, Samantha brought a cup across to where Miss Beasley sat fiercely cleaning her spectacles.

"That was great, Miss Beasley," she said. "Well done. I'm afraid my effort will sound a bit pallid."

"If you can use words like 'pallid,'" said Ivy, "and what's more know what they mean, I should think you're on the right lines, dear."

At lunchtime, Ivy once more sat at a table surrounded by young people. One of them asked if she felt a bit out of it, being so much older than the rest. She did not bother to answer, pretending to be deaf, but asked Samantha if she would like a little walk around the garden before getting back to class.

"Of course. And I can help you find your way back inside, since you're so old, Miss Beasley."

Ivy smiled. She was, in fact, beginning to feel quite at home at Manor House College.

BACK INSIDE FOR the afternoon, the question and answer session began enthusiastically. After a discussion about describing the weather and the landscape, and how boring this could become, Ivy asked how much other students had noticed about their surroundings, here in Barrington village.

"Good question," said Rickwood. "Anyone?"

Several students offered answers, and then Ivy said she had noticed a footpath across the field to Spinney Close. Had others gone that way at all? Samantha said she used it every day, as it was a shortcut to college. The others shook their heads. Mostly, they said, they went down to the pub.

Then Alexander, the know-all student with a heart of gold, said that he had actually gone that way once or twice. A friend he'd met in the pub lived in the new houses. They'd gone that way for a walk, and he had noticed the disused farm buildings. The others teased him, asking if he had an ulterior motive. But Ivy brought them back to the footpath. What had they thought of the field, and had they noticed the lame sheep?

"I tell you one thing I noticed," said Samantha. "There's one of those old henhouses in the spinney. I can see it from my bedroom window. Somebody goes in there occasionally. I keep meaning to have a look inside. Yesterday, for instance, I could swear I saw you, Rickwood, leaving the henhouse and walking across the field?

"Well spotted," said Rickwood. "I was collecting eggs. No, but seriously, I do escape there occasionally. It's clean and tidy, and peaceful when I have work to do. My mother is a little deaf, and loves the telly turned up loud. Aunt

Eleanor never came that far away from the farmhouse, so no risk of upsetting her."

"Perhaps it would be a good idea, Rickwood," Ivy said, seeing a good way of useful observation, "to get us to go for a field exercise on Monday afternoon to see how different our descriptions would be? Don't forget the lame ewe. Somebody's feeding it. Then when we get back to base, we can discuss how we handle what we've seen," said Ivy.

Rickwood the tutor hesitated. He thought his students might think this too childish an exercise. On the other hand, it could produce results. Something to vary the monotony, he thought. He would not need to get permission, of course. If anyone questioned them being there, he could say his aunt had said he could go where he liked on the farm. There was nobody to contradict that now! He cheered up, thinking it could work. He would have to be careful and keep his eyes open.

One or two said they hadn't suitable shoes, but most of them liked the idea, and it was agreed they would assemble on Monday afternoon and set off through the farmyard and into the field.

"Anyway, I'll ring you, Ivy and Samantha, if it's cancelled," said Rickwood, "otherwise assume it's all go!"

"No need for Samantha and myself to come in to college," said Ivy. "We'll wait for you others by the gate."

Thirty-four

IVY'S TELEPHONE RANG early next morning, and she was not pleased to hear Deirdre's voice, bright and breezy, asking if she and Gus had been missed.

"Don't be ridiculous, girl," she said. "We've scarcely had twenty-four hours since you last left a whiff of Chanel in our noses."

"Same old Ivy!" said Deirdre. "We thought you might like a report on what we've been doing."

"Go on, then. I haven't finished my cup of tea yet, so you'll have to put up with slurping."

"Well, we've found the pork butchers, but they are no longer Winchen's. A man called John Jones bought the business. We talked with his son for quite a while, and discovered what he knew about the last of the Winchens."

"Who were they?"

"Eleanor and her sister, Mary. After Mary left, there are no records of what happened to her. Until she turned up in Barrington at some stage, but relatively recently. We shall go through the local archives, of course.

"We're all set, Ivy. More to report later. Our return will depend on what we find out. Oh, and Gus wants a word."

Ivy sighed. Her tea was cold, and she could hear sounds of other residents going down to breakfast.

"Hello, yes?" she said.

"Morning, Ivy," answered Gus, also sounding very chipper. "I wanted to ask a favour. Could you go down to Miriam Blake's in Hangman's Row, and make sure Whippy is all right? Not pining for her master? Thanks very much. Looks like being a lovely day, so you'll enjoy the walk."

"Thanks very much!" said Ivy. "I'll say good-bye now. Roy is knocking on the door. Good-bye, both of you."

"SO THEY THINK they're on to something?" said Roy. He turned to thank Katya for a plate of crispy bacon, fried egg and bread, all slightly burned, as he liked it.

"Deirdre sounded quite excited. Mind you, that might have had nothing to do with the hunt for the Winchens. I spoke to Gus as well, and he was worried about Whippy, but otherwise sounded sunny."

"Dear things," said Roy. "Obviously enjoying themselves. And so shall we, in a few weeks' time. I have received confirmation from the best hotel in Blackpool, as requested. I shall make sure you are excited and sunny on our honeymoon, my dear."

"Roy! That's quite enough of that! Now, let us plan our day so that we have something useful to report when the others return."

"Do you think we might have a trip into Oakbridge estate agents and pretend to be interested in Blackwoods Farm? I hate to see it all run-down and neglected. We could perhaps get in touch with an old friend of mine. He owns the big estate agents in town, and they specialise in farm sales."

"Excellent idea! Are you thinking of buying it, if it

comes on the market? There is one snag. Neither you nor I look young and fit enough to be working farmers."

"Me? I ran four farms when I was younger, and you don't grow out of being a farmer. But you have a point, Ivy," he added, seeing her crestfallen face, "and we shall say we are looking around on behalf of my grandson. He will have to be fictional, since poor Steven died, and he was my only living relation."

"Exactly right, Roy dear. What shall we call your fictional grandson?"

"Anthony, Anthony Goodman. Now, I shall finish my breakfast."

ELVIS ARRIVED ON time, as always, and came into Springfields reception to ask for Ivy and Roy. Mrs. Spurling was in the office, and she came out to intercept him.

"And where are they off to this time?" she said. "Sooner or later one of them is going to drop down dead from exhaustion, rushing about from pillar to post, and giving me no warning of when or where they are going. And, of course, I shall get the blame."

Elvis nodded. "They are marvellous for their age, aren't they?" he said, completely missing her point. "And now we're off to Oakbridge. They love the coffee shop there, so I am sure that will be first stop."

Mrs. Spurling sighed deeply and returned to her office, where she sat staring at her computer. She brought up a website of situations vacant for nursing home managers, and looked for a free position miles away from Barrington. Then she saw Miss Beasley and Mr. Goodman, arm in arm, following the taxi man out of the door, and they were all smiling. I must be doing something right, she thought. She closed down her computer, and went off to bully the girls in the kitchen.

* * *

HALFWAY TO OAKBRIDGE, Ivy tapped Elvis on his shoulder with her umbrella. "Do you know anything about a family named Winchen?" she said.

"Winchen? No, I don't think so. Oh, wait a minute, wasn't the woman from Blackwoods Farm a Mrs. Winchen Blatch? That's the only one I can think of. Poor soul. They don't seem to have made much headway with finding her killer. If she was killed! Fell to her death, didn't she? It was all over the local paper for a while, but now it's the floods in Summer Meadows in Tresham that's making the news."

"Oh dear, that sounds bad. Anybody drowned?" said Ivy.

"Yes, a couple of lads who were mucking about near the river bridge. The water's running very high, and neither of them could swim. Tragic, really. Now, is it the coffee shop first?"

Ivy nodded. Roy said they could unload him and his trundle from the taxi, and he could park it on the pavement outside the café.

"Back here about twelve?" Elvis said. "Behave yourselves, and not too much sugar in your coffee!"

They parted laughing, and Ivy and Roy were then welcomed into the café as regulars, and ordered their usual milky coffee and jam and cream scones.

"Excuse me, dear," Ivy said to a pleasant-faced woman who was serving them. "Can you direct us to Botham's estate agents?"

The woman raised her eyebrows. "Are you thinking of moving away from Springfields, once you are married?" The entire staff in the coffee shop were well acquainted with the several-times-postponed wedding day.

"No, no. We are just enquiring about a property,

Blackwoods Farm in Barrington. On behalf of Roy's grandson."

"Isn't that where that poor woman died? Is the place up for sale now?"

Ivy shook her head. "We are not sure. You don't happen to know who owns it, do you?" she asked casually.

"Oh yes. Wasn't it them Blatches? Maybe the one who's just died. She came from up north. Lincolnshire, I think. They'll probably sell it off now. The young ones don't want to go into farming these days. Anyway, the agents are round the corner, on the market square. You can't miss it."

Roy thanked the waitress politely. "I suppose Mrs. Winchen Blatch used to come in here for your excellent coffee now and then?"

"Once or twice, I think. It's coming back to me now," she said. "She came in one morning, years ago, when I first came to work here. She was looking very down-at-heel, and didn't speak to anyone. I remember because she made a bit of a scene about the bill. And she lit up one of them cigarillo things, and our manageress asked her politely to put it out. She said she wouldn't, and it was all very unpleasant. No law against it in them days. She never came in again, thank goodness!"

"How long ago would that be?" said Ivy quickly.

"Oh, years ago, dear. As I said, she never came in again. Now, is there anything else I can get you?"

Ivy shook her head politely, and when the waitress was out of earshot, she looked across the table. "Come along, Roy," she said. "Time we went on our way. We shall be back next week, God willing."

Once outside, with Roy safely back in his trundle, Ivy set off for the market square. With only fifty yards to go, they were quickly there. Roy climbed down to the pavement, and followed Ivy into the impressive offices of Botham, Son and Lords.

Roy's old friend was in his office, and greeted them with pleasure. "Long time no see, Roy old man. And have I heard whispers that you are breaking the habit of a lifetime and getting wed soon? And this is your lovely fiancée, I presume."

Ivy was introduced, and coffee was offered but turned down politely.

"Strange you should come in this morning, Roy," said the agent. "I had a call from someone called Smith this morning, making preliminary enquiries about selling a farm in Barrington. Rickwood Smith, his name was. A new one on me. But I know the farm. Blackwoods, isn't it? Old Ted Blatch ran the place very well, but he died years ago, and I believe his widow died in unusual circumstances recently?"

After more reminiscing, the agent said he planned to go and have a quick look around the old place this afternoon. Perhaps he could meet Ivy and Roy there?

Ivy explained her brief acquaintance with Rickwood Smith, who would also be there, and the expedition was confirmed with another telephone call.

Thirty-five

"YOU'RE NOT GOING out *again*, Miss Beasley? Wouldn't you like a quiet afternoon by the fire? I have collected some new magazines, and I'm sure there will be one or two to interest you. And you, Mr. Goodman?"

Before Ivy could get in a tart reply, Roy thanked Mrs. Spurling kindly, and said they were only going as far as Blackwoods Farm, where Rickwood Smith had agreed Botham's could have a preliminary look around. Ivy had also given him a quick courtesy call to check that he was happy about them going round the farmhouse with the agent.

Rickwood had agreed. There could be no harm in it. He had asked local cleaners to go through the house and leave it all clean and tidy, and they had once more achieved wonders. He was not at all decided on what to do with the house and land. He might very well choose to stay there himself. But a valuation could do no harm.

The fire escape, which had been left open when Eleanor had been found, was shut off with padlocks and warning tape wound around it. And the little room, where he knew his aunt had occasionally had a quiet smoke, was also locked, on his own orders.

Now Roy set about placating Mrs. Spurling. "I am enquiring on behalf of my grandson, Anthony," he said. "At present, he lives in the West Country, but is interested in buying a property over here in Suffolk."

"Very well, then. But do try to be back here before the sun goes down and the east wind takes over."

As Ivy and Roy set off for Blackwoods, they discussed the interesting snippet they had heard from the waitress in Oakbridge. "If Eleanor was looking witchy," said Ivy, "then the relationship with the lodger must have broken down some while previously."

"Deirdre said Eleanor hadn't been seen for years. Certainly not in town, smoking a cigar in a café."

"Next time we have coffee, we'll ask the waitress for more details."

THE AGENT JUMPED out of his car and advanced on them, hand outstretched. "Hello again, Miss Beasley, Mr. Goodman, lovely Saturday afternoon now, isn't it?"

"Shall we go and have a look around?" said Ivy.

"As I told you, we are interested on behalf of my grandson," added Roy, "and there's Mr. Smith waiting for us."

They opened the yard gate and walked in. "We'll go in the back way," said Rickwood. "The front door is temporarily stuck. Easy to fix, though, I can assure you."

"I should get it fixed if I was you," Ivy said. "Makes a bad first impression, doesn't it?"

The house was cold, but there was a pleasant smell of air freshener. The police had, of course, been in, carrying out extensive tests, but the furniture was still there as Eleanor had left it. Ivy walked over to the window overlooking the yard. It was muddy and untidy, as if half the village had been in, helping themselves to anything of use.

"Upstairs, then," she said. "Anthony has a family, and so will want several bedrooms." The agent went up first, and began with the main bedroom.

"Very nice," said Ivy. "Good view over the yard and the field beyond. Now the others, please."

The smaller ones, including the one which Gus had occupied, were examined.

"Plenty of room for a family," said the agent, smiling at Ivy.

"And the other one?" she said.

"Sorry?" said Rickwood.

"The other bedroom, along there. I'll go and see."

Before the agent could reply, she was off, heading for the dark chamber.

"It's locked," she said, returning quickly. "Can I have the key?

"Mr. Smith?"

"Sorry, Miss Beasley. We seem to have lost the only key. I shall have to find a locksmith."

"May I try my magic opener, Mr. Smith?" said the agent.

Rickwood reluctantly agreed, but the magic did not work. "It's only a glorified broom cupboard, anyway," he said, "where the bed linen used to be kept. Let's go down now, and have a quick look round the farmyard. Then you can make a report to your grandson, and he can ring me any time if he is interested."

The yard was of no interest to Ivy. All the outbuildings must have been searched by the police. Roy went straight to the barn, and saw that the Ferguson tractor was still there.

"I'd like to put in a bid for that tractor," he said. "I expect there'll be a yard sale?"

"And how about that old sheep?" said Ivy. "Does it go with the rest?"

The agent laughed. "I am sure it will be taken care of, one way or another," he said with a knowing look.

Ivy did not laugh. "It would make a nice pet for someone," she said. "Needs to have a comfortable billet for the rest of its life."

The agent sighed. "Of course, Miss Beasley," he replied. "Now, are we all done? The sun has gone, and it's getting really chilly. I am sure you two will want to be getting back home. Shall we meet tomorrow to inspect the broom cupboard?"

He could not quite keep the irritation from his voice, and Ivy stared at him.

"Of course," she said. "Anthony will want to have a complete report. Good afternoon. We shall see you tomorrow."

LATER THAT EVENING, Gus telephoned. "Good stuff to tell you," he said to Ivy, "but we plan to come home tomorrow, so it'll be best to keep it till then. Sunday tea at Springfields?"

"Fine," said Ivy. "We'll have something to report as well. But before you go, you did see into the dark chamber a while back, didn't you? Before Eleanor died?"

"Oh yes, certainly. And I noticed the fire escape, too. Remember? Why?"

"I'll tell you tomorrow," said Ivy. "And make sure you drive carefully. Bye."

Thirty-six

AT ROY'S INSISTENCE, he and Ivy decided on Sunday being a day of rest. It was also a good opportunity for Ivy to do some serious reading of her course work. She was not usually one for spending hours with a book, preferring to be on her feet doing something practical. Long years of her mother asking her what she thought she was doing sitting about had engrained the habit.

Now, at the beginning of a new week, she was pleased to see a bright sun shining through her curtains. "Fine before seven, rain before eleven," she said, adjusting the old saying to suit herself, and then remembered she had two walks to make today. Up to the Manor House College, meeting Rickwood for a peep into the dark chamber—if he had found the key—and then across the field behind Blackwoods Farm with the other students, and to discuss what they had seen. She planned to walk back to Springfields for tea. She sat up in bed, and then lowered her legs to the floor. She pulled up her nightdress and examined her calves and feet. Not too many knotty veins, and her

ankles, her best feature, were as slender and trim as ever.
So were they up to tramping across fields?

"Of course they are," she said. She stood up and walked
round the room. All muscles working well. She must select
a good pair of walking boots, and nice thick stockings.

A tap at the door heralded Katya with morning tea. "Up
already, Miss Beasley?" she said.

Ivy returned as athletically as possible into bed and said
she was looking forward to early-morning biscuits and a
cuppa. She had been searching for a pair of woollen stockings, she said. "I have quite a lot of walking to do today,
and my feet will need support!"

"The forecast is for rain this afternoon, so don't forget
to take a brolly. And your mobile phone, so that we can
come and get you if you're miles from home."

"Oh, I shall be only as far away as the college."

"Morning, Ivy!" said a voice from the landing. Roy
stood there grinning at her, and looking rather handsome
in his paisley dressing gown and velvet slippers, his silvery
hair pleasantly tousled. "Nice legs, if you don't mind my
saying so, Miss Beasley," he added.

"Roy! How long have you been standing there?" Ivy
quickly pulled the covers over her lower half.

"Long enough, my love. Morning, Katya. I shall leave
you two ladies to your machinations, and see you at breakfast very shortly."

"PERHAPS YOU SHOULD call your Mr. Smith and see
if he's found the key," said Roy, greeting Ivy from the breakfast table. "If not, we won't waste any more time with it. You
won't want to miss the field walk with the other students. We
could perhaps meet the agent at lunchtime at Blackwoods,
and then you could be in time for the walk. Or will that be
too much for you? Do you know, it's at times like this that we
could do with another seat on the trundle."

Thirty-seven

IVY HAD ALREADY told the college she would not be in on Monday mornings, but she would be there for the afternoon walk, she had said, and added that she hoped everyone would enjoy it. Rickwood the tutor had mapped out the morning's work, which was to consider how well students looked around them, noting down what they saw.

By the time Ivy, Roy and Gus arrived outside Black-woods Farm, the agent was waiting for them.

"Good day, sir," said Gus. "I see you've brought your brolly. The weather's a bit uncertain today."

Roy smiled. He could see that Ivy was impatient to get on and into the farmhouse, so he said nothing. Rickwood took charge, and after one or two more pleasantries, they walked into the yard and up to the back door, which he opened with a flourish.

"Here we are again, then," he said.

"I am assuming," said Ivy, following into the kitchen, "that you have the key to the little chamber? Otherwise, I know you were going to cancel this meeting."

Rickwood looked uncomfortable, and pulled a large bunch of keys out of his pocket. "I am reliably informed," he said, "that the key to the broom cupboard is among this lot. I'm afraid I haven't had a moment to check, but I am sure we shall find it."

Gus raised his eyebrows. "I do hope so," he said. "You wouldn't have wanted to waste three people's time, I am sure."

"Perhaps you would like to have another quick look at the rest of the house, before we open the cupboard?"

"No, thanks," said Ivy. "Straight upstairs, if you please."

They trailed up the stairs and stopped outside the dark chamber. Rickwood fumbled amongst his keys, until Ivy got cross and said he clearly had no intention of finding the key.

"Shall I have a go?" said Gus, and Rickwood handed over the keys. In very little time, the key was found and put smoothly into the lock. Then Gus pushed the door. It remained shut, and he pushed again, this time with knee and shoulder. It remained shut.

"Let me try," said Rickwood, but he, too, had no luck.

"Bolted inside the door," said Ivy. "We'll have to force it."

"I think not, Miss Beasley," Rickwood objected. "There is a fire escape leading to it, and I am prepared to go up and see what I can find. If it is only a walk-in cupboard full of sheets and pillowcases, as I think, I hope that you will be happy with leaving the bolted door until I can arrange for professional help."

Gus cleared his throat. "Mr., er, Smith," he began. "I myself, in my right mind, and in broad daylight, have seen the interior of this room, accessed by this door, and the exterior fire escape, locked top and bottom. I suggest you believe me, and arrange for someone to show the interior to Miss Beasley and Mr. Goodman as soon as possible."

While the others were walking back along the landing

and downstairs, Ivy bent down with her eye to the keyhole. Nobody there, then. She continued to look for a few seconds, but there was no movement detectable inside the chamber, and she followed the others downstairs and out into the yard.

RICKWOOD SMITH SAID an edgy good-bye to Roy and shook hands with Gus, and said he would be in touch as soon as he had freed the door into the broom cupboard. He called the college office and reported that he and Miss Beasley would be returning straight away for the field expedition.

Ivy said good-bye to Gus and Roy, and walked away to join the students gathering outside the college. The sun was again struggling through the clouds, and it looked promising for what Rickwood the tutor insisted on calling their "Awareness Experience."

Thirty-eight

SOME TIME WAS spent, once all the stragglers had been accounted for, going from one empty stable to another. The big barn was still locked, Ivy noticed, so Gus's tractor was safe from marauding vintage Ferguson fanciers. She had decided to hang back, in order to encourage the students to be first through the gate and into virgin territory.

"Hey, look at this!" shouted one of the girls, emerging from a small loose box with a pail full of—what? Ivy had an idea, but one of the lads walked over to the girl. "Sheep nuts, you dope! Everybody knows that!"

There was a chorus of contradiction, some saying that of course not *everybody*, and some pronounced the contents of the bucket as chicken corn, all squashed into pellets and containing every vitamin that a hen could possibly need to lay an egg a day.

Then, having exhausted that amazing discovery, another girl was exclaiming at the sight of a lame sheep approaching from the other side of the gate.

"It's heard you rattling the bucket," said the boy who knew all about farming. "Best give it a few pellets on the ground. It may have been fed this morning already."

"Do you think it's laid an egg?" said one joker. The little group moved through the gate and into the field, and Ivy followed. She had made a small note. "Sheep well fed. Who is feeding it?"

The sheep was not stupid. It singled out the girl who had held the bucket and butted her back. She screamed, giving a predatory male the excuse to hug her close.

"Oh, for God's sake!" said the knowledgeable student, "It's only a sheep! And a lame one at that!"

The students were now walking in single file across the field, keeping to the muddy path that led straight to the spinney. Rickwood had lingered behind with Ivy and Samantha, saying he wanted the students to have a completely new confrontation with what the field could offer.

Ivy resisted the temptation to say that it was only a field, wasn't it? Both she and Rickwood were rewarded with a sudden yell from one of the lads. "Hey! Look at this!"

He was holding up high what looked like a dark-coloured rag, and Ivy and Rickwood hurried to look. By the time they caught up, one of the girls had turned away in tears, and a hush had fallen over the rest. "It's a dead cat, I think," said Samantha, bolder than the rest.

Ivy marched forward and looked closer. "It's a hot water bottle cover, you sillies," and took it firmly away from the girl. "Probably dropped by a child. I'll take it back and wash it out. Then we can put it in the shop, in case anyone claims it."

"Very reassuring, Miss Beasley," said Rickwood under his breath. "Why don't we put it under the hedge and collect it later. Now, shall we move on?"

All were busily noting down the discovery of a hot water bottle cover in their notebooks. Ivy did the same, and added, "Nicely made cover. Finders keepers?"

They were now two thirds of the way across the field, and the pace quickened. As they reached the spinney, one of the girls announced her intention of going back the long way round, by road.

"I'd feel safer, Rickwood, with houses and cars and people to look at. I don't mind going off on my own, and I'll make lots of notes."

"Sorry, can't allow that," said Rickwood. "Rules, rules. We all have to stick together. We'll go to the other side of the spinney and then turn round."

"But it's starting to rain, so please can we all go back round the road? We can walk faster, and it will be just as interesting. More interesting than a stupid sheep and a hot water bottle cover, in fact," said the girl.

"I have seen you all taking copious notes, so I am sure our expedition will have been profitable. And we're more than halfway through. So come on, adventurers, storm the spinney and then we'll turn back."

The thought of being more than halfway round seemed to buck up the group, and they set off through the trees at a good pace, Ivy and Rickwood bringing up the rear. The rain was not so heavy under the leafy trees, but as they emerged into the field, the wind was now driving it, almost sleet, horizontally across.

"Can we shelter in Rickwood's old henhouse over there? Or we can go back to my house?" shouted Samantha.

"I have a key to the henhouse, so we could shelter in there," said Rickwood, "but from the look of the sky, the rain has set in for the rest of the day. Shall we take a vote? Everyone has rainwear, and we can dry out when we get back to college."

"But I think Miss Beasley should go back to my house," persisted Samantha. "My mother's at home, and would be only too pleased to see her."

Ivy smiled, and took the girl's arm. "Very sweet of you, my dear," she said, "but we'll share my umbrella and be perfectly all right. Come on now, everybody, best feet forward!"

Eventually, damp and grumbling, the group began to walk the muddy path, even muddier now, back towards the farmhouse. Suddenly the leader stopped. "Hey, everybody!" he shouted. "First to notice something different gets a free pint in the pub tonight!"

All dutifully looked round the rain-swept field, shaking their heads. But Ivy smiled. She knew exactly what was different. The hot water bottle cover which had been put under a hedge had disappeared into her large brown bag.

BACK IN COLLEGE, dried out against radiators, the group once more assembled in the tutorial room. A watery sun had emerged, cheering up the assembled group.

"Coffee all round?" said Rickwood. "And tea for Miss Beasley. And then, while memories are still fresh and notes decipherable, we will reveal what we have seen."

This was more productive than Rickwood had hoped, and as each read out their notes and elaborated on them, he was delighted with the range of what had been spotted by a group of chiefly urban youngsters. Ivy, too, was pleased that in spite of the mud and rain, it had been a successful expedition.

There was one left to present her notes, apart from Ivy, of course, and that was Samantha. "It was a familiar route for me," she said. "But strangely enough, looking at the field through the eyes of the others, I noted several previously unnoticed things. The hot water bottle cover I mistook for a dead cat, of course, and that was not there when I came to college this morning. I am sure of that. But when we were trying to get into the henhouse, I noticed footmarks. It was really muddy where we had been walking round, and most of the marks had been sludged together. But round the back, off to one corner, I noticed prints heading off in the opposite direction towards the corner of the spinney. Did anyone go out that way?"

All the rest claimed they had followed the route they had already taken. Rickwood said he had counted them all as they set off to return, and none had been missing. "Very well spotted, Samantha," he said. "Whose prints do you think they are?"

Samantha smiled at him. "Yours," she said. "I've been watching you, sir."

"Indeed," said Ivy approvingly, and making another note in her own little book. "Perhaps we can investigate further," she added.

"Another day?" said one of the girls anxiously. "And in our own time? And when it stops raining?"

ROY WAS EXTREMELY glad to see the college vehicle draw up outside Springfields, and Ivy nimbly alighting. He limped over to greet her in reception, asking her tenderly about the heavy rain, and had it all been too much for her?

"Quite the contrary," she said. "It was most revealing. There was grumbling, of course, but we all arrived back in college in one piece. Even Rickwood Smith was impressed with the success. It was most amusing at times to hear the students' notes, and as always, one clever-clogs had clearly made it all up."

"Like what?" asked Roy. He saw from Ivy's pink cheeks and shining eyes that she had had a great time.

"He noted a half-hidden unexploded wartime bomb over by an oak tree, and also a gap in the hedge where he had seen an enormous bull looking through, and so on."

Roy laughed. "Let's hope he *was* making it up, then. Perhaps we should avoid the field path in future."

"Oh yes, and then there was a real dead body halfway across the field."

"Don't be silly, Ivy! Come on, tea awaits. Who was it, anyway?"

"It wasn't a who. It was a cat. At least that's what the students thought. I thought for one awful moment it was Tiddles, my very own Tiddles! But it wasn't. It was a furry hot water bottle cover. We put it under a hedge to deal with on our return. But it had gone!"

"Probably the fox came back for it," said farmer Roy. "Come along now. Anya has made us lemon tarts for tea."

Thirty-nine

ALMOST AS SOON as Roy and Ivy sat down to tea, Mrs. Spurling advanced on them with a red face. "It's Mrs. Bloxham," she said disapprovingly. "She says it is urgent." She thrust the phone into Ivy's hand and waited, lips pursed.

"God, Ivy, what an old dragon!" said Deirdre. "Anyway, before she locks you in your bedroom, I am longing to hear what happened on your student walk? Can me and Gus come over this evening, about half six? More convenient for me. Would that be allowed by La Spurling? . . . Okay? Bye."

Ivy handed the phone back wordlessly to Mrs. Spurling.

"Thank you, my dear," said Roy, smiling his sweetest. Sometimes he felt quite sorry for their manager. He could see that Ivy's fierce independence made life very difficult for the poor woman, and he tried to alleviate the tension it created all round.

Mrs. Spurling walked away, thinking for the umpteenth

time that she could not for the life of her understand what nice Mr. Goodman saw in the impossible old baggage.

"Gus and Deirdre are coming at half past six," said Ivy to Roy. "They want to hear what my student walk produced. It will be nice to see them, so perhaps you could exert your charm and order coffee—and one pot of tea—in my room ready for them? Thank you, my dear!"

Roy was not at all sure that Ivy wasn't mocking him. He could see a glint in her eye, but decided to ignore it. She could outwit him without effort.

IN THE FALLING twilight, the old sheep limped over the field towards the henhouse, and stopped a few yards from it. It baa-ed several times, and then settled down to wait.

Usually around this time, a handful of sweet-smelling hay was brought out, but so far it had not appeared. After a while, the sheep gave up, and wandered back to the other side of the field.

Samantha, walking back from college, where she had stayed for a social gathering of students in the bar, shone her torch over the muddiest patches on the path. She did not notice the sheep coming up behind her, and suddenly felt a strong push in her back, and she screamed.

When she turned around and saw what had shoved her forward, she shouted angrily at it, and vowed not to return home this way again. It was a foolish thing to do, anyway, she decided, and quickened her pace. Almost up to the spinney, she stopped. She could see the henhouse through the trees, and was certain the door opened and then quickly shut. Oh Lord, keep me safe, she said to herself. Then the door opened again, and she ran.

"Samantha! It's Rick! Don't be afraid. Come back."

She had only a few yards to go to the other side of the spinney, and reached her garden gate with relief.

"What on earth is the matter with you, Samantha?" said her mother, as she flopped onto the living room sofa without taking off her Wellingtons. "Those muddy boots! You surely didn't come back over the field path in the dark?"

Samantha nodded. "It is the last time I do," she said. "It's not only the mud. There was someone in the henhouse. The light was on, so I came on home as quickly as possible."

Her father came in and asked what was up. Samantha gave him a brief account. She did not own up that she knew all along that it was her tutor who worked in there at odd times. She rather wished she had stopped when he called. He had such a lovely warm voice . . .

Her father nodded wisely, and agreed that she shouldn't go that way until the field would be dry, and the evenings lighter. "It is private property, Sam. We are trespassing when we use that path, although it has been a shortcut for years, so the villagers say. But as long as you are not threatened in any way, it is nothing to do with us if the henhouse stores the instruments for the town band."

"A person, Dad," said Samantha. "Our tutor, Rickwood Smith, works in there. Not trumpets."

Her father shrugged. "Same difference," he said. "You did well to steer clear. Come and watch the telly and calm down."

IVY'S ROOM HAD once more become a meeting place, with extra chairs for Gus and Deirdre, and a tray of coffee and biscuits on a small table in front of them.

"How pleasant!" said Deirdre. "I don't know why you grumble about Springfields, Ivy. They always seem most accommodating. And where on earth did you get that furry thing? Don't tell me it's a nightdress bag?"

Ivy shook her head. "Hot water bottle cover. I found it and brought it back to be company for Tiddles. Sleight of hand, dears, and none of the others noticed. But let's talk about my expedition this afternoon. The students did well and enjoyed most of it."

"Never mind the students! We want to know what you learned about the farmyard and the footpath. The spinney, too, if you got that far."

"Who was with you on the expedition?" Gus asked Ivy. "Anyone we would know?"

"None you would recognise, I doubt," said Ivy. "Except, of course, Rickwood Smith. He was leader for the afternoon. Nice chap. But then, you've met him, Gus."

"Mm, I'm reserving judgement until I have seen more of him. He's been very uncooperative about the dark chamber. I'm certain he could open the door, and probably does when there's nobody about. He's acting as if he owns the farm already. Very proprietorial, he is.

"You've probably seen most of the students in the pub. There's one who always has a lot to say for himself. And then there's another knows all about farming. And, of course, young Samantha, who is my special friend."

"Smiley-faced girl?" said Gus. "Lives in the village? I think she's been down to the pub with some other girls. That could be Samantha. I think she's usually called Sam by her friends."

"Very pretty," said Ivy. "If I'm not mistaken, the poor child has developed a crush on our tutor, Rickwood Smith. Not a good idea, I think, but it is none of my business. On the other hand, I would not like to see her come to harm."

Gus nodded sagely, but in fact was deep in thought about how he could get his hands on the Ferguson tractor. He said he was sure Samantha's parents would be on the lookout for her, but who was keeping an eye on the Fergie?

"Somebody has locked the barn, but I can see it's still there. That peephole in the door is useful. Smith is very cagey about it. He says he has plans for the place when

everything is finalised. He seems pretty sure now that he
will be the new owner. Could be his mother, I suppose,
but since she is very disabled it might well be him in all
but name."

"Ye gods," said farmer Roy. "And we know he is thinking of selling up. If he stays, anything could happen.
There'll be donkey rides and rare breeds on show. School
parties, and reptile houses!"

"Tour buses and car parks!" said Ivy. "Tree walks and ice
creams. At a price! I know all about diversification, but these
hobby farms are a waste of time, using up good pasture land
that could support proper farm animals. And," she added,
"he'll be too busy to continue with the writing course, I
suppose. Always supposing he stays in the village."

"And if he moves into the farmhouse, I shall call with
my collecting tin," said Deirdre. "A very good way of
snooping! What say you, Ivy?"

"You snoop with your tin, I shall proceed more stealthily. First, I shall ask at college if anyone knows about the
new owner of Blackwoods Farm. I still think it is too soon
for Rickwood or his mother to have been legally approved
as Eleanor's sole beneficiary."

Roy groaned. "I do hope you spend a little time on your
memoirs, dearest. I suspect your class is becoming a useful
offshoot of Enquire Within!"

"Of course!" answered Ivy. "Why else do you think I
applied for the course?"

Roy laughed, and then smothered a yawn.

"We must go," said Deirdre. "It's been a great evening,
both. See you in church on Sunday, maybe? Meanwhile,
I'm off in the morning to see a client in Spinney Close.
Social services have asked me to visit."

"Who's that, then?" said Ivy.

"Mrs. Winchen, of course. Who else?"

Forty

"SO WHAT ARE you two dear things up to today?" Miss Pinkney smiled fondly at Roy, as he and Ivy sat reading the newspapers after breakfast.

"Oh, a quiet day, I think, Pinkers," he said. "This and that, you know."

"And a spot of the other?" said his friend Fred, propping himself up on the back of a chair. "You two must be close to being spliced."

Ivy nodded. "Not long to go now," she said. "But we've sort of decided not to talk about it too much, in case it should have to be cancelled again!"

"Possibly for good," said Roy, uncharacteristically gloomy.

"Cheer up, friend!" said Fred. "And hey, have you heard the latest?"

"Tell us," said Ivy.

"Blackwoods Farm, the old Blatch place. People are saying the new owner is moving in himself and turning the place into a safari park. How d'you fancy lions next door to you, Ivy?"

"Not at all, Fred. It's not so much the lions I object to. It's all the charabancs and hordes of so-called wildlife enthusiasts. I think I preferred the hobby farm rumour. In any case, you'll be able to say good-bye to peace and quiet in Barrington."

"Is that what's bothering you, too, Roy?" said Fred. "Not like you to have a miserable face. Mind you, I can see you, being a farmer, you'd not like that kind of thing where there should be native sheep and cattle, and the odd sheepdog running round the fields with his shepherd. Nor me, chum! Nor me. Let's hope the planning application gets turned down."

"Who is the rightful owner, then, Fred?" said Ivy, hoping this precious piece of information would drop into her lap.

Fred shook his head. "It was Eleanor Blatch's, of course. But folk say she didn't leave no will. Next in line would be that Rickwood chap's mother. She what was Eleanor's sister. So I suppose it's hers. He's been swanning around like he owns the place, so I expect he's running it for his mum."

Ivy's mobile rang, and she rummaged in her big handbag for it. After she finally located it, her face broke into a smile when she heard Samantha's voice on the phone.

"Hello, dear," she said. "How can I help you?"

"You know that dead cat that turned out to be a furry hot water bottle cover? Well, as you probably know because you keep your eyes open, it disappeared before we walked back to college. We reckon someone picked it up when we weren't looking."

"Ah, yes. Well, I have a confession to make. It was me. I picked it up, brought it back to Springfields, gave it a bath, and now it is curled up with Tiddles on my bed."

There was a small silence, and then Samantha began to laugh. "You are full of surprises, Miss Beasley!" she said. "I am sure it could not have a better home. So what are you planning for the weekend?"

"Well, I had a dream last night, and it was like a rerun of something that happened to me when I was a nipper. I thought I would spend this afternoon writing it down. I am planning to ask Roy to edit it for me."

"Best of luck, Miss Beasley. I hope we shall be allowed to read it?"

"We shall see. And what are you up to?"

"I thought I would go with my mop, broom and duster over to the henhouse to see if Rick needs a cleaner. You know how men are! It'll be my good deed for today."

"You will be careful, my dear, won't you? Good-bye."

"ME EDIT YOUR notes? Not me, Ivy, not likely!" said Roy. "Your memoir should have the voice of Ivy Beasley in all of it. And as for editing, you'd best ask our Gus to do that for you. He's a properly educated chap."

"No, I want you to read it and approve it, whatever its mistakes. Please, Roy."

"Very well, dearest. You get busy this afternoon, and perhaps I will do the same and write down some of my memories, too?"

"No need, we'll have plenty of time to sit by the fire and reminisce when we're old."

Mrs. Spurling, passing by, heard Ivy's last few words, and raised her eyes to heaven.

FOR THE REST of the morning, Ivy and Roy decided to take a walk across the Green and down Hangman's Row to call on Gus and Whippy. Roy climbed into his trundle and they set off into the sunlit Springfields garden. As they went through the gate into the road, a loud voice hailed them.

"Good morning! Beautiful morning, isn't it?" Peter Rubens approached and asked them where they were going. "May I accompany you as far as the pub?" he asked. "We have been so busy with our first year of courses and students, and I have neglected my contacts with neighbours. How are you both keeping?"

"Pretty well, thank you," said Roy. "And yourself?"

"Oh, splendid, thank you, Mr. Goodman. Miss Beasley will have told you about our successful expedition, teaching us to keep our eyes and ears open."

"Yes, indeed. She told me they found a hot water bottle cover that resembled a dead cat and a lame sheep. All very useful for potential writers, I am sure."

"Ah, yes, the lame sheep," said Peter. "You aren't feeding it, are you? Not a good idea with sheep."

"Changing the subject," said Ivy, "have you been told about the safari park at Blackwoods Farm?" Ivy's face was all innocence, but Roy knew exactly what she was up to.

"Rumours, Mr. Rubens," he said. "But there's no smoke without fire, as my old mother used to say. There's another memory for you, Ivy," he added with a smile.

"I heard a family called Winchen were taking it over. Does that name mean anything to you?" Ivy replied, still smiling encouragingly at Rubens.

"Only one of the names of that poor woman who was murdered. I suppose they'll make the most of that in the safari park publicity. 'Visit the haunted house that even the tigers won't go near!' I can hear it now."

"We heard that it hasn't actually changed hands, as old Mrs. Winchen, Eleanor's sister, is still alive. But her son, Rickwood, could be involved. Doesn't he work for you, Mr. Rubens?" said Roy. "I shouldn't think he will want that sort of thing."

"He's a good fellow and tutor, so I hope he won't be leaving us. Very popular with the girls, too. Can't see him tangling with tigers, though!"

They were at the corner of the Green, and Peter Rubens left them, heading for the pub.

"So there we are," said Roy. "Not a lot further forward."

"Hardly anywhere," said Ivy. They continued down Hangman's Lane, waving to Miriam Blake as they went.

"Now," said Roy, "are you going to knock on Gus's door? No point in my detrundling if he's not there."

Gus had seen them coming, and appeared at his door, smiling broadly.

"Hi, you two, come on in? I wasn't expecting you this morning. Deirdre's coming in later. Let me help you, Roy."

Ivy said Roy was perfectly capable of managing by himself, and walked in, followed by Whippy. Ivy was not particularly partial to dogs, but she stroked the smooth head dutifully, and sat down on one of the least rickety of Gus's chairs.

"How about lunch here?" said Gus. "We can phone La Spurling and I can invite Miriam. She always cooks enough for an army. There's a great deal to talk about, and Miriam may well have something to contribute. Look outside! There's heavy drops falling already. I'll push the trundle under cover, and have a word with Miriam."

AN HOUR LATER, they welcomed Miriam bearing plates of steaming curry, and all managed to sit round an unsteady folding table. Pronouncing it to be the best curry he had ever tasted, Gus poured glasses of primrose wine all round and suggested they tell Miriam what they knew.

"Not all of it," said Ivy. "It will take too long. But I wonder if first, Miriam, I could ask you if you have had any contact with Mrs. Winchen, who lives in the old persons' bungalows, or her son, Rickwood Smith?"

Ivy said that it was Mrs. Winchen who they were really interested in. Mary Winchen, who was now disabled, and had her son staying with her at present. "We know quite a

lot about them currently," she said. "I have met the son at
college. He's a tutor. And Mrs. Bloxham, who does volun-
tary work for social services, as I expect you know, she is
visiting Mrs. Winchen to see if she is okay and happy an'
all that, or needs help."

Miriam shook her head. "The only Winchen I really
remember was poor Mrs. Eleanor. Her second name was
Winchen. She was older than me, of course, but us kids
used to go round the farm after school and Mr. Ted would
give us sweets. I think he liked kids, and they didn't have
none of their own. Mind you," she added, moving her chair
closer, "there was talk of a miscarriage, and my mum said
the poor woman wouldn't try again. Know what I mean?"

She paused, deep in thought. The others waited, and
then Gus said, "Go on, Miriam, tell us more."

"O' course, it would be before any of you lot came to
live in Barrington," she said. "But, believe it or not, after
Mr. Ted died, Mrs. Eleanor took a lover. Well, to be honest,
he came as her lodger, but ended up, everyone said, as her
lover. You could tell, y'know. Then, poor woman, he did
a runner, taking all her savings an' that. Never came back,
the rotten sod, if you'll pardon my French."

"Granted," said Ivy. "We have heard about the lodger.
But didn't Eleanor have a sister Mary? A younger sister?"

"Yes, there was one. Prettier than Eleanor. Would that
be the one living in Spinney Close now?"

"Yes, we think so. Deirdre will tell us more." Ivy shifted
in her seat to give her a better view of the lane outside.

"If you don't mind my asking, Miss Beasley," Miriam
said slowly, "why do you want to know all this? A case
you're working on, is it?"

"And my memoirs," said Ivy quickly. "I am writing my
memoirs, and have become fascinated by village history
here in Barrington. You have such a good memory, Miriam, and it's all so interesting."

Roy coughed, and said he was sure Miriam would

remember a poor young mother expecting, and then no baby to show for it. "It happened with cows sometimes," he said, "when I was a working farmer."

"I didn't hear much about it as a child," Miriam said. "Though I used to get under the table and listen to grown-ups talking. I used to like that. I did hear them talk about a 'miss,' as they used to call it. Didn't understand it, quite, but I knew we never saw no baby. Oh yes, it's coming back to me now. That's when the sister came to stay for a while. Very pretty, she was. She was nice to us kids, too, but she got sent back to Lincolnshire, my mum said. Too pretty, she said, and all her friends sitting round the table laughed like drains. There's a memory for you, Miss Beasley!"

"Wonderful, Miriam. You should be the one writing your memoirs. Wonderful recall of times past. It's valuable stuff, you know. Oral history they call it at the college. There's a course on it. Perhaps you should have a go?"

"I have quite enough to do with looking after my cottage, and keeping an eye on Gus here, and his Whippy. I'll leave the studying to you, Miss Beasley, thanks very much. I shall look forward to reading your book, when you've finished it."

Deirdre arrived outside, and came in with a long face. "Sorry, friends," she said. "No Miss Winchen, I'm afraid. There was a note addressed to me, pinned to her front door saying she had gone to a doctor's appointment at the surgery in Oakbridge."

"I hope you weren't late," said Ivy in a disgruntled tone of voice. "We were hoping you'd have great revelations for us. Miriam here has been wonderful remembering things."

"Good-o for Miriam," Deirdre said nastily, and Gus's well-meaning neighbour got to her feet and departed in a huff.

Forty-one

INSPIRED BY THE fruitful nature of Miriam's memories, Ivy's writing session in the afternoon at Springfields had gone very well, and now she produced a sheaf of papers and handed them to Roy.

"Chapter one," she said triumphantly.

"How many chapters to go?" said Roy, taking it with a smile.

"Lord knows. And I mean that literally. I expect I shall carry on with them until the time comes for me to account for myself at the gate of heaven."

"Very poetic, Ivy, my love! Have we discovered a hidden talent to add to all your others?"

"I doubt it," said Ivy. "But it is a nice thing to do, looking back over a long life. I remember so much, good and bad, funny and sad. It is amazing how much comes back, once you start. Remember Miriam yesterday?"

"So where have you begun," said Roy, shuffling the papers.

The Blackwoods Farm Enquiry   217

"Don't mix them up! I'll never get them back together again."

"Have you ever thought of starting from now, and working backwards?"

"If you have nothing more constructive to say, Roy Goodman, you can give it here at once!" Ivy reached out her hand, but Roy evaded it.

"Only teasing, beloved," he said. "Actually, I'm jealous. I tried to think of a single interesting memory yesterday, and my early life, and the rest of it, was as boring as hell! Village school, boarding school, agricultural college, Young Farmers Ball, rugby football, farming, retirement, and then Wham! I meet Ivy Beasley! That's it, so far. Now, I shall read this after coffee, in my room, in peace and quiet, away from the hurly-burly of daily life in Springfields."

Ivy laughed. "Have you noticed, dear, how our conversation becomes quite literary when we're talking about such matters? But aren't we going to church?"

"It's holy communion, with that visiting canon in the pulpit. He could do with an editor when writing his sermons. There's Evensong we can go to, with our own nice vicaress. Let's do that."

ROY WAS SITTING peacefully in his room with Ivy's memoir on his lap. It had fallen from his grasp as his eyes had gradually closed and he had drifted into sleep. Two pages had fallen on the floor, and as his telephone began to ring he jumped awake and sent the whole lot, sheet by sheet, tumbling off his lap.

"Hello? Um, no, I am not expecting a call, Mrs. Spurling. What name did you say? Jones? Well, better put him through."

When Mr. Jones said he was calling from Boston,

Lincolnshire, Roy snapped properly awake, and asked him his business. Mr. Jones proved to be the pork butcher Gus and Deirdre had met and talked with about the Winchens. When Roy asked how he had got this number, Mr. Jones said Gus had given him four numbers to contact, and this one was the first to answer.

Having straightened that out, Roy listened avidly to what Mr. Jones had to say.

"I was interested after talking to your friends about the Winchens, and decided to do a little research myself. Difficult family to track down! But one thing puzzled me more than anything, and that was what happened to Eleanor's sister, Mary. Then I found amongst the old butcher's accounts, a letter from, I think, Eleanor's mother to a cousin—I think it was a cousin—in Australia. It was an old carbon copy, dropped in there by accident, I should think. Do you remember when we used a piece of carbon paper to keep a copy of our letters? The burden of this one seemed to be that she was sending a young woman—no name given—to live with the cousin's family and settle down as an Australian citizen."

"Good gracious! And do you think that young woman was Mary?"

"As I said, no name given. No trace thereafter of Eleanor's sister. That's it, all I could find. Your friends might like to trace it further, but I don't know how. Perhaps you could pass it on? If I find out more, I'll let you know."

Roy thanked him profusely, and took his number. Then he picked up Ivy's papers and set himself to finish her memoirs so far. It was more than his life was worth to return to the lunch table without having restored them to order and read them properly.

"WE SHOULD CERTAINLY get Gus and Deirdre along to tea," Ivy said. "Better than trying to remember it all in a phone call. Pinkers is on duty all day today, so no problem there. What an interesting morning!"

"Not too interesting to forget about a certain person's memoirs," said Roy. "An excellent start, beloved! Really gripping, and I couldn't put it down until I reached the end. It was rather sad, though, the way your father was sent out to sober up in the garden shed with nothing to sit in but the dog basket."

He forbore to mention that Ivy had always maintained they had cats, as her mother couldn't abide dogs. The story was a good one, and who was he to quibble?

At teatime, Gus and Deirdre arrived promptly, and they settled once more in Ivy's room.

"So what's this important news?" Gus said.

Roy related simply and accurately what Mr. Jones had said to him. "Nice man, I thought," he concluded. "Very friendly, and interested in everything you'd told him. I asked him why he rang me, and he had tried all four of us, and I was first to answer. So what do you think about this mystery person growing up in Australia?"

Deirdre pretended she had something in her eye, and dabbed away a tear. "It is very sad, isn't it, whoever the young person was. Sent off to another country like a parcel. I wonder why? There must have been something very serious behind it. Think of the terrible journey she must have had. Probably ended up in the outback, working like a drudge on a remote farm."

"Your imagination does you credit, Dee-Dee," said Gus. "But equally, she may have been sent as a nursemaid, and settled in a leafy Sydney suburb with a charming doctor's family. Ended up marrying the son of the house."

"In that case," said Ivy, "we must wait until you, Deirdre, make another appointment and ask Mrs. Winchen some important questions."

"But where is this leading us, folks? What lead are we following? I really do think I shall have to ask Frobisher straight out if he thinks Eleanor tripped and tumbled to her death, or was pushed. To put it baldly. The results of an autopsy could be attributed to either, I reckon."

"You weren't here to listen to what Miriam said yesterday," said Ivy. "The most interesting revelation was that Eleanor became pregnant, lost the baby, Mary came to look after her afterwards and went back home in—some said—disgrace. We need to know why, when and how."

"In other words, I have to encourage poor Mrs. Winchen to forget her aches and pains and search her memory for some answers. Right?"

"Right, Deirdre love," said Gus.

"And then shall we have another trip to Boston, Gus? Call on Mr. Jones again?" said Deirdre, looking hopeful.

"Good thinking," he said. "We could take another look at the baptismal records in the Stump. Wonderful church, Ivy. You should take a trip with us and see it. From the top of the church tower you can see for miles and miles. From up there they used to have a beacon to guide travellers across the fens. There are still treacherous marshes on the edge of the Wash. Lonely country, where anything might happen."

"Don't get carried away, Gus," said Deirdre. "Shall I book us in to the hotel again then? Two nights?"

"If you two ever get married," said Ivy acidly, "you'll know where to go for your honeymoon, won't you?"

Forty-two

IVY WAS FIRST to arrive at college on Wednesday morning, and Peter Rubens greeted her enthusiastically.

"Good morning, Miss Beasley! A fine day and my favourite student has made an early start. Excellent example to set to the other slackers."

"I've got a reason, Mr. Rubens. Can you spare a minute? I want your permission to ask one or two of the day students if I could talk to their local families? They need to be in Barrington, or nearby. Not to put too fine a point on it, I want to pick their brains. How about it?"

"Is this concerning your own memoirs?"

"Yes, sort of. I need some farming background material, as instructed by Rickwood Smith. I myself come from the Midlands. Ended up here because of my cousin Deirdre. Lives at Tawny Wings—you must have met her?"

Peter Rubens's eyes sparkled. "Oh yes, young Mrs. Bloxham. Very lovely person. We've met on a committee in Thornwell. Social work, with an emphasis on old people. I like to keep abreast, you know."

"Right, well, I thought I should ask you. I hope there will be no objection?"

"None at all, Miss Beasley. I'll get Stephanie to write a note of introduction for you. And if I can be of any help, do speak to me. I shall soon be staging a small drinks party for neighbours and friends who have been so kind to us since we opened up here. Perhaps Mrs. Bloxham might like to come along?"

Not a chance, you old idiot, thought Ivy. Mrs. Deirdre Bloxham is a rich and merry widow, and she has much bigger fish to fry than you, Peter Paul Rubens.

Thinking she would start with the young student who knew about farming, Ivy asked his name and planned to approach him at coffee time. Adam Broadbent, Rubens had said, and he confirmed that the lad was a day student and lived locally.

The first session of the day concerned source material for the memoir writer. Friends and relatives, old diaries and photograph albums, back copies of newspapers and magazines. In Ivy's case, her contacts were few, and she had never kept a continuous diary. Her one very precious photo album was kept in a bag under her bed, and was seldom taken out. Perhaps this was the one occasion? She could show it to Roy, and hope that he was not dismayed by the small girl with skimpy pigtails and dark eyes hiding behind goggle-eyed spectacles.

And she was bandy legged! Over the years she had developed a habit of always wearing long skirts, well down her legs. "My skirts," she would say, "cover a multitude of sins."

She would do her best to remember what went on in the outside world, but back in Round Ringford, a tiny, isolated village in the middle of England, Ivy's memoirs would chiefly concern her mother and father, and after her father's death, life with a domineering, cruel-tongued mother.

Coffee time arrived, and Ivy sat down at the same table as Adam Broadbent. He held her chair for her and said politely that he had enjoyed the expedition she had suggested.

"A sad-looking place, though, isn't it, Blackwoods Farm? Such a shame it has been allowed to deteriorate."

"I agree. I did have a fancy that my dad might like to buy it for me, but times is hard and he couldn't manage it."

"I suppose your father remembers it as a useful going concern?"

"Not sure. You'd have to ask him."

So, given this perfect opening, Ivy explained that she needed some background material for her memoirs. "You remember that Rickwood said we should interlace our own experiences with background material concerning the world at that time," she said.

"Yeah, Dad'd certainly remember a lot about that."

Ivy continued, saying that she needed someone with a farming background who could describe life back then, and Adam agreed to ask his grandmother if she could help. "She'd remember more than Dad. She lives with us, so you could come and have a cup of tea."

BY LUNCHTIME, THE group were becoming well versed in extracts from other memoirs, especially those where a certain amount of "embroidering" had gone on. Dialogue would be encouraged, as long as the voice provided colour and authenticity.

"The Suffolk accent is wonderfully mellifluous," enthused Rickwood.

"It sounds nice, too," said Ivy.

"It's quite singsong, really," volunteered Samantha. "Not like in the West Country, but Suffolk and Norfolk are very recognisable."

"Remember the Singing Postman?" said Ivy. "Ha' y'got a loyt, boiy?"

"Yes, well, we must get on," said Rickwood, with an

uncomfortable feeling he was being sent up. "My watch tells me it's nearly lunchtime."

"I expect Adam can produce a true Suffolk accent?" Ivy was enjoying herself.

"Oh, yeah. Here goes. 'Where y'bin?' 'Bin t'swaff'm, t'do some thrashin'. All f'nuth'n. That's s'uthn.' Will that do, Miss Beasley?"

AFTER CLASS FINISHED, Adam suggested Ivy should come along with him straight away.

"Dad always comes in for a cup around four," he said. "He'll be only too pleased to have an excuse to stay in the kitchen for longer, and he can get Gran going."

"Shouldn't you first ask your parents if they mind my coming?"

Adam pulled out his mobile with a flourish, had a few words with his mother, and smiled. "Fine. You'd be very welcome," he said. "Grannie loves to talk about the old days."

THE KITCHEN OF the old farmhouse was warm, and smelt of generations of good cooking. Ivy sat comfortably in an old chair that left white dog hairs on her skirt, and listened to Grannie Broadbent reminisce.

"How clear your memories are!" she said, after a while. "I couldn't possibly remember so much. Perhaps it should be you writing your memoirs!"

"It's the farming community, I reckon," he said. "We all know each other and swap stories when we meet."

"I suppose you remember Ted Blatch and his family? Didn't they live at Blackwoods Farm?"

"Oh, yes, Ted was a one with the ladies. He married an outsider. That's what we called anyone coming in from more than twenty miles away! Pretty girl, Eleanor was, too. Shame she came to a sticky end."

"Did she settle in all right?" persisted Ivy. "Must have been difficult, with her family coming from up north?"

"Yes, though we never met them," said Adam's father. I think her young sister, Mary, came down once, when Eleanor had a miss. Then the Blatches never had no more children, and that was a sore disappointment. No sons. Nor no daughters, either. Speaking of which, you would have loved a daughter, eh, missus?"

"Not too late, mind," Grannie Broadbent added slyly.

Adam looked embarrassed, but Ivy laughed. "Never too late," she said. "I suppose the Blatches went on trying?"

"Not sure."

Ivy had a feeling they were clamming up on the subject of the Blatches, but ploughed on. "Eleanor must've needed friends. My mother always used to say you made friends at the school gate, waiting for little 'uns to come out."

"Miss Eleanor died recently, as I'm sure you know," said Adam's mother, clearly attempting to draw a line under the subject.

"And Mary?" said Ivy. "What happened to her?" She held her breath, waiting for an answer.

With a quick look at Adam's father, Mrs. Broadbent shook her head. "Mary who?" she said.

"Winchen. Eleanor's sister," Ivy reminded her. Goodwill was ebbing away.

"Oh, her," said Mrs. Broadbent. Both she and her husband shook their heads, and even Adam looked absently out of the window.

"Don't know nothing about Mary," old Grannie Broadbent said finally. "As I said, we never met the Winchen family. Now, Miss Beasley, how about another cup of tea?"

"I AM SURE they were hiding something," said Ivy, as she sat with Roy in her room. "Definitely shifty, all three of them. Not hiding, so much as unwilling to talk about her. They would surely know about Mary Winchen now, though. A disabled lady living in Spinney Close?"

"Very likely. But village politics can be very tricky, as I'm sure you know. Still, you did your best, my love. Deirdre and Gus might have more luck up in Boston. I myself have not been idle."

"Roy, my dear, of course you haven't! Tell all."

"That, Ivy, is an expression you have picked up from young Katya, and I am sure would be frowned on by tutor Rickwood. But I will tell you all that I have discovered from sitting in the lounge and listening to our fellow guests here in Springfields."

Suitably subdued, Ivy pecked him on the cheek. "Never thought of that," she said. "Old folks' memories on our doorstep! Who did you speak to?"

"Well, I decided to tackle the dreaded Mrs. Cornwall. Very large, very fond of lavender water, and with a very loud voice and loud opinions. Mrs. Cornwall, the very same."

"Oh lor, Roy. Very brave of you. How did you get on?"

"Well, as usual, my dear, with bullies, face up to them and they crumble. She was very pleasant and extremely helpful."

"Has she always lived in Barrington?"

"Yes, from being born in a barn one winter's night when her mother hadn't time to get back to the house."

"Very colourful," said Ivy. "So come on, Roy, did she remember anything about Mary Winchen?"

"Yes," said Roy. "She did." He turned to adjust the cushion behind his back.

"Roy, I am breaking off our engagement if you don't tell me exactly what she said!"

"We talked about the sad death of Eleanor, and then Mrs. Cornwall volunteered the information that Mary would get the money, after all. That's all she said. Dropped off to sleep, then, or pretended to. I touched her hand, but she didn't wake up."

"Roy! That is very important. And fits in with what Mrs. Broadbent said to me not two hours ago. She mentioned the younger sister, Mary. We've always thought Eleanor was the eldest of the two, haven't we, so we were right there."

"Elder of two, eldest of many. I mention that only because you are now in the writing game."

"Mm, but you don't know that there weren't more children than Mary and Eleanor. There might have been Tom, Dick and Harry as well."

"There you are, then," said Roy.

Forty-three

WHEN GUS TELEPHONED from Boston, he was anxious to know how Ivy and Roy had progressed with their enquiries. He explained that he and Deirdre had drawn a blank so far. They would not be able to look at the registry office records until tomorrow, and so had wasted time wandering around graveyards and accosting elderly people in the street asking if they remembered the Winchen family.

"Bad luck," said Roy. "You'll be glad to hear that Ivy and I have not been idle. I'll put her on."

"Hello, Gus. Oh, it's Deirdre now. Hello, dear, how are you enjoying Boston?"

"We're not here to enjoy it, Ivy, as you very well know. But I must say the keen east wind is enough to freeze you solid. Turn a corner of a street and you run slap into it. You'd never know it is still summer! It *is* just like a slap in the face. We did find some Winchens in the graveyard, but all from the nineteenth century. Quite posh graves, so I imagine they were a wealthy family. One of the gravestones praises a Walter Winchen for his charitable acts in helping the poor."

"Very interesting. Anything else?"

"No, but we've got a special dispensation to look in the register records tomorrow, and let's hope that will be more fruitful. Now, how about you and Roy?"

"Well, I didn't have much luck, either, talking to a farming couple, parents of one of the college students, and his grannie. They were friendly, and knew Eleanor, of course, and also—and here's the nugget of gold. Apparently Eleanor was once pregnant, but lost the baby, and Mary came down to look after her. But according to the farmer and his wife and the grandmother, she never came again. At least, not to their knowledge."

"That *is* interesting, Ivy. Did they say anything else?"

"No, only polite conversation."

"And Roy?"

"He did better. Talked to one of our residents, who remembered the Winchens visiting Barrington. One sister married Ted Blatch, and the other went off somewhere else. She was a bit hazy about that, apparently. But then she said, out of nowhere, that now Eleanor was dead, Mary would get all the money, *after all*."

"Doesn't that make sense, if Mary was younger?"

"That's what we have to find out. But there was a problem, that's for sure. We'll talk about it tomorrow when you get back. Can you come here in the evening? Or come to tea?"

"Depends on how we get on in the registry office. We'll ring you."

IT WAS LATE by the time Peter Rubens, up at the Manor House, had finished his paperwork and gone round locking doors and putting out lights. His electricity bill was enormous, and he planned to give a lecture to students on putting out lights in unoccupied rooms.

His daughter, Stephanie, was playing loud music in her room, and from across the yard he could hear voices talking and laughing. All going well, he thought. How lucky he was, to have come across the Manor House, being exactly what he was looking for. His thoughts turned to Rickwood Smith and all the rumours surrounding him. He had proved a very useful tutor and had said nothing about leaving. He hoped the farm would be sold and Rickwood become a fixture at the college. The loud music dimmed down, and was eventually switched off. With a sigh of relief, Peter drifted into sleep.

NEXT MORNING, ROY woke early, and thought he would toddle along to Ivy's room to share a cup of tea and plan their day. He climbed out of bed, reached for his stick, and limped slowly along the landing. Bright sunlight streamed through a window, and he could see the sky was blue and cloudless. His spirits rose. Perhaps he and Ivy would be able to take Elvis and his taxi into town, and do some frivolous shopping. The Winchen Blatch case was moving along. Slowly, certainly, but after Deirdre had had her interview with Mrs. Winchen, things should be a lot clearer. And even more so if she was able to extract information from Inspector Frobisher. So they were all waiting for Deirdre.

A gentle morning in Thornwell would take their minds off it and clear the air for both. Perhaps Ivy would allow him to buy her a present! She was very strict about such things, being unwilling that he should spend money on her until they were formally married. And that was not long to go now, so perhaps she would relax the rules.

Ivy heard his tap on her door, and called to him to come in. She sat up in bed, whipped off her hairnet, and did her best to adjust her nightdress neatly. First impressions are most important, she told herself, and the thought made her smile. She and Roy had been more or less permanent companions for so long now that short of seeing her totally naked, he was familiar with her every mood and appearance.

"Good morning, beloved!" he said. "You're looking as beautiful as ever. The sun is shining, I am pleased to say, and I have come to share an early cuppa with you. I saw Katya on her way up the stairs, so she should be here in less than a minute."

"How did you sleep, Roy?" Ivy said. "I couldn't go off for ages. Winchen Blatches kept passing before my eyes in ever increasing numbers! Anyway, I made a few notes—here, take the book—so that we know exactly what we are doing. Please add anything you think I've missed. Then we can get going straight away."

Roy shook his head. "No, not straight away, Ivy dear. This morning I am ordering Elvis to pick us up at ten o'clock and take us into Thornwell, where we shall have our favourite coffee and doughnuts, and visit my friend the jeweller, where I am going to buy you a sparkling jewel to wear on your bosom."

Ivy stared at him. "Are you feeling all right, Roy?" she said.

"Never better," he said. "Ah, here's Katya with our tea. Morning, my dear, how's the bump coming along?"

Katya smiled. Roy was a specially nice resident in her eyes. "I think he was playing football last night," she said. "Kicking away for hours. I could actually see his little feet making small humps on my stomach! Isn't it exciting?"

"Did he win?" said Ivy, also smiling. "Oh, good, you've brought two cups."

"I spied Mr. Goodman on his naughty way to your bedroom," Katya replied.

After she had disappeared, Ivy returned to the attack.

"We cannot possibly afford the time to do all that," she said. "I plan to go down to the church, to find Miriam Blake, who is always there on a Saturday morning, busying herself about God knows what."

"I expect he does," said Roy mildly. "May I ask what you plan to say to her?"

"I'm going to search her memory. She hasn't got much sense, but her memory is unusually good."

"How old do you reckon Eleanor was when she died?" Roy said thoughtfully. "I would have said sixty-ish."

"Difficult to say. When we first met her, when she came to ask for our help, she looked dreadful. Old and unkempt. But after she came out of hospital that time, and got herself together with Deirdre's help, she looked years younger. Probably sixtyish, I would say."

"So this sister, Mary, who is younger, would be anything from midfifties to sixty? Miriam Blake is well into her forties, and so could possibly remember something, but not much, I would say."

"Are you trying to say it is not worth my going to see her?"

"I think she has already told us more or less all she knows. Other more urgent things for us to do. Like booking Elvis for Saturday, and getting out of Barrington for a few hours. It will still be here when we get back. What do you say, dearest?"

Ivy frowned. She wanted to say that his suggestion was rubbish, but she was learning, and so nodded instead. "Perhaps you're right," she said.

Forty-four

ON SATURDAY, ELVIS turned up promptly at ten o'clock and loaded Roy and his trundle into the taxi. Ivy sat in the front, and they went off smoothly through the sunlit village, while Elvis warned them not to be fooled, there was a chill in the air. "There's a rug in the back there, if you're chilly, Mr. Goodman," he said.

They assured Elvis that they were indeed warm enough, and chatted idly until Roy said something about Ted Blatch being a tough old farmer if he'd lived in that derelict house for many years.

"Ted?" said Elvis. "Ted Blatch? He was a nice bloke, never mind about being tough. A bit mean, maybe. He and his wife, they were a pleasant couple. The number of times I've given him and her a lift into town, but neither of them ever had any change to give me. I gave up hoping in the end, and decided I'd get a bonus point on the day of Judgement!"

"Perhaps they were really poor," said Ivy. "The place is certainly derelict now. Nobody in the village really knows what's going to happen to it."

"They were certainly poor. Ted sunk all his savings into the place when he took it over. His uncle was a bank clerk, with the National in Thornwell. I think that's how Ted got a loan to do what he wanted to the place, and he really worked hard at it. He was a good-looking man, was Ted. Tall and dark-haired. Wiry build, and kind of loped along, like a cowboy! Him and Eleanor made a handsome pair. But after he'd gone, she lost heart, I reckon. Let the place go. It'll take a bit of capital to put it right."

"How do you know all this, Elvis?" asked Roy.

"Ah, you'd be surprised what I hear in my job. People don't reckon I'm human. A deaf human at best! Conversations, arguments, threats and courting couples. All human life is here, Mr. Goodman. I hear it all."

"So I suppose Ted had to sell up, in the end?" said Ivy.

"No, he said he'd never sell. He told Eleanor one day in the back of my vehicle that although it was a millstone around his neck, he intended to carry on until he died, and then it would be her millstone to do what she liked with. Left it to her in his will, so he said."

"And you never heard a whisper about it being sold?"

"No, nothing like that. Why are you so interested, Miss Beasley, if you don't mind my asking?"

"Oh, no reason, really. It's only that I'm doing this writing course at the Manor House College, and am interested in background material to the life of the farm, then and now."

"I see. That's really clever of you, at your age. Do I get a copy when it's published?"

"Of course. Perhaps you know of some knowledgeable person I could talk to? Everything that's told to me is confidential, and I'd never use any names an' that."

Elvis was quiet for a moment, and then came up with a real person, a lady he took every so often to her chiropodist. "She has always lived in Barrington, with her family at Church Farm. I think they have been in the village for generations. I could ask her if she would have a talk with you, Miss Beasley?"

Ivy thanked him kindly, and said she could walk along to Church Farm, if Elvis would make the introduction.

They wandered around the market, and Roy persuaded Ivy to let him buy a little black cat brooch. Then a happy half hour in the café with coffee and doughnuts worked its magic, and by the time they returned to Springfields they were back to their happy relationship. Elvis promised to be in touch in a couple of days, after he had spoken to the farmer's wife, Mrs. Coleridge.

Forty-five

ELVIS WAS AS good as his word, and on Sunday morning around eleven o'clock Ivy's phone rang.

"Morning, Miss Beasley!" he said. "Hope I didn't interrupt anything? Good. I thought you'd like to know I talked to Mrs. Coleridge, and she says her memory of the old days is pretty good, and she'd be happy to see you for a chat. Here's her phone number."

Ivy wrote it down in her clear, precise handwriting, and thanked him kindly. Then she looked at her watch and decided to ring the number straight away. Roy was still upstairs, and she planned to fix an appointment before he appeared. Gus and Deirdre had not been in touch since a quick call saying they would be back around four this afternoon, so she might have something useful to tell them.

"Hello? Is that Mrs. Coleridge? Ivy Beasley here. Elvis spoke to you, I believe. Well, that's very kind of you, I'm sure. Around half past two, then? No, no, I shall be

perfectly able to walk that short distance! I look forward
to meeting you."

ARRIVING OUTSIDE CHURCH Farm, Ivy could not
help comparing it with the sadly neglected Blackwoods.
A shallow stream ran parallel to the road, crossed by a
small bridge with a freshly painted white handrail. The
house itself was clearly very old, but well maintained, with
window frames and a simple front door also painted white.
The general appearance was of a busy, hardworking family
farm.

Mrs. Coleridge was waiting at the door with a welcoming smile, and Ivy stepped inside with a pleasant feeling
of familiarity. This was exactly how a farm should be, she
thought, and was reminded of her own grandparents, who
had farmed in the Midlands.

"Do sit down, Miss Beasley. My daughter will bring us
tea in a couple of minutes. I do hope you take tea? I am
afraid I am not a coffee lover."

A woman after my own heart, thought Ivy, and relaxed
into a comfortable, plush-covered armchair. "This is very
kind of you," she began.

"Not at all. I love talking about the old days. Don't ask
me the name of the man who brought the bread yesterday!
But where shall we start?"

Ivy explained about her writing course, and said she
was interested in the history of Blackwoods Farm, but
could find nobody who could remember, or wanted to
remember! "It is such a neglected old place," she said. "I
wondered what could have happened there in the past?"

Mrs. Coleridge heaved a deep sigh. "Ah, Blackwoods
Farm," she said. "Not a happy tale, I'm afraid, Miss Beasley, but a very interesting one. I must think carefully and
make sure I get it right."

"Perhaps if I tell you what I have found out already? I know Ted Blatch lived there, and his wife was from a family called Winchen, from Lincolnshire. Eleanor Blatch was, as everybody in Barrington knows, found dead from a fall down that fire escape recently."

Mrs. Coleridge looked at her, paused and smiled. "Miss Beasley," she said, "shall we get this clear straightaway? You are, I know, doing a writing course up at the Manor, but you also run a private enquiry agency from Springfields? Now, that doesn't make any difference to me. In fact, it is more interesting than putting words together in the right way. Can I suppose you need to know about the Blatches because you're on a case there? Did she fall or was she pushed?"

Ivy frowned, and then her face cleared and she broke into a rare cackle. "Got it in one, Mrs. Coleridge," she said. "What a relief to talk to someone like you! Yes, you are quite right. Eleanor Blatch came to us before she died, quite a while before, and said she thought she was being persecuted by the ghost of her husband. We thought she was a bit batty, but took her on. My colleague, Mrs. Bloxham at Tawny Wings, got to know her, and said she was perfectly sane, and actually became a good friend. Then this awful thing happened, and we felt duty bound to help find the truth surrounding her death. We suspect there is something to do with a family feud that goes a long way back. And that's why I'm here. Is that still all right with you?"

Mrs. Coleridge told her a great deal about the rumours that began almost as soon as Eleanor Winchen came into the village as Ted's fiancée. It seemed it had been common knowledge that there was another Winchen girl, who was much prettier than Eleanor, and who was reputed to have turned down Ted when he proposed to her first. So Eleanor had been second best, the village decided, and waited to see what would happen. They waited in vain for trouble,

and when Eleanor said she was pregnant, everybody
thought they must be getting on all right together.

And then the miscarriage," Mrs. Coleridge ended.
There was a pause, and she passed a hand over her eyes.

Ivy got to her feet. "I have taken up quite enough of
your time," she said. "Perhaps we can talk again soon. I
don't have to tell you how useful your recollections are.
Such a shame about the Blatch baby," she added, as she
put on her coat and hat. "Things might have been so different if it had lived."

"Yes, indeed," said Mrs. Coleridge. "But they always
refused help, you know. None of us ever found out whether
the baby was a boy or girl. And in fact, it must have been
an early miscarriage. Eleanor never showed. Poor little
thing."

Ivy walked home with her thoughts busily turning. An
early miscarriage? Eleanor never showed a bump? A prettier younger sister who had turned down Ted?

"So here you are, my love. And with roses in your
cheeks from cosy conversation. I hope you gleaned some
useful information?" Roy was sitting comfortably by a
sunny window, with the Sunday newspapers on his lap.

"I have, I think. Useful but sad. Anyway, I can see
you've been busy," she replied sharply. "Any more news
from Gus and Deirdre?"

"Oh, yes. They did ring about an hour ago, and said
they were nearly home. They would come and see us after
tea this evening. Will that be all right?"

"Yes, of course. I shall have quite a lot more to tell
them. In fact, if you don't mind, Roy dear, I will keep it
all until then. Meanwhile, you can tell me what's been
happening at Springfields."

Roy smiled at her sweetly. "Well, my dear," he said.
"After you had gone, a small jazz trio arrived, and Mrs.
Spurling, clad in a short skirt and dancing pumps, got us
all doing the cha-cha-cha. Then Mrs. Cornwall said she

would like to sing 'Summertime' from Porgy and Bess, and the jazz trio provided the backing."

Ivy stared at him. "And then what?" she said sternly.

"And then Katya went into labour and produced twins in the dining room, while La Spurling acted as midwife. After that, you came home, which was the most exciting happening of the afternoon."

IVY HAD TAKEN exception to Roy teasing her, and had stomped off to have a rest, she said, in the peace and quiet of her own room. She did not invite Roy to go with her, and the air was distinctly cool when she reappeared for tea. However, by the time Gus and Deirdre arrived, good relations were restored, and Ivy greeted her cousin warmly.

"You look tired, girl," she said. "Come and sit down and tell us everything."

Gus looked at Deirdre, and they both laughed. "Nice to be home," Gus said. "And I am sure you have lots to tell us, too."

Ivy said she would start, as her afternoon's visit was still fresh in her mind. When she got to the wedding of Ted and Eleanor, and the rumours surrounding it, Deirdre was all ears. "Honestly, Ivy? Did Ted really fancy the young sister first?"

"And she turned him down?" said Gus. "That begins to make some sense, doesn't it? I don't suppose sister Mary was very welcome at the farm. Eleanor would not have wanted to risk it!"

"And the baby, Ivy, how far gone was Eleanor when she miscarried? And why did she? Did your Mrs. Coleridge know any details?"

"Not many. She said the Blatches kept themselves to themselves at this time, and shut themselves off from friends. They didn't seem to have much in the way of family, either. The sister never came to see them again, until

Ted's funeral. And then she didn't turn up, although she was apparently expected."

"We didn't get round to that, but we know Mary might have been in Australia, or perhaps already disabled. But you are going to see Mary Winchen, aren't you, Deirdre? Now you know some of the background, it might be easier. Mrs. Coleridge has offered to see me again, so I shall take her up on that. We got on very well. A very nice woman."

"Well done, Ivy," said Gus. "There are several leads there for us to follow. Now, Deirdre, you're next."

"Nothing as interesting as Ivy's report," she said. "But we did find the birth of Mary Winchen recorded in the registry. After Eleanor. About four years after."

"Four years after the birth of Eleanor Winchen. It is strange, imagining Mary as a tiny squalling baby, arriving in this world with an already jealous big sister."

"You don't know she was jealous, Ivy." Roy had listened to all that was said, and now considered all that was new, what was surmise and what fact.

"I think Ivy's right," said Deirdre. "My sister was four years younger than me, and I remember tipping her out of her pram in a fit of jealousy. The neighbours had been in to bill and coo over the new arrival."

"Did she survive your attack?" said Roy anxiously.

"Oh yes, my mother held on to the handle of the pram and it only tipped very slightly. Baby yelled, but was quite safely tucked in."

"So sister Mary remains the most important unsolved mystery in our case so far," said Roy. "We're pinning our hopes on you, Deirdre. And let's hope Mrs. Coleridge has remembered more when you go to see her again."

"Did she talk to you about the lodger who must have figured largely in Eleanor's life at one time?" Gus was interested in encouraging Ivy to remember everything before it faded.

"She mentioned him, but couldn't tell me any more than we knew already. So now, Gus, anything else to tell us?"

"That's all, I'm afraid. I am sure if Deirdre finds Mrs. Winchen cooperative, a lot of all this will fall into place. Meanwhile, I propose we take time to consider what we do next, not forgetting one important piece in the jigsaw."

"Rickwood Smith," said Ivy. "Now, it seems, master of all he surveys."

Forty-six

ROY WAS STILL asleep, but surfaced when he heard Ivy's voice, in a stage whisper, outside his door.

"Roy! Are you awake? I'm coming in, dearest."

Bolt upright now, Roy called to her to come in. He was more or less decent, he said.

The door opened quickly, and was equally quickly closed behind her, and she put her finger to her lips. "La Spurling is on duty today, so we have to be quiet, unless she goes to my room and finds me gone. I had to come along to talk about something urgently, before I forget it!"

Roy pulled the bedcovers back, and indicated for Ivy to sit in beside him. She hesitated.

"Come along, Ivy. I shan't ravish you, and you'll get cold in your nightie."

"Oh, very well," she said, blushing furiously. "As long as you promise not to compromise me."

Ivy climbed in beside him, insisting on leaving a wide stretch of bed linen between them. "It's that premature baby of Eleanor's," she said. "She might have been one of those women who don't show for months. But when it was born, and either was born dead or soon after birth, where was it taken? I'm sure Eleanor would have wanted to mark its brief sojourn in this world."

"Ivy! That's a beautiful thought. You are quite right, and it's more than likely there was a note in the church register."

"Right! First thing after breakfast, we walk up to the church and have a good look around the churchyard and cemetery."

Roy pricked up his ears. "Do you hear what I hear, beloved?" he said.

"La Spurling, calling my name," said Ivy. "Move over, and sit on the edge of the bed! Quickly!"

Roy muttered that he had every right to have his fiancée in his bed if he so chose. But Ivy gave him a push, and then dived down under the bedclothes behind him. Then she flattened herself out under the covers and was still.

The expected knock on Roy's door came within seconds, and Mrs. Spurling called that she was coming in. She stood at the entrance to his room, and said she was sorry to intrude, especially as he was about to get up, but had he seen Miss Beasley?"

"Good heavens, no, Mrs. Spurling. As you see, I am in a state of undress, and I would hate to frighten my beloved into ending our engagement! Have you thought of looking in her bathroom? Or perhaps she has gone downstairs to feed Tiddles. I know that is one of her first chores in the morning."

Apologising again for bursting in on him, Mrs. Spurling left, and her footsteps were heard going down the stairs.

"Wow! That was close!" Ivy said, popping her head out from under the duvet. She began to move to her side of the bed, when Roy turned swiftly and put his arm around her shoulders. "Whoa!" he said. "Too good an opportunity to miss, Miss Beasley!" and he pulled her back into his arms . . .

MONDAY MORNING BREAKFAST time was usually late, as new staff coming in and changing of rosters and diet sheets, et cetera, took time. Even so, Mrs. Cornwall, already on to her last cup of coffee, noticed that Ivy and Roy came downstairs hand in hand, and looked, she said to her neighbour, decidedly shifty.

"If I didn't know Ivy Beasley better," she said, "I should suspect hanky-panky!"

"I reckon she's had her moments," said her friend. "Dark horses are always the worst."

"Or best, depending how you look at it," said Mrs. Cornwall sadly. "It's so long since I had the chance. Anyway, don't stare. You know what she's like. You'll get the rough end of her tongue, else. Here, have another piece of toast and we can linger a bit longer."

AS SOON AS they had finished breakfast, Roy and Ivy set out up Cemetery Lane.

They were at the main gate now, and Roy began to dismount. "Nobody around," he said. "We can take our time. Those shouts are coming from the sports pavilion. I can hear the dulcet tones of Miss Pinkney hitting an ace. Now then, Ivy dear," he added, "shall we wander round and see what turns up?"

"The baby's grave? Yes, well, in we go."

They walked slowly round, reading the epitaphs and commenting on extraordinary ones. "Look here," said Ivy. "Not what we were looking for, but interesting. It's Ted's grave."

Roy stood looking at it without saying anything. Finally,

he turned to Ivy, and said, "Poor old Ted. He had many good years in front of him when that tractor went in the ditch. He was quick-tempered, but always ready for a game of darts or shove ha'penny."

"Was the tractor the same one that's in the barn? The one you sat on and played at being a farmer again?"

"And the one Gus and I are going to restore to its former glory. I do remember that it was hardly damaged at all when it took Ted into the ditch. He died outright. Broken neck, so they said."

"He's got no flowers," said Ivy. "Nobody to care, I suppose." She walked across to a new grave, covered with wreaths and bunches of flowers. She picked up one with a mixture of yellow and white chrysanthemums, and returned to put it on Ted's weedy patch. Then she cleared out dandelions and chickweed, and stood back to admire her handiwork.

"That's better," she said. "Now, let's continue our search."

They looked very carefully, and got excited when they saw a small mound with a stone angel on it, right next to Ted. "Can you see what it says?" said Ivy.

"It's almost rubbed away," Roy said. "But it looks like 'Louise, gone to live with Jesus.' That's all. The rest is indecipherable."

"What's more, you can't read it," said Ivy, who couldn't resist. "But is she right next to her father, maybe?"

"Could be, but we should perhaps look around more."

"I think we've looked everywhere," said Ivy, after twenty minutes or so. "Let's go and see if we are allowed to look in the baptismal register. They're sure to have recorded her."

"Right. Come on then, then we'll go back to Springfields for coffee. Enquire Within meeting later on, and it would be nice to have something to tell them. I feel really sad about baby Louise. I bet Eleanor would have loved a little girl."

Forty-seven

AFTER SECOND THOUGHTS, Ivy had decided that she would not bother Mrs. Coleridge on a Monday afternoon. "It'll be washday on the farm," she said, and would not be persuaded by others that in the modern age of washing machines and dryers, any day could be a washday.

Roy smiled. "But we must keep up to date, Ivy," he said. "Though I must say I used to love washday as a child. That smell of soapsuds and everything blowing in a lovely fresh wind."

"Huh! You didn't have to scrub dirty collars and cuffs, nor have wrinkly hands from being in water too long!" said Ivy. "Still, if you think it would be all right to approach Mrs. Coleridge again so soon, I'll give her a ring. I'd decided not to go to college at all today, anyway."

"I'VE INVITED HER for tea," she said, after lunch. "Do you have anything special you'd like to ask her? I'm sure she'll be pleased to meet you."

He shook his head. "Not really," he said. "Most of the time I've been thinking about my early-morning visitor, and wondering how I could persuade her to repeat her visit."

"Mm," said Ivy. "Best forgotten. I was thinking about the little grave in the cemetery. Very close to Ted Blatch's grave. I am certain it was the poor little soul who never made it to this old world."

"Well, we'll see what emerges from your tea party this afternoon. Might turn up something interesting."

When Mrs. Coleridge arrived, walking briskly and smiling at residents that she knew from earlier days, Ivy and Roy welcomed her warmly and led her to a small alcove already allocated by Miss Pinkney for their guest.

"So nice to see you," the assistant manager enthused. "We love to have visitors, and Mr. Goodman and Miss Beasley brighten our lives already with their adventures around the village."

"Perhaps I'll apply for a job with Enquire Within," said Mrs. Coleridge, laughing at Ivy. "We are two of a kind, I suspect."

They settled happily with tea and cake, and Roy, of course, having been part of a farming county community, had many reminiscences to share with their visitor. After a while, Ivy, who was feeling a little left out, said she had been so interested in what Mrs. Coleridge had had to say about the Blatch family, and now she had a new question or two for her, if she didn't mind.

"Good gracious me, no," she said. "Ask me anything you like! Fire away, Ivy. I may call you Ivy, yes?"

"Of course," said Ivy, "and he's Roy, as you know."

Roy shut his eyes and held up a hand. "No, don't tell me. I've nearly got it. Pamela! Pamela Coleridge. Am I right?"

Seeing that this might send them off into yet more memories of their youth, Ivy said firmly that since they were so good at remembering, did Pamela remember anything more about Ted Blatch before he became involved with the Winchen family?

"Well, not much. As I think I said to Ivy, they were an odd family, and didn't always join in with the rest of us in the village. Ted was very good-looking, you know, and clever. I think part of the time he knew he'd failed at farming and wanted to go on to higher education."

"I expect you fancied him when you were young," said Roy with a smile. "I seem to remember you were a pretty young thing."

Ivy groaned inwardly. "Why do you think he looked outside the village for a wife? I know farming families often intermarry," she asked Pamela, offering her another piece of coffee cake, and taking one herself. "I wonder how he met the Winchens?"

"Ah, now let me think," Pamela said, wiping coffee cream from the corners of her lips. "It was a Young Farmers public speaking competition. Goodness knows why they thought young farmers need to know how to get up and make a speech. But there it was. A party of us went in a bus to Lowestoft, and Ted, being clever, was somehow persuaded to make the speech. I had to second the vote of thanks, and I remember how I dried up completely, and let them all down." She stopped speaking, lost in the memory of humiliation.

"After the competition," she continued, "we had refreshments, and we mingled with other club members. I was really soft on Ted at the time, and tried to get him to talk to me. But there was this stunning girl from a Lincolnshire branch, and guess who she was?"

"Eleanor Blatch?"

Pamela shook her head. "No. It was Mary Winchen, and I could see Ted was smitten. Of course, as I told Ivy, it came to nothing, and Eleanor was waiting in the wings."

"So did Ted leave the village and go to college, like he

wanted?" Ivy said. It occurred to her that Roy should surely have remembered some of this himself, being a local farmer. But then she recalled him saying that he did not live in Barrington, but grew up on another of his family's farms. Nevertheless, she thought crossly, he had remembered Pamela was a pretty young thing! Or was it just her dear Roy being his usual gentlemanly self? She decided on the latter.

"He did go away for a year or so, I think. I know I gave up all hope, and married my John Coleridge, who was a good and kind husband for the whole of our marriage."

So, thought Ivy, back to the Winchens. "I expect the first you knew of Ted's failure to catch Mary was when Eleanor turned up as his fiancée?" she asked.

"Well, it's a long time ago. But because I had been sweet on him, I do remember the word got round that Mary had turned him down, and I thought maybe I'd have a chance, as I hadn't teamed up with John by then. But no, the next thing we knew was when Eleanor appeared, bold as brass and very pleased with herself. Mind you, I'm not sure she didn't draw the short straw. He wasn't very kind to her, so people said."

Ivy's nose quivered, like a mouse smelling the scent of cheese. "So he was rough with her, was he?"

"Shouldn't speak ill of the dead, Ivy, I know. But Eleanor could be very irritating. I suppose he was never really reconciled to making her his second choice."

At this point, Mrs. Cornwall limped over to where they sat, and said, "It's Pammie Coleridge, isn't it?"

Pamela turned and looked up at her. "And you are Irene! Irene Cornwall. How lovely to see you again. Why don't you sit down and have a cuppa with us?"

Ivy gave up.

Forty-eight

SAMANTHA HAD WOKEN with a headache, and so was late in setting off for a day at college. Since the expedition with the dead-cat hot water bottle, she had given up using the footpath over the field, and taken the longer road route through the village. But she looked at the clock and decided that the sun was shining and she would go by the footpath, for one time only. With luck, she would meet Rickwood!

As she entered the spinney she quickened her step and so did not see the snaking bramble across the path. She caught her foot, and went down heavily. Cursing everything and everybody, she sat on the hard ground and examined herself for injury. Then she heard footsteps behind her, and saw Rickwood approaching, looking anxious.

"My dear Sam," he said, crouching down beside her, "Let me have a look." His hands were gentle, and he found a clean white handkerchief in his pocket, which he tied neatly round the graze. "We'll get someone to look at it in college, unless you want to go back home. Are you feeling steady enough to get up?"

He put his arm around her waist and helped her up, then let go immediately.

"I'm fine," she said. "It really wasn't much. Caught me by surprise, that's all."

"Come along, then. We are a little late, but the class will probably be fine, even without Miss Beasley in charge. Bless her!"

"Actually, we're not a bad lot, and she is really nice at heart. Hides her light under a bushel, as they say. And it's amazing how well she's fitted in. Perhaps I could hold your hand for a minute or two to steady me?"

NEXT MORNING, BRAVE, warmhearted Ivy Beasley was conducting a major row with Mrs. Spurling, on the subject of curbing the escapades of Enquire Within.

"At least as far as you and Mr. Goodman are concerned," said the manager, her face scarlet with annoyance, "you two are my responsibility, however hard you may argue around that fact. I care for you, and if anything happens to you, I shall be accused of negligence in my duty."

Roy sat up very straight in his chair. He had been with Ivy in her room when Mrs. Spurling had burst in, having discovered that they had been out in the rain before breakfast, and had returned wet through, with squelching feet and damp clothes.

Ivy began to speak, but Roy interrupted. "You are quite right, Mrs. Spurling, and we are at fault. I know Ivy will join me in apologising sincerely. We were so keen on an early-morning constitutional—my father swore by it—that we forgot to tell staff, and were caught in a shower of rain. But look at my Ivy's rosy cheeks, Mrs. Spurling," he said. "Fresh as a daisy, she is, and ready for anything."

Mrs. Spurling was mollified and said shortly that she hoped "anything" would not include such foolish behaviour which upset the whole Springfields community.

"Rubbish!" said Ivy. "You're making a mountain out of a molehill, and all we did was nip out for a short stroll and run into a small shower. And now I shall go and change m'feet. Come along, Roy. You'll need clean socks. I mean to catch Samantha on her way to college."

After which, Mrs. Spurling returned to her office and in desperation telephoned the local job centre, saying she would take anything, any job, even scrubbing floors, whatever they had on their books.

Ten minutes later, Ivy set off and met Samantha coming along the road.

"Good morning, Miss Beasley! Just the person I wanted to see!"

As they walked along, Samantha told her about her fall and how helpful Rickwood had been. Ivy frowned. She recognised signs of a girl halfway to falling in love!

"Do you know, Miss Beasley, I hope you won't mind my asking, but do you know if Mr. Smith, Rickwood, has a wife? Or girlfriend? We girls at college are curious, as we know he lives with his mother, but is tutoring on a more or less temporary basis. And now the rumours are all of his taking over Blackwoods and turning it into a wildlife park. The girls said you would probably know, as you keep your ear to the ground."

"That's a long speech, Samantha! Can I summarise it by asking if, following his gallant rescue of a pupil caught by a bramble, that young student is fancying him rotten, to use current parlance, and would like to know what are her chances?"

Samantha blushed deeply, and nodded, crestfallen. "I know what you're going to say, Miss Beasley," she said. "I am a silly young girl who should be thinking about working hard at my writing course and not wasting time fancying men old enough to be my father. But I know he works respectably in the old henhouse, and is always extremely careful about chatting up girl students. That is, he doesn't. Chat them up, I mean. And that includes me. He gets plenty of opportunity! He's very interesting to talk to during break times. Did you know he'd spent most of his early life in Australia?"

Ivy stopped in her tracks. "Australia? What was he doing there?"

"Not sure. He never actually says where he lived, or anything like that. Mostly he tells us about the wildlife. Kangaroos and snakes. That kind of thing."

"Don't even think of him, Samantha. Not only is he much too old for you, but still an enigma. You girls are not the only ones wanting to find out more about him. No, my dear, steer very clear of that one. But if he should let slip what he was doing in Australia, make sure to let me know."

They walked on, and although Ivy changed the subject, she was not at all sure that Samantha would act on what she had said.

Forty-nine

"AN INVITATION FOR you, Miss Beasley and Mr. Goodman," said Miss Pinkney happily. She had taken over from her superior after Mrs. Spurling had gone off, saying she had an important interview to attend.

"Invitation?" said Ivy, who had come back from college feeling very perky. "It's like I am on the verge of discovery, Roy dear. Of what or who or where, I do not yet know. Now, Pinkers, who is this invitation from?"

"Mrs. Bloxham, of course. She asked if you two would like to go up to Tawny Wings for supper this evening. You were out, Miss Beasley, and Mr. Goodman was asleep in his chair, so I said I was sure you would accept, but I must confirm with you."

"How kind!" said Roy. "She is a busy lady, you know, with all her social work. It will be a nice change, don't you agree, beloved?"

Ivy grinned. "Let's hope she's got something decent for us to eat. Another one of Deirdre's appalling slimming salads will be the death of me."

"She does her best, Ivy," said Roy firmly, "And her invitation could be a genuinely kind and sincere offer to two old folks locked up in an old dodderers' retirement home."

"Well said, Mr. Goodman," said Pinkers, "except the old dodderers bit! Now, Miss Beasley, can I help you to change into your best dress?"

"No, thank you, dear," she said. "I am quite capable of dressing myself, and in any case, so long as I don't wear my old mother's squirrel coat that smells strongly of mothballs, I am sure I am smart enough for supper at Tawny Wings."

Elvis was ordered to collect them at a suitable time, and they retired upstairs for a short rest. "I wonder if she's invited Gus?" Ivy said.

"I have no idea. But if, as you suspect, she wishes to know more about your tête-à-tête with Pamela, then yes, it will be an informal Enquire Within meeting, and he will probably be there."

Ivy patted his arm. "Not deliberately leaving you out, dear," she said. "Our tea party was such a damp squib that I need time to sort it out. As you know, Pamela's visit drew a complete blank, but my chance encounter with Samantha today has been more fruitful. I am rather worried about that young one. She has obviously fallen hook, line and sinker for Rickwood Smith. So far he seems to have been the perfect gentleman, but I'd hate for her to get hurt."

"I wouldn't worry, dearest. I have one small suggestion, before we set forth," said Roy. "Speaking of Samantha, we seem to have lost all interest in the henhouse. The one on wheels, in the spinney."

"Should we be especially interested in the henhouse? One of us looked at it once, but could see no signs of life, except that, as we know, Rickwood works in there, when he can't get any peace in his mother's house. I don't think there's much more to say about the henhouse? I think I'm right in saying that, but we can check with Deirdre." She paused, and then added, "I remember Samantha saying something about her father warning her that the field and the henhouse are private property, to be left alone."

DEIRDRE WAS WAITING at the open front door for her guests. Roy accepted Elvis's arm to be escorted into the house, and as they had expected, they found Gus already in the best armchair in front of the fire.

"A chill in the air this evening," he said, rising to assist Roy, and bending to risk a peck on Ivy's cheek. "This is very nice of you, Deirdre," he said. "Wonderful smells coming from the kitchen."

"Roast beef with all the trimmings," she said. "I don't often get the chance to cook a really splendid piece of beef, and the butcher has done me proud."

"So is this a purely social occasion?" asked Ivy bluntly.

"It can be, but as the four of us are here together, we'll probably talk Enquire Within business, won't we?"

"After supper," said Gus with a smile. "I mean to enjoy the beef with no thoughts of graveyards or cigar smoke."

In spite of his declared intentions, it was not long before Ivy asked if Deirdre had ever walked through the spinney and across the field. "I know you go everywhere by car," she said.

Deirdre bristled. "Of course I have," she said. "When my Bert was alive, we often walked that way on Sunday afternoons. Across the field and up past the Manor House, and then back across another footpath farther out of the village. Bert loved a good walk, and we had an old spaniel who always went with us."

Her chin wobbled, and Ivy reached across and took her hand. "Don't take any notice of me, duckie. Come on, now, eat up your beef. Best I've ever tasted."

As always, it was Roy who poured oil on troubled

waters. "A good old boy, your Bert," he said. "He could examine a car engine like a doctor does his patient! Many's the time I've seen Bert with his head under the bonnet, his ear cocked, as if the engine were speaking to him."

Deirdre gave him a watery smile, and said if everyone was finished, she had an enormous sherry trifle in the fridge, needing to be eaten up and the bowl licked clean.

It was not until coffee was poured out in the drawing room that the subject of Blatches and Winchens was introduced. Gus said he would like to sum up things so far, and then they could discuss their next moves.

"The case we were asked to take on was the apparent manifestation of Eleanor's deceased husband Ted, in Blackwoods Farm. Eleanor Blatch was frightened by evidence of his ghostly presence in her house, appearing at night and instructing her how to kill herself and join him in paradise. And she swore it was Ted."

"Who," said Ivy, "as we now know, could be unkind and possibly quick tempered. Violent, do you think?"

"I'd forgotten that bit," said Deirdre. "Carry on, Gus."

"We were supposed to get rid of this ghostly person, and for this reason, I spent a couple of nights there. In the meantime, following a supposed attack on Eleanor, we set out to investigate the background to Eleanor's family in Lincolnshire. We have discovered she had a sister, a younger sister, Mary. We can trace no other early record of this Mary Winchen, except for a letter suggesting she might have been sent to Australia as a young woman, to be adopted and given work by a suitable family."

"And it is no coincidence that Samantha told me this morning that Rickwood told the girls at college that he had spent some time in Australia. With his mother, presumably."

"And now Mrs. Mary Winchen is living in Barrington,

with her son, Rickwood. And there has been a family feud between the two sisters for many years."

"Thanks, Deirdre. All coming together, isn't it? That is a very important point. To continue, on my second morning at Blackwoods, I came downstairs and found Eleanor, stone cold dead at the foot of the fire escape."

"Did you tell the police about the stone cold bit? I know autopsies can decide the date and time of death, but this would confirm that she died some time the previous evening, wouldn't it? Don't forget the police have been involved in this from the moment you found her."

"I'm not likely to forget that, Ivy. The police then arrested me and took me to the station to be interrogated. I was, of course, released after questioning. But not before Miriam Blake had seen me in the police car, and burst into tears."

"I don't think that's important to our investigation," said Deirdre. She asked if Gus was going on much longer, because she wanted to fetch refills for the coffeepot.

"Not long, Dee-Dee," he said. "Because I knew you were fond of Eleanor, and admired her courage, I more or less agreed to continue looking for a possible killer, supposing he was not a wraith but does exist in person in this world and in Barrington. Future enquiries to be in conjunction with the police, of course."

At that point, the house telephone began to ring, and Deirdre went off to answer it. When she came back, she looked upset.

"What's wrong, girl?" said Ivy.

"That was my friend, Inspector Frobisher. He thought we'd like to know that a dead sheep has been found in the farmyard at the back of Blackwoods farmhouse. Some lads were trespassing and playing football in the field. When they came back through the farmyard to go home, they noticed it, lying by the door into a feed store. Very old, said Barry Frobisher, and one front leg shorter than the other. Lame, he said."

A stunned silence greeted this, and then Ivy said briskly, "Did he tell you how long it had been there, dead?"

"Not long," he said. "Possibly the natural end to a very long life. For a sheep."

Fifty

AFTER ELVIS HAD taken Ivy and Roy home to Springfields, Gus stayed behind to help Deirdre clear up.

"Bags I stack the dishwasher," he said.

"Fine," Deirdre replied, grinning. "I see the overgrown
schoolboy is back."

"A turn of phrase, my dear, to keep our feet on the
ground. Suppose I get on with stacking, and then we can
have a cosy bed talk."

"I don't recall inviting you to stay the night. Are you
sure you wouldn't rather get back to the tearful Miss
Blake?"

"I have no idea what her overnight hospitality is like,
but I know yours is top of the range."

"Well, actually, to be serious, I would like a little
reassurance in all this. There is still someone out there
who perhaps killed Eleanor Blatch, and may be responsible
for others, for all we know. And does not at all like what
we are up to."

"Who also fed a lone lame sheep? It's hard to square a

vicious killer with somebody soft enough to bother with a poor old animal, don't you think?"

"Yes, I do. In fact, I think the dead sheep is a red herring. Don't laugh, Gus!"

"But seriously, I suppose it depends on the circumstances. The night before Eleanor died, I was in the house, but admittedly not quite my sharpest self owing to a couple of splendid pints of Old Hooky. And, of course, as you know, Deirdre, I did have earplugs in. I don't think even screams from her as if from the fire escape would have penetrated my heavy sleep! I'm afraid we must plod on patiently."

"You've done very well, Gus. Not many would have bothered. Why don't we plod on upstairs?" said Deirdre, taking his hand.

AT MIDNIGHT, IVY woke. The wind had risen, and was whistling loudly through a crack in her window frame. She would have to tell Mrs. Spurling in the morning.

Now, as she lay wide awake, thoughts of Winchens and Blatches came back into her mind. There was something she had forgotten when talking to Roy. Something to do with Mary? Or Eleanor?

Eleanor's baby. That was it. They had talked a while back about the possibility that little Louise in the graveyard might be Eleanor's, and she and Roy were going to check in the church records. Tomorrow they would go.

As she drifted back into sleep, Ivy dreamt of a young woman, lovely and light at heart, bundled off at a moment's notice to Australia, like a convict expelled for life.

Fifty-one

IVY HAD AGAIN been woken early, this time by a cockerel crowing persistently in the garden below. She slipped
out of bed, and without putting on her slippers, pushed
open her window and shooed as loudly as she could.

"Miss Beasley!" said a voice from behind her. "What
do you think you are doing by that open window and with
no dressing gown or slippers?"

Ivy turned and saw Katya, carrying a tray of morning
tea, and beaming at her, her smile belying her tone of
voice.

"A little fresh air won't hurt me," she replied. "And how
blooming you are looking! The bump seems to get bigger
every day. It's big enough to use as a shelf for your tray!
Do you think it is a boy?"

Katya blushed. "We have decided to wait for the birth
before we find out. Now then, let me help you on with your
warm dressing gown."

When Ivy was sitting up in bed, Katya lingered to make
sure she was all right. "Guess what I saw this morning,

Miss Beasley," she said. "A removals van stopped outside Springfields, and asked the way to Blackwoods Farm. Apparently there is a new person moving in today."

"Do you think it is the person who has inherited it? So many rumours have been around. It was going to be a rare breeds farm or a wild animal safari park. Rickwood Smith would be the new owner, that's another one. What's the latest in the village?"

"I have heard it is a man on his own, and it is the person you are talking about. Still, nobody knows what he is going to do with it. A great deal more to discover!"

"I hope he won't close the footpath through to the spinney. Such a nice walk, and several people use it to get to work in the Manor House College."

"We shall see," said Katya. "It is not so long to go now until I shall be pushing a pram and having to stick to the roads!"

RICKWOOD SMITH, NOW assured by his mother that she considered him to be in charge of the Blackwoods estate, decided to go for a walk along the footpath to the farmhouse. He had dropped the idea of selling up, and decided his life would be in Barrington from now on. His mother was delighted, and said that though she would stay put, he would be always within call.

Now he had the decorators in, some new furniture delivered and the painter should be arriving for work. He wished to brief him on colours and textures sympathetic to the old house.

Halfway across the field, he met a familiar pair, one silver-haired and limping and one striding out in buttoned waterproof overshoes the like of which he had seen only in early photographs of smart ladies' rainwear. "Miss Beasley and Mr. Goodman! No college for a couple of weeks, of course, and so you decided on a morning stroll? Am I right? I am so pleased to have run into you, as I've had good news this morning and am dying to tell someone. And who better than you two? Here, Mr. Goodman, please use my shooting stick while I tell you. You can sit on it and have a moment or two's rest."

"Out with it then, Mr. Smith," said Ivy. "We have heard so many rumours about this place."

"Some wrong, some right, I expect. Well now, as you probably know, Mrs. Eleanor Blatch was my mother's sister, and therefore my aunt. After she died, poor soul, the matter of inheritance became very simple, though, of course, very sad. My mother is next in line, with the whole estate willed to her by Aunt Eleanor, and as you may have heard, she is unfortunately very disabled after a riding accident in her youth in Australia. In the outback, you know! She has therefore handed over responsibility for Blackwoods to me, and as soon as I can arrange it, I shall be moving into the farmhouse, still being close to my mother, of course."

"Wonderful for you!" said Roy, putting out his hand in congratulation.

"And for the rest of us, we hope," said Ivy. "What are you going to do with it all, Mr. Smith? You will presumably be giving up your tutoring at the college?"

"Not so, if it can be arranged. I love the work there, and you know yourself, Miss Beasley, what fun we have, and how interesting your fellow pupils can be."

He then outlined his plans for keeping rare breed cattle and sheep, and restoring the old barns to be a centre for the performing arts. "I went to drama school myself in Australia, years ago, so that will be a bit of self-indulgence! So, now, Miss Beasley, what do you think of all that?"

Roy looked at Ivy, who, he thought, for once in her life was speechless. But no. She took a deep breath, pursed her lips and said, "I'll let you know, Mr. Smith, when I have seen how it all turns out. Good day to you."

Roy, who felt Ivy had been less than gracious, handed the shooting stick back to Rickwood, and said, "I wish you luck, sir. And if you want to know anything about breeding cattle, you know where to come."

Fifty-two

DEIRDRE HAD RISEN late, and had a quick breakfast before checking her diary. First thing she had to do this morning was ring Mrs. Winchen and make an appointment to call and have a chat.

"Hello? Is that Mrs. Winchen? Oh, good. My name is Deirdre Bloxham, and I'm glad to catch you at home."

"I'm never anywhere else," said a soft voice. "How can I help you?"

Deirdre explained her social services role, and asked if there was a convenient time when she could pop in and see her. "Only for a chat, to make sure you have everything you need, and are comfortable. I know you have your son living with you, but sometimes it's nice to chat with a fellow female!"

There was a small silence, and then the quiet voice said, "He's not going to be living with me for much longer. But he won't be far away. Now, do you want to come this afternoon? It is my best time, so why don't you come and have a cup of tea around three o'clock?"

Easy, thought Deirdre. Not at all the old dragon I was expecting. She sounds very amiable. Very different from her sister, Eleanor! Although she had liked Eleanor, and admired her for her spiky courage, there was something unreliable about the older sister, always an uncomfortable feeling that she could turn against you at any minute. Perhaps the result of a reclusive life, thought Deirdre, and hearing the gardener's knock at the door, she went to organise her new rose bed.

THE OLD PERSONS' bungalows were almost within shouting distance of Tawny Wings, and Deirdre stepped out along the road, cheerfully looking forward to meeting Mrs. Winchen at last. She had no idea what to expect. She knew the poor woman had had a riding accident in her youth, and was severely disabled. Not so severely that she could not produce a son. But maybe Rickwood had come along before her accident. Something to find out.

Number three, Spinney Close, was bathed in sunlight, and as Deirdre opened the gate and walked up to the front door, she noticed that the garden was trim and colourful. In the centre of a small green lawn a fountain trickled tunefully over an umbrella held over two children sitting on a bench. It was charming, worked on solar panels, and was in full view of the person sitting in a chair by the window.

The door was ajar, and Deirdre pressed the bell, at the same time announcing her arrival in a loud voice. The poor lady might be deaf, as were many of Deirdre's clients.

"Come in, dear!" replied Mrs. Winchen. "I'm not able to get up, but you'll find me in the front room. I saw you coming," she continued as Deirdre entered. "And I think I recognise you. Aren't you the lady who lives in Tawny Wings? I look across the field from my bedroom at the back, and often see you in the garden. Am I right?"

After that, it was plain sailing as the two women found topics of conversation interesting to both. Finding a suitable point at which to introduce the subject of Rickwood and Australia, Deirdre asked how long Mrs. Winchen had been in this country.

"I believe you spent many years abroad?" she said. "You must find Barrington rather dull after your travels?"

"Well yes, Mrs. Bloxham, I do, in a way. But Rickwood is my only relative, and it is nice to be close to him. Sons are always a little special, and we have come together only quite recently. Do you have any children, my dear?"

Deirdre made an excuse for being childless, and brought the subject back to Mary Winchen.

"But wasn't Mrs. Blatch your sister?" she asked. "Forgive me if I am intruding on your grief. Poor Eleanor's death must have been a terrible shock."

To her acute embarrassment, Mary Winchen laughed.

"Oh dear, Mrs. Bloxham, what will you think?" she said, putting her hand in front of her mouth. "It is only that Eleanor had become a complete stranger to me and to Rickwood. She banned us from her sight when we returned from Australia. I was already very disabled, and she found a cottage for us on the farm, and then when the bungalows were built, moved us into this one. And, to be fair, she paid the rent then and did so right up until her death. I had had no contact with her since first arriving back in this country."

"And Rickwood? Would she have nothing to do with him, either? You must tell me to mind my own business, you know, if I go too far. We do like to have some kind of background information, as it can be quite useful in the ways we can help."

"Well, as I said, I hadn't seen her for years and years, and that is how it continued. It was easy for her, because as long as she didn't come near Spinney Close, there was no risk of her seeing me. Rickwood has only come to

Barrington recently, and she would not have recognised him if she saw him, though . . ." She stopped speaking, and adjusted her position in her chair. Deirdre could see that her spine must be very twisted, and felt so sorry for what was clearly considerable pain.

"And are you going to move with him into the farmhouse?" she said.

"Oh no, this bungalow is specially adapted for me. I live in this wheelchair, or curled up in bed. Carers come in and look after my intimate needs! I am very fortunate."

"The village is very curious about what he plans to do, but from what I gather he won't be doing any of the outrageous suggestions going around the gossip shops!"

"Indeed no. He has always wanted to farm. And he has plans for rare breeds. The old barns he will restore and use for a variety of purposes. I think he will be very happy here in Barrington now. Oh, yes, and I know he hopes to continue helping students at the college."

"Sounds good," said Deirdre. "He will have many strings to his bow."

"Except one," said Mary Winchen.

Deirdre's pulse quickened. "Which one is that?" she said.

"I quote," said Mary Winchen. "'It is a truth universally acknowledged, that a single man in possession of a good fortune, must be in want of a wife.' The divine Jane."

Deirdre stared. Was the dear thing rambling? Perhaps she had overtired her and it was time to go. But one thing she wished to know more than anything else was the name of Rickwood Smith's father. Who was Mr. Smith? The last piece of the jigsaw. She stood up and was encouraged by her client's smiling face.

But Mary Winchen got in first. "Time to go, Mrs. Bloxham, I think," she said. "It has been so pleasant talking to you, and you can assure them back in the office that my carers are working well and I lack for nothing, at present.

Do come again when you can. Good-bye, my dear. I shall wave to you over the field!"

GUS WAS WAITING for her as she walked into her driveway. "Don't tell me you have been for a walk!" he said. "Our Ivy will be really pleased with you. I have just met the two dear things coming out of the church. I accused them of sloping off and getting married without telling anyone, but they denied it and said they had found a useful piece of information from the churchwarden."

"Come in and tell me all. I've some news for you, too."

They took long drinks of lime juice and soda out to the terrace by the pool, and Deirdre said Gus should go first.

"Ivy was quite excited. Remember they told us about the little gravestone they found in the churchyard? Dedicated to Louise, with an angel on top? Next to Ted Blatch's grave? Well, apparently Ted Blatch years ago bought a largish plot for the whole tribe he planned, and little Louise was buried before Ted. So that makes it certain that she was the baby born prematurely to Eleanor."

"How sad, Gus," Deirdre said, sniffing. "Do you want a drop of gin in your glass? It has been a very emotional afternoon. I have been to see Mrs. Winchen, at last."

"And?"

"And she is a very nice lady. Very twisted, and obviously suffers a lot of pain, but doesn't grumble. She is still pretty, you know. Silvery hair and the bluest eyes I've seen. And a nice soft voice, not like the strident tones of poor Eleanor! In spite of her disability, she seemed quite a bit younger than her sister."

She then told Gus the rest of the story, including the strange rift between the sisters. "Though she carefully avoided telling me the cause. But she included Eleanor's charitable act in paying their rent ever since they came back from Australia."

"Will you go again to see her?" Gus poured a generous slug of gin into both their glasses.

"Oh, yes. I've thought of several more questions for her already. Though I shall have to approach her stealthily. She's a bit like a little faun, and darts away when I get too close."

"Not very apt, dear Deirdre. Shall we go and see Ivy and Roy tomorrow and pool our findings?"

"Good idea," said Deirdre. "Ivy will be at college until around four, but we could call for a cup of tea. Perhaps we should take flowers for Mrs. Spurling?"

"You can if you like, Dee-Dee. If I arrive with a bunch of red roses, she might get the wrong idea."

Fifty-three

ROY WAS WOKEN by a knock at his door soon after seven. Shaking himself out of sleep, he hobbled to the door, anxious not to lose an opportunity if it was his beloved up so early. It was not. He looked up and down the corridor, but could see nobody. Then he realised the kitchen staff were banging about downstairs, and so he returned to bed, where he decided to do some useful thinking.

The result was constructive. He was determined to walk up to the farmyard at Blackwoods. With any luck, as the painter would be there, he would find the barn door open and be able to have another look at his tractor. At least, he hoped it would be his. He must get Rickwood to name his price, and then he and Gus could arrange to have it removed to where they could work on it. Rickwood would be teaching on a Friday, so he should catch him at lunch-time if he came back to check on décor progress.

AT BREAKFAST, ROY announced his intention to go up to Blackwoods, where he would be busy assessing with the painter/engineer what work should be carried out next to get the tractor on the road again. "I might even have a chance to nobble Rickwood Smith about a possible price," he added.

"And Roy," Ivy said, suddenly becoming animated, "we do need to find out more about Rickwood Smith and his background. I am still worried about Samantha, dear thing. She is besotted, and her infatuation cannot come to good."

"I wouldn't worry, Ivy. Surely Smith will handle it properly? Seems a sensible chap to me. He is very good-looking, and probably has a suitable girlfriend waiting in the wings. If I see him this morning, I shall tactfully bring up the subject. You can rely on me, Ivy dear, to be diplomatic. At Samantha's age, broken hearts mend quickly."

Ivy said no more, but was reminded of her beloved Roy's adventurous youth. Adventurous with the girls, anyway. But she mustn't mind, she told herself. It was even more remarkable and wonderful that he should finally have chosen her to be his wife.

LUNCHTIME CAME, AND Roy was still in the barn at Blackwoods. The painter had proved to be an expert on old tractors, and the two had spent the whole morning looking for rusty tools and old sacks to kneel on as they delved into the inner workings of the Ferguson.

"Well, well! I didn't expect to find a couple of mechanics in my barn," said Rickwood, returning home. "I hope you won't charge me for your time!"

The two men described in detail what they had discovered, not noticing that Rickwood's attention had been suddenly taken by a car turning into the yard. The tall, angular figure of Inspector Frobisher got out and approached them.

"Inspector!" said Roy. "Good morning, sir. May I ask how things are going?"

Frobisher did not smile. "That's exactly what I have come to ask you, both of you. Not the painter, of course. Shall we go into the house, Mr. Smith?"

Fifty-four

THEY STOOD IN the kitchen, the three men, until Rickwood had finished telephoning his mother, and then to Roy's surprise, the door opened and Ivy walked in. She did not seem in the least surprised to see Frobisher, and suggested they find somewhere to sit down, but before they moved out of the kitchen, another car drew up and Deirdre got out. She opened her boot and took out a folded wheelchair, which she opened and helped Mary Winchen to sit in it awkwardly.

Frobisher went to the door, and the others followed, helping and getting in the way until they had negotiated narrow doorways and bumpy floors to assemble in the sitting room.

"This is beginning to look like the end of an Agatha crime story," said Ivy sourly. "But shouldn't we have Gus bounding in through the French windows?"

"No, I'm here." Gus's voice was heard coming through from the kitchen, and then he appeared. "I hope this is not going to take long, Inspector," he said. "I see Mr.

Goodman has started work on the tractor, and I am anxious to conclude a sale with Mr. Smith here."

"All in good time," said the Inspector. "I apologise for any inconvenience I may have caused you, but new information has been received, and I need to have your help. Mr. Smith has already been assisting us with his recollections of that fateful day when Eleanor Blatch fell to her death. It was, by the way, a fatal blow to the head, probably suffered on her way down the fire escape. There is nothing to suppose anyone else was involved. Not closely, anyway."

"Get to the point, Barry, do," Deirdre said crossly. "Mrs. Winchen is not at all comfortable in this chair, and it would be very good if she could be allowed to go home as soon as possible."

"Then we will begin with you, Mrs. Winchen. Perhaps you will tell us a brief history of your sad life so far, and I would ask the others not to interrupt. Each of you will get a chance to have your say."

Mary Winchen, usually pale-skinned, now looked as if all her blood had drained away. "Well, I expect you all know Eleanor was my older sister. We came from Boston in Lincolnshire, from where the *Mayflower* sailed long ago to a life in the new world. Well, Ted Blatch from here in Suffolk fell for me at a young farmers' do, and though he was nice and handsome, when he proposed I turned him down. I was very young, not quite sixteen, and I knew my parents wouldn't approve. Then Eleanor, who had met him at the same time, stepped in and made a play for him. If you remember my sister, you'll know she was hard to refuse! So he married her instead."

"Didn't you mind that?" Deirdre said, and the inspector frowned at her.

"Yes, I did, but that didn't make any difference. Then Eleanor got pregnant, and I was pleased for her. But she lost the baby, and afterwards asked for me to look after her until she was stronger."

"And Ted?" said the inspector. "Was he upset about the miscarriage?"

Mary Blatch looked near to tears now. "Of course he was," she said. "I tried to comfort him as best I could."

"Mother! You don't have to go on, if you're too upset," said Rickwood, moving to stand by her and hold her hand.

"Oh, you might as well know all of it," she said. "We comforted each other, and the result was that I became pregnant. We had to tell Eleanor, as Ted would not hear of an abortion, or anything like that. I was still under age, you see. He wanted to adopt the baby and bring him up as his own. But she was angry and hurt, and said with some venom that she would not ever see me again, and would arrange for me and the little bastard to be sent to Australia to distant relations, where the child would be taken away and adopted and I could work for my living. Ted gave in, eventually. Eleanor was very strong, and always got her own way. And, in a way, she was the wounded one."

"And so that's what happened?" Deirdre's voice was soft and reassuring.

"Yes. I was too young to disobey my parents, and they sided with Eleanor, anyway. Everybody said I had behaved unforgivably, and I could see the only way out was to agree to Eleanor's plan. I had nobody to support me, and I knew nothing about babies. Rickwood was adopted by a nice couple, Mr. and Mrs. Smith, and I did not see him again, from the moment he emerged, wrinkled and newborn, until two years ago, when he had discovered his roots and came to find me."

Silence descended on the room, and nobody spoke until Gus cleared his throat, and said this was a terrible story, and he was sure Mary Winchen had the sympathy of all present. "But, Inspector, I don't see why we have been brought here together. We shall do all we can to make life for Mary and Rickwood as pleasant as possible. There are great plans for the farm."

Rickwood nodded in thanks, and said it was his turn to speak. "I shall keep it as short as possible, but the inspector has asked me to describe once more the night of Eleanor's death. I had been in the pub with Samantha and friends. They were all students who had come before classes started. A bonding couple of weeks, according to Mr. Rubens! Anyway, I left early, as I was going back to college where I had a spare bedroom allocated for my use. As I approached Blackwoods, I saw a light in the window of what Mr. Halfhide has christened the dark chamber. The curtains were open, and I could see the figure of my aunt moving round the room."

"Was she smoking?" asked Ivy.

"Please, Miss Beasley," said the inspector. "Carry on, Mr. Smith.

"Yes, Miss Beasley. I knew that she used it as a smoking room, and loved to sit there with the window open. The one leading to the fire escape, that was. I stood looking at her and thinking about my mother. On an impulse, I scrambled over the cage onto the steps, and made my way to the top." He paused, and seemed to choke back tears. "I was not sober, I must confess. We had had a very merry evening at the pub. At the top, I hesitated, the climb having sobered me up a little. Then I hopped into the room, intending to make a dramatic entrance and introduce myself as her long-lost nephew. But before I could say anything, she stared at me and then screamed, a horrible scream. I moved to reassure her, but she backed away round me and stepped out onto the fire escape, yelling that I should leave her alone. I went to restrain her, but before I could reach her . . . Oh God, she missed her footing and fell heavily, cracking her poor head as she went down, into the cage at the bottom. It was horrible, horrible, and I'll never ever forgive myself. I rushed down after her, but when I got to the bottom, I could see that she had already stopped breathing. So I scarpered. Very cowardly, I know

now. But I was scared. Scared of what everyone would think. I am afraid that's why I was so reluctant to let you into the dark chamber. Fingerprints and that sort of thing. I have been a real idiot, I see that now."

Once more silence fell heavily on the listeners. Then the inspector spoke again. "I am anxious to know now," he said, "to complete my enquiries, why exactly did Eleanor Blatch recoil from her personable young nephew, with such disastrous results?"

"I can tell you that," said Ivy, matter-of-factly.

"Miss Beasley?" said the inspector, looking surprised.

"She thought he was the ghost of her husband, Ted, returned from the dead to claim her. Look at him, Mrs. Winchen. Isn't he the image of his father? We have seen photographs, but you remember the man himself. The short-tempered young farmer with a second-choice wife and a baby in the graveyard."

"Ivy! Don't say another word!" Roy banged his stick on the floor. "I will not hear any more of this. You, Inspector, can take yourself and your suspect out of this house and away. And the rest of us will reach a place of calm as soon as we can. Terrible things have been revealed here. Too much to be absorbed without time for some of us to recover."

Frobisher raised his eyebrows, and sniffed. "All in good time, Mr. Goodman. Most of what needs to be said has been said. And as for my suspect, provided he does not leave this village without telling us, I shall not be requiring his presence at the station. There are one or two open questions, but that will do later."

He looked across at Deirdre, but her face was streaked with tears and she held on tightly to Mary Winchen's hand. He shrugged. "Good day all, then," he said, and left the room.

Fifty-five

"WELL," SAID GUS, looking at Deirdre across the break-fast table, "I still think he *could* have given her a push. Revenge, Dee-Dee. He was drunk, he admitted, and not thinking straight. His father was known to be quick-tempered, and it would only have taken half a second for him to act on a sudden impulse."

"But why? What would he gain by it? Nothing that he wasn't going to get, anyway. He must have known his mother would inherit when Eleanor died. Years later, prob-ably, but . . ."

"But he was possibly in a hurry. And, don't forget, it was only two years since he discovered his real mother, and the circumstances of his birth. That must have made him furiously angry with his cruel aunt. That's how he must have seen it, and when the moment, the opportunity, presented itself. Wham!"

The telephone rang, and Deirdre went into the hall to answer it. When she came back, she was frowning.

"That was Ivy," she said. "She says an important

development has come up. I really honestly thought the whole thing had been wrapped up! Not sure I can take any more, Gussy."

"What does she want us to do?"

"She says the inspector is to be at Springfields at eleven o'clock, and she wants us to be there."

"Three-line whip? I suppose we'd better go, then."

GUS AND DEIRDRE walked arm in arm down the road towards Springfields, and as they approached they saw Inspector Frobisher disappearing through the door.

"Why does my heart sink at the thought of more revelations?" Deirdre said, squeezing Gus's arm. "Do you think they've found some real evidence of Rickwood's guilt?"

"We shall see, my love. In we go, and chin up! At least we're not in the firing line."

"No, but think how awful this must be for Mary Winchen. No sooner has she found her long-lost son, but he is about to be arrested for murder!"

"Hey, slow down! You might be completely wrong. Let's wait and see. Ah, good morning, Mrs. Spurling. You are looking particularly smart, I must say! Busy weekend?"

"I'm always busy, Mr. Halfhide," she said. "And, as I am sure you appreciate, much busier since dear Miss Beasley arrived. Now, here is the inspector."

"*If* you are ready, Mr. Halfhide, perhaps you would be good enough to follow me?"

Inspector Frobisher had been enjoying a leisurely breakfast when he received a message from Miss Beasley. Now he saw his free day turning into another Enquire Within marathon. Rickwood Smith was chatting to Miss Pinkney, and one of the college students, a fair-haired girl he thought he recognised, sat close to Miss Beasley.

The conference room was more crowded than usual, and at last they were all settled. All except for Mary Winchen, who was wheeled in by Miss Pinkney.

"Right," said the inspector. "I am a patient man, and I have been asked by Miss Beasley to meet you all again here. She stressed it was important, and so here I am. And here are you, Mr. Rickwood Smith, and your mother, Mrs. Winchen, Mrs. Bloxham and Mr. Halfhide, Mr. Goodman, and, of course, Miss Beasley. And you are?" he said, turning to the girl.

"Samantha Earnshaw," she said. "I am Miss Beasley's friend, and a student at the Manor House College."

"And an important witness," added Ivy, dropping a bombshell in their midst.

Rickwood Smith stared at her, a questioning frown on his face. Deirdre and Gus looked at each other. Another of Ivy's shots in the dark!

Mary Winchen leaned forward to speak to the girl. "How do you do, Samantha," she said. "We have met once or twice in Spinney Close, and I am very fond of your mother."

Roy, who had said nothing at all, now cleared his throat. "Ivy, my dear, I think that as it is the inspector's free day, we must come to the point." Not for the first time, Inspector Frobisher thanked God for Roy Goodman.

Now Samantha took over. She addressed herself exclusively to the inspector, and her voice was firm. "On the night that Eleanor Blatch died as a result of falling down the fire escape, I had been with the other students and Rickwood Smith in the local pub, having a jolly evening. Rickwood got on well with us, and we were looking forward to the writing course starting. We liked him, to put it simply."

She paused and looked round to where he sat. "But that has nothing to do with what I am about to tell you. That night at the pub, Rickwood left before the rest of us, but I thought he looked a bit wobbly as he went. Not drunk, you know, but wobbly. I knew he wouldn't want me to follow him, so I kept well back so if he tripped over, something like that, I would be able to help him. I saw him go into the garden at Blackwoods and stand looking up at the fire escape. Then he did a great leap over the cage and onto the steps. I was standing with a very good view of the open window. I saw him reach the top, and disappear into the room. Then I saw Mrs. Blatch standing alone at the open window. She was yelling in fright at someone called Ted, and I saw quite clearly that she stepped out onto the little platform at the top, looked back, missed her footing and fell. Rickwood must have been away at the other side of the room because I could see quite clearly that nobody was behind her. Then I saw him coming fast down the escape, and I hid behind a bush until he had gone. That is exactly as it happened, and I am telling the honest truth."

There was a silence, and the inspector nodded. "Thank you, Samantha," he said. "She was yelling at someone called Ted, did you say? That is a very important point. You have given us a clear picture of what you witnessed. I have no reason to doubt the truth of your statement, though I shall have to ask you to come into the station later. Now, have any of you anything to ask?"

Rickwood Smith moved over to his mother and put a hand on her shoulder. He looked at Samantha, and said simply, "Thank you, Sam. That *is* how it happened, and I shall have the responsibility for the result of my foolish action to bear for the rest of my life. Looking back at my family history, it is so sad that the loss of a tiny speck of human life should have sparked such a dreadful series of events. I will take my mother home now, if that is okay with you, Inspector, and in the coming years I hope to make amends here in Barrington."

MM, VERY SMOOTH, thought the inspector. And was the light of love shining in Samantha's eyes? He shrugged, and drove off in his car. At least he would be in time for his round of golf with his wife.

Gus and Roy walked together to the gate of Springfields, and Gus suggested a stroll up to Blackwoods to have a quick look at the tractor and perhaps catch Rickwood in a good mood and willing to sell. Ivy and Deirdre reluctantly approved, and said they were not to be late for lunch.

Rickwood was standing outside the barn, deep in thought. Hearing the two men approaching, Roy in his trundle, and Gus with Whippy at his heel, he turned with a smile.

"Welcome," he said. "What a morning! And that dear child! It must have cost her a great deal of courage to come forward. Now, I know what you are about to ask, and as I owe you a great deal for all your support, I am giving you the old tractor and hope you have fun with it. My painter says it is roadworthy after your tinkering the other day, so now's the moment!"

DEIRDRE AND IVY sat in the Springfields lounge, not speaking much, but thinking a great deal. Finally Ivy looked at her watch, and said wouldn't it be a good idea to walk up to Blackwoods and make sure Roy returned for lunch on time.

"We've had enough excitements for one day, without a lecture from our gaoler," Ivy said.

As they set off up the road, they suddenly stopped short on the path. With one accord, they said "What's that!?" as down the road came the old Ferguson tractor, making the most extraordinarily loud noise, with Roy in the driving seat and Gus with Whippy standing precariously behind him.

They drew to a halt beside the ladies, and Ivy took a deep breath. "Roy Goodman!" she said. "Take that thing back at once!"

Roy smiled broadly, touched his forelock, wished them a polite good day, and drove on into the village.

"If anyone asked me," said Ivy, hands on hips, "I would say that my Roy is a stubborn old idiot, and the most wonderful man I've ever met. Come on, Deirdre, let's go back and face the music."

Fifty-six

IVY HAD NOT been able to sleep, with all the revelations and conclusions revolving in her head, and she had tiptoed along to Roy's room and crept into bed beside him. He had, needless to say, welcomed her into his arms, where she had gone immediately to sleep.

Now it was morning, the doves cooing outside the window, and sounds of kitchen activity coming up from below.

"Morning, beloved," Roy whispered into Ivy's ear. She stirred, stretched, and said quite clearly, "Morning, Tiddles. Time to get up?"

Roy laughed, and Ivy woke up properly. "Ah, now, my love," he said. "You must be gone before La Spurling catches us in flagrante delicto."

"Or," said Ivy, "in plain English, catches us red-handed!" She planted a kiss on his forehead and slipped quickly out of bed. She opened and closed the door noiselessly and sped along the corridor. Pushing open her door, to her dismay she saw a figure standing by her bed.

"Miss Beasley? Please come in and help me." It was

Katya, and she was clutching her stomach. "Aaaah! Please could you get Mrs. Spurling? I think the baby is coming, and I could not find anyone awake. I was on duty last night instead of going home. It was a favour, as the other girls are on holiday. Oh, oh, aaaaah!"

"Sit down here, dear," said Ivy calmly. "Take some deep breaths, and try to relax." She picked up her phone and summoned Mrs. Spurling and Miss Pinkney, and Katya's husband as an afterthought, and then sat down beside her and held her hand. "Is it too early for the baby to come?" she said.

"A little, but I was not too certain about my dates. Oh, I think I hear Mrs. Spurling on the stairs. Sorry if I alarmed you, Miss Beasley. May I stay here with you until the ambulance comes? I do not think I am very well into labour yet."

Then it was as if all hell was let loose. Mrs. Spurling bustled around, moving things from one place to another, fetching cushions for Katya's back, and telling Miss Pinkney to fetch a cup of tea, when her assistant had already arrived with a steaming cup in her hand.

Ivy, still in her nightdress, but with a woollen stole put round her shoulders by Miss Pinkney, sat solidly beside Katya, telling her a long story about when she was at her village school and the nurse came to deal with nits. "We all got them in the end," she said.

"What are nits, Miss Beasley?" said Katya, her attention fully focussed on Ivy's story.

"Fleas, my dear. Fleas in your hair. I don't suppose children get them now. Now, I think I hear the ambulance, and here's your husband, so time to go. You have a bag ready? Good girl. Best of luck!"

AT BREAKFAST, ROY was loud in praise of his Ivy's presence of mind.

"I must say," said Mrs. Spurling, sniffing, "that for someone with no personal experience of childbirth, Miss Beasley was magnificent."

"Damned with faint praise," whispered Ivy to Roy. "Little does she know that I once sat up all night with a sheep in labour. Beautiful little lamb, she had, when we had cleaned it up. Can't be that different, can it?"

Roy's mobile rang, and he handed it to Ivy. "It's Deirdre," he said. "Inviting us to lunch today. What do you think?"

"Deirdre? That would be very nice, dear. About half past twelve? Thank you. And do I hear Gus's voice? So we shall all be together. How pleasant."

"Better tell La Spurling we shall be out. I have a small errand to pursue, but can take care of that this afternoon."

"Not the tractor!" said Ivy.

Roy smiled blandly. "Right first time, my love," he said.

Lunch at Tawny Wings was as delicious and considerable as always, and after a short doze in the garden, Gus and Roy got to their feet, and announced that they had an urgent task.

"At Blackwoods Farm?" Ivy said. Deirdre groaned. "I've heard of a golf widow, and now it looks as if you and I, Ivy, are to be tractor widows."

The two men slid away like naughty schoolboys, and walked swiftly out of the drive and on their way. When they were a hundred yards away from the farmyard, they could see an unfamiliar figure standing by the barn.

"It's not Smith," said Gus. "Definitely not Rickwood Smith."

"Never seen him before," said Roy. "At least, I don't think so."

"G'day, gentlemen," the man said, as they approached. "Can you help me?"

"Ask away," said Gus. He stood protectively against the barn door, closed with the tractor still there.

"I wonder if you could tell me where I can find Mrs. Eleanor Blatch," he said.

Gus and Roy looked at each other. "And who are you, if you don't mind my asking," said Roy, frowning suspiciously.

"My name's Sturridge," the man said. "I remember you, Mr. Goodman. You used to farm over near Oakbridge. How's life with you? Hope you're not rotting away in that Springfields place down the road!"

"I am afraid I don't remember you," said Roy stiffly. "We are very busy, I'm afraid, and will have to get on."

"But you haven't answered my question," said the man, still smiling. "I can see she isn't here anymore. I lived with her a few years ago. She and I were, well, you know how it is. I thought I'd look her up, maybe stay for a week or two."

Gus, annoyance rising sharply, decided to wipe the smile off the intruder's face. He was a short man, stout with approaching old age. "I can direct you to where you will find Mrs. Blatch," he said, pointing back down the road to the village. "Up Cemetery Lane," he said. "The graveyard is on your right as you come to the top of the hill. You'll find her there."

"And," said Roy, "we know exactly who you are now, and I advise you to get out of here as soon as possible, before we call the police." Shouting that there was no need for that, the man turned on his heel and disappeared at speed.

Neither Gus nor Roy had anything to say for a few minutes, and then Gus said, "Right, come on, Mr. Goodman, let's open this door and get to work."

"It was him, wasn't it?" said Roy. "T'was Roger the lodger, the sod."

Fifty-seven

SUNDAY EVENING WAS always a quiet time at Springfields. Everyone sat in the lounge, watching television or playing games. Ivy and Roy usually set themselves to do the quick crossword in the Sunday *Telegraph*, and when that was finished—they always finished it—they would retire to Ivy's room to work on a jigsaw puzzle permanently set up for the odd idle hour.

Tonight, the crossword proved to be more difficult than usual, and in the end Ivy said she was fed up with it and was retreating up to her room to have an early night. Roy agreed, and they were halfway up the stairs when Miss Pinkney called from the hallway.

"Miss Beasley! Good news from the hospital. Special message for Miss Beasley, the nurse said. Are you coming down?"

Ivy turned and joined Miss Pinkney in the office. She picked up the telephone and a familiar voice said, "Is that Miss Beasley, yes?"

"Katya! My dear child, is that you?"

"Yes it is. And I shall be home soon, bringing with me my beautiful baby daughter! All went well, and she weighs seven pounds, ten ounces! And my husband says it is a good thing that girls can play football professionally nowadays."

"Congratulations to you all," said Ivy, laughing. "And what are you calling her? Have you got a name ready?"

"Oh yes, she is Elizabeth Ivy, of course. Miss Beasley, are you still there?"

Ivy sniffed hard and rubbed her eyes with her cuff. "Yes, my dear Katya, I am here and so is Roy, and we can't wait to see the new resident at Springfields. Take great care, all of you. Good-bye."

Roy took the receiver from her, and held her hand tightly as she sobbed. He had never seen Ivy in such a flood of tears. It was a new Ivy, and he loved her all the more. "Elizabeth Ivy," he said. "And you are . . . ?"

She finished his sentence, "Ivy Elizabeth Beasley, soon to be Goodman."

He handed her his snowy-white large handkerchief, and together they went up to bed.

FROM NATIONAL BESTSELLING AUTHOR

ANN PURSER

The Sleeping
Salesman Enquiry

An Ivy Beasley Mystery

Ivy Elizabeth Beasley is ready to share her golden years
and plans to wed Roy Vivian Goodman on the fifth of
May. A spinster no more, the private eye is in for marriage, murder, and mishaps galore . . .

PRAISE FOR THE SERIES

"Purser's Ivy Beasley is a truly unique character, a kind
of cross between Jessica Fletcher, Miss Marple, and Mrs.
Slocum from *Are You Being Served?*—just a delightful,
eccentric old darling that readers are sure to embrace."
—*Fresh Fiction*

"[A] firecracker of a senior citizen sleuth."
—MyShelf.com

annpurser.com
facebook.com/TheCrimeSceneBooks
penguin.com

M1400T1013

FROM NATIONAL BESTSELLING AUTHOR

ANN PURSER

THE IVY BEASLEY MYSTERIES

The Hangman's Row Enquiry

The Measby Murder Enquiry

The Wild Wood Enquiry

The Sleeping Salesman Enquiry

The Blackwoods Farm Enquiry

❧

"Purser's Ivy Beasley is a truly unique character, a kind
of cross between Jessica Fletcher, Miss Marple, and Mrs.
Slocum from *Are You Being Served?*—just a delightful,
eccentric old darling that readers are sure to embrace."
—*Fresh Fiction*

"A delightful spin-off."
—*Genre Go Round Reviews*

"Full of wit, venom, and bonding between new friends."
—*The Romance Readers Connection*

annpurser.com
facebook.com/annpursercrimewriter
facebook.com/TheCrimeSceneBooks
penguin.com

M1231AS1013